# CIGAR CLUB

JA Armstrong

ISBN-13: 978-0692083710
ISBN-10: 0692083715

# PROLOGUE

## FROM OPEN TAB

Fallon Foster pulled into Riley Main's driveway and looked out at the small house in the distance. Why had she come here? What kind of person looked to cry on the shoulder of the woman she had fallen in love with over the loss of her lover. "Only you, Foster." Maybe she should turn around. For some reason, she couldn't. Fallon made her way toward Riley's front door.

It was nearly midnight. Riley couldn't imagine who would be at her door. Her heart stopped. When she opened it. "Fallon?"

"It's over, Riley."

Riley was confused.

"Me and Andi. It's over."

Riley was stunned. Fallon's eyes were swollen. She led Fallon inside and enveloped her in a hug. Fallon's tears started fresh.

"Come on," Riley cooed. "Come sit down with me. Tell me what happened."

Fallon let Riley lead her to the sofa. Why was she here? Of all places, why had she come to Riley's? Regret and confusion overwhelmed her.

"Hey," Riley called softly. "What happened?"

"Nothing," Fallon replied. *And everything. I love you. That's what happened. She knows it. I love her too. How can that happen?*

Riley sighed. Andi made many denials to Riley about how she felt for Fallon. Andi loved Fallon. Riley guessed that Andi was in love with Fallon. Some part of Fallon was in love with Andi. An ending had always been inevitable. That didn't make it easy. "I'm sorry, Fallon. I know how much you care for her."

Fallon nodded. "She's right. I know she's right. Why does it hurt so much?"

"Because you love her."

Fallon's eyes filled with tears again. What was wrong with her? Were these tears endless? Is this what her mother was afraid of? And, Riley? God, she loved Riley. That hurt most of all. It was all her fault—again. Andi had quelled her loneliness, given her a place to fall and feel—feel something beyond momentary arousal and gratification. Why did she insist on falling in love with people who would never be able to give her what she desired? Riley? Just perfect, she'd broken Andi's heart, splintered her own by stupidly falling for a woman who could never love her—a straight woman. *Well, that takes the cake, Fallon.*

"Fallon," Riley whispered. "It'll be okay. I know it doesn't feel like it right now, but things will work out."

"I'm not sure what that even means," Fallon confessed.

"Andi loves you," Riley offered.

"I know."

Riley kissed Fallon's forehead. "What do you say I make us some cocoa?"

"Cocoa?"

"I'll throw some Bailey's in it for good measure."

Fallon smiled weakly. *How do you do that; make it better?*

"It's my remedy for the blues," Riley explained.

"I'm sorry, Riley."

"For what?"

"For dropping in at midnight and crying on your shoulder. I just... I didn't want to be alone."

"You don't have to be." Riley started for the kitchen and stopped. "There's a pair of your sweats in my room," she said. "From when I stayed over. Why don't you go change?"

Fallon stared at Riley.

"Well? I have extra blankets too. Go on. I seem to recall you telling me that turnabout was fair play once. I guess it's my couch's turn to host you."

Fallon chuckled. There was no point in arguing. Riley wouldn't force her, but the offer was sincere. Fallon wanted to accept. She didn't want to be alone. Somehow, she knew Riley would understand. She nodded and headed off to find the sweats.

Riley made her way to the kitchen, filled a tea kettle with water, and lit the burner. She took a deep breath and let it out slowly. A quick glance to make certain that Fallon was out of earshot and she picked up her phone.

Andi looked at the caller and sighed. "Hi, Riley."

"Are you okay?"

"She's there; isn't she?"

"She is."

"Good."

"Andi... Are you okay there..."

"I'm all right, Riley; I promise."

"Is it okay if I tell you that I think you're full of shit?"

Andi laughed. "I'd expect nothing less."

"What can I do?" Riley asked.

A tear washed over Andi's cheek. "Take care of her, Riley."

Andi's simple reply made Riley's chest ache. "I will; I promise."

*I know you will, Riley. You just need figure out what that means.* "Don't worry about me."

"Too late."

Andi chuckled. "I'll see you soon, Riley."

Riley couldn't speak. She placed the phone on the counter with a sigh.

"How was Andi?" Fallon asked as she stepped into the kitchen.

Riley looked up regretfully.

"It's all right." Fallon smiled earnestly. "I don't know if you realize it, but Andi thinks of you like a daughter."

Fallon's observation should have delighted Riley. Tonight, it aroused a sense of guilt, although Riley wasn't sure why. "I didn't know."

"Mm. Like you feel about her."

"I guess I do," Riley admitted. "Or a sister."

Fallon grabbed the kettle off the burner when it whistled. "So? How is she?"

"Hurting," Riley answered honestly. "Just like you."

"We'll be okay, Riley." Fallon wasn't sure if she spoke the words for Riley's benefit or hers.

"You will be," Riley agreed. "Let me get the cocoa."

"And the Bailey's."

"And the Bailey's. Fallon?"

"Hum?"

"It really will be—all right, I mean. I know it doesn't feel that way. It will be."

Fallon nodded. *I hope so, Riley. I hope so.*

**May 24th**

"What are you up to?" Carol asked Fallon. Fallon's playful grin made her giggle. "Off to torture Riley?"

"Torture? I'm not bringing any silly string." Fallon was sure that Riley remained grateful Owen's party had taken place at Fallon's house. Fallon had been finding trails of silly string ever since the birthday party. *Still better than dealing with that talking dinosaur.*

"What?"

"Never mind," Fallon said. "You missed that part."

"Oookaaay."

Fallon shrugged.

"What are you up to, Fallon?"

"I'm not *up to* anything. I'm just picking up dinner for a friend and surprising her."

Carol stopped drying the glass in her hand, set it down and put her hands on her hips. "I don't believe it."

"What?"

"You're wooing Riley."

"Wooing? What is that; some kind of weird bird call?"

"Ha-ha. Tell me I'm wrong. You're trying to get in Riley's pants."

Fallon sobered. "No."

Carol knew which buttons to push to get the information she desired. She ought to. She spent more hours with Fallon over the last eight years than anyone. *I knew it.*

"What? Why are you looking at me like that?"

"She's terrific, Fallon."

"Who?"

"Who? Riley, you idiot."

"Yeah, she is."

"Well, I hope it all works out."

"What's that?"

"Riley."

"I'm not... Carol, we're not..."

Carol smiled. *Not yet.*

Riley had been struggling to concentrate all day. She had tried successfully to ignore thinking about the milestones of this day. The only thing staying home seemed to accomplish was making he think about it more. She'd gone as far as to pull out her wedding album. It surprised her that she felt little sadness in flipping through the pages. The images made her laugh and smile. She did miss Robert. She missed his laugh, and the way he would wink at her from across a room. She missed his off-key singing in the car and the shower. She missed his arms around her and his lips on hers. Most of all, she missed his friendship. She massaged her temples. Owen was at a friend's house. She was bored. Boredom led to thinking and that was the last thing that Riley wanted to do. She was relieved when her phone rang. An adult conversation—hell, any conversation would be welcome right now.

*Jerry. Well, he is an adult.* Riley answered the call. "Hi, Jerry."

"Hi. Busy?"

"Nope."

"Good. Well, not good, but, well, you know."

"What's up?" Riley asked.

"I was just wondering if you were busy, you know, later, not now, because you already said you're not busy now."

Talking to Jerry sometimes made Riley dizzy. He was very sweet. *Sweet. He is sweet.* "Other than fixing Owen dinner and probably being forced to listen to taking dinosaurs or traveling through Storybook Village, I'm open."

"Oh... That sounds... Well, I hate to intrude on your time with Owen and dinosaurs."

"Jerry? What are you asking me?"

"Oh, I was wondering if you might like to have dinner at Josiah's. I have some friends staying in Essex. Jan, she and I've known each other since birth. She and her husband, Steve wanted to catch up."

"I don't want to intrude."

"You wouldn't be. It's always a little awkward."

"Third wheel?" Riley guessed.

"Who happened to date the second wheel all through high school."

"Ah... Sure. I'll have to see if Marge is around. I'd call Andi, but... Well, Jake in home and..."

"I get it. Just let me know. I'll pick you up around six if it works for you."

"Pretty sure it will be fine. Plan on six. If something changes, I'll let you know."

"Oh, great. Thanks, Riley."

"I'll see you." Riley set down the phone. *Very sweet. Well, you get to be the fourth wheel for a change. Stepping up in the world, Riley.* She chuckled.

Andi slid the papers across the kitchen table to her husband. Jake Maguire looked at them and shook his head. "Why?"

"It's time, Jake."

"Time? Is this about Fallon?"

"This is about us. It's about me."

"And Fallon," he guessed.

"I'm not seeing Fallon anymore, not the way you mean."

Jake nodded. "She broke it off?"

"Sign the papers, Jake."

"Why? Why now?"

Andi sighed.

"Because I want to move to Arizona? Why wouldn't you want to go? What's left here, Andi? The kids are gone most of the year. Don't you think we deserve to make a change now?"

*We? A change?* "What kind of change do you mean, Jake?"

"What?"

"It's a simple question. What kind of change? Are you planning on retiring early?"

"No..."

"Are you planning on staying home—with me?"

"Andi, you know that my job entails travel."

Andi nodded. "So, you'll be keeping the same lifestyle only we'd have our house in Arizona."

"You make it sound like a punishment."

"Is it? Is it a punishment for me?"

"What are you talking about?"

"This is my home, Jake. You aren't interested in a home."

"That's not fair," he said.

"Isn't it? It's the truth. You want to roam the world and explore all it has to offer," she said.

"I'm not the only who's had affairs."

"No."

Jake rubbed his face. He was frustrated and confused. "Twenty-six years of marriage, Andi. Why now?"

Andi wasn't sure how to answer that. Being with Fallon had reminded her that she could feel deeply for someone other than Jake Maguire. Ironically, watching Fallon and Riley fall in love had awakened her as well. Andi didn't want to become a bitter old woman. She loved Jake. He'd been part of her life for most of it. He'd given her two children who continued to be the center of Andi's world. She was no longer the center of any of theirs. She needed to figure out who Andi was—not Andi Maguire—Andi Sherman, the young woman she'd left behind so many years ago. What part of her still existed? What did Andi Sherman want from life? If she ever hoped to discover that, Andi needed to be alone. This was her home. Whiskey Springs was the place Andi needed and wanted to be. Perhaps Fallon was not her lover, she still loved Fallon. She loved Riley and Owen. She adored Ida and Carol. She even loved Pete and Dale. This was home—her home. That was the one thing Andi did know.

"This is what I need, Jake. You don't need me."

"How can you say that?"

"For what?" Andi asked. "You're gone more than you are here. You don't have one mistress waiting for you; you're like a sailor." She chuckled. "A girl in every port."

"Don't exaggerate."

Andi sighed. "I still love you."

"Tell me what you want, Andi and I'll do it."

"This is what I want. You are who you are, Jake. That's who you've always been. I don't want to change you. I can't follow the path you want to keep walking. I can't."

Jake studied his wife's expression. Andi had always been as intelligent and confident as she was stunning. He sighed heavily. He did love her. He'd always love her. He'd taken for granted that she would always be there. "You're sure?"

Andi nodded.

Jake took a deep breath and signed the papers. He pushed them back to Andi. "I wish you'd reconsider this."

Andi squeezed his hand. "I wish I could."

Fallon drove across town to Tony's Pizza to pick up dinner. Riley loved Tony's pasta and meatballs. Fallon couldn't blame her. There weren't many choices for dining in Whiskey Springs. Tony's hole in the wall pizza joint could easily deceive an unknowing visitor. People from across the area made the drive to Tony's for pizza, grinders, salads, and pasta. That's all Tony had made for the last twenty years. The worn façade of his building added charm in Fallon's opinion. The food was amazing and inexpensive. *Double win.*

She had devised the perfect plan. Riley had absently commented that she had no plans for the next few days. Fallon would arrive around six with dinner—cheese pizza for Owen. Okay, that might torture Riley slightly. But Owen was so cute when his face was covered with sauce, it was worth it. She'd offer to clean the Owen up while Riley picked up from their dinner. They would read with Owen for a little while, and when he finally went to sleep, Fallon would suggest they have a glass of wine. Then she would give

Riley her gifts and say, 'happy birthday." Riley deserved to be celebrated.

Fallon had spent hours online searching for the perfect gift; something that sparkled and something that Riley would treasure. Riley often left her computer open when she had stayed with Fallon. Fallon had noticed one image that flashed across it repeatedly. She'd considered a million possibilities for the perfect gift. Riley was an avid reader. She read anything and everything she could get her hands on. Fallon would have thought that her friend would be tired of reading after editing books all day long. Riley explained that it was different. She loved to immerse herself in book and escape into some foreign land with colorful characters. Fallon had seen her read everything from *Harry Potter* to Toni Morrison. Books lined the built-in shelves of Riley's living room. Every novel by Austen and King, Rowling and Tolstoy adorned the shelves. One day, Fallon hoped the shelf would hold a volume by Riley Main. And, that is how she decided on the perfect gift.

She turned the corner and started down the winding road that led to Riley's house. A stupid grin curled her lips. Was she trying to "woo" Riley? She wanted to make Riley happy, to see Riley smile. And, yes, it was true she hoped somewhere beneath it all that one day she might just be rewarded with a sweet kiss—with Riley. Fallon took a deep breath as Riley's house came into view. Who was that on the porch? Jerry? Oh, no. Riley? Riley was saying goodbye to Marge. Fallon stopped the car. *She has a date. Jesus, Fallon, how stupid are you. It's her birthday. Of course, she has a date.*_Fallon felt sick. She put the car in reverse and pulled away. *What now?*

"I thought you said Fallon was spending the night with Riley?" Charlie asked Carol.

Carol nearly groaned. Her eyes found Fallon across the room with a group of young women who had been in the bar several times in the last week. She wasn't sure what was going on with Fallon. She'd gone out back and found Fallon tossing a bag and a pizza box in the dumpster. Fallon's expression told her to leave it be. Next thing she knew, Fallon was behind the bar pouring herself a beer. Moments later, the three women had walked in. Fallon had been in the corner with them ever since. *That has no good place to go.*

"I'm not sure what happened," Carol told her fiancé. One of the women had been eyeing Fallon for days. Carol had noticed it. Fallon had seemed oblivious to the attention. That was rare. Even if Fallon chose not to act on a woman's advances, she always noticed them. Carol sighed. Fallon's moods had been fluctuating like tides for days. One minute she would seem upbeat and positive, the next she was sullen, and before you could blink, Fallon would snap over some trivial bit of information. It was wholly unlike Fallon. Part of it, Carol was certain, stemmed from the relationship she had with Andi ending. Andi hadn't been in the pub since. Carol hadn't needed to ask why. She'd gotten a call from Andi. Andi knew Fallon better than anyone except Ida, even Carol, and Carol had a close friendship with her boss. Andi's voice held both concern and sorrow.

Fallon's feelings for Riley had been apparent to Carol for months. At Owen's birthday party, she'd found herself wondering when they might be headed to the altar. Fallon had been almost giddy about her plans for the evening. Something had happened. As much as Carol dreaded Fallon's wrath, she thought it was time to find out. It wasn't the cute, flirtatious blonde hanging on Fallon's every move that Carol sought to save Fallon from; it was herself.

"Do me a favor?" Carol asked Charlie.

"Sure."

"Watch the bar for a minute?"

"Where are you going?"

*Probably to my death or the unemployment line.* "I'm going in."

"You're kidding," Fallon laughed. "You're renting the Bath's cabins at the pond?"

"Yeah, why?"

Fallon shook her head. "Oh nothing." She wondered what Dora and Dick Bath might think if they knew lesbians were enjoying the fruits of their labor. She sniggered. If the night went the way she expected, Fallon would be enjoying some fruit in the Bath's cabin. That brought her a degree of sick satisfaction.

"Hey," Carol tugged on Fallon's arm.

"Oh, hey. Carol. This is Deb, Trish, and Aubrey."

"Hi," Carol greeted the trio evenly.

"They're renting those two cabins the Bath's own down at Morton Pond."

"Oh? Nice," Carol said a bit dismissively. She wanted to roll her eyes at the way Aubrey's hand not so subtly fingered Fallon's arm. *Ugh. You aren't in the same league as Andi or Riley.* "Can I borrow you for just a minute?" Carol requested.

"Sure," Fallon said. "I'll be right back," she told Aubrey.

Aubrey stretched to place her lips in front of Fallon's. "I certainly hope so."

Carol thought she might wretch. *I can't believe that works.* She walked a few feet to the side door of the pub and stepped outside.

Fallon followed her friend. "What's up?" Fallon asked.

"I don't know; you tell me."

"Tell you what?"

"What's going on with you?" Carol asked.

"I was enjoying a beer."

Carol stared at Fallon. "Why aren't you at Riley's?"

Fallon's face contorted. "She's busy."

"She's busy?"

"Yeah. You know—busy."

"Uh-huh. What did she say when you showed up?"

Fallon was growing anxious. Talking about her trip to Riley's unsettled her for reasons she had no desire to explore with Carol or anyone else. There were things she was eager to explore—things called Aubrey. "She didn't say anything."

"What?"

"I didn't talk to her."

"Lost me."

"I pulled up; she was walking out with Jerry."

"Jerry? Jerry Walker?"

Fallon made no comment.

"So, you just left?"

"I dropped some things off on the porch after they were gone."

"So, she went out; so, what?"

"Exactly. It's her life."

Carol sighed. "You know, Fallon, you really can be thick."

"What the fuck does that mean?"

"If you're so crazy about Riley, maybe you should tell her."

"I'm sure Jerry has that covered. Is there anything else?"

Carol took a step toward the door. "You know; if she means that little to you that you'll just walk away because she happens to spend time with someone else, maybe she'd be better off with Jerry." She shook her head. "Go play with Aubrey."

"I will."

Carol shook her head again. *Sometimes, Fallon – sometimes.*

"I'm glad you were free," Jerry said.

"I'm glad you called."

"Really?"

Riley grinned. "Yes, really. I needed to get out."

"I can't believe that Charlie and Carol set a date for the wedding already."

"I can."

"Really?"

Jerry certainly like the word really. *Not like Fallon's kerfuffle.* Fallon seemed to have fallen in love with the word kerfuffle. She would use it whenever the opportunity presented itself. Riley had asked why she had so much affection for the word.

*"I don't know," Fallon told her. "I just like the way it sounds – like I'm smart."*

*Riley chuckled. As if Fallon wasn't intelligent. She suspected Fallon found the word fun to say. "You know, there are a plethora of or underutilized words, Fallon."*

*"Ohh, could there be a plethora of kerfuffles, though?"*

*"I don't think so."*

*Fallon huffed. "That would be fun to say."*

"Riley?"

"What?"

"The wedding?"

"Oh, yeah." *That could turn into a kerfuffle.* She chuckled.

"Did that wine go to your head?" Jerry asked as he pulled into Riley's driveway.

"No. I'm sorry, Jerry. I was just thinking about something."

"It's okay. Listen, I had a nice time."

Riley smiled. Everything about Jerry was nice. Electric? No. Nice? Very. "Me too," she said.

He leaned over and placed a light kiss on Riley's lips.

Riley offered him another smile. *Nice. Just – nice.* "Thanks for dinner."

"I'll call you."

"Sounds good," Riley said as she stepped out of the car. *Oh, Riley… He is a very nice man. What is wrong with that?* She chuckled. *I think It's prefer a kerfuffle.*

Fallon followed Aubrey into the cabin. Before she could speak, Aubrey's mouth claimed hers with a desperate kiss. Fallon welcomed it. Fallon welcomed anything that might have the power to banish images of Riley Main. Who needed love? Where did that lead? It led directly to loneliness, that's where it led. How many lessons did a person need? She shed her jacket and tossed it carelessly aside. Aubrey's hands were everywhere all at once. Fallon immersed herself in the sensation that was pure, unapologetic lust. She wasn't seeking tenderness. She intended to touch every inch of the woman kissing her. She'd tear away the cloth barriers between them if need be.

"Mmm." Aubrey moaned into Fallon's mouth. She'd been watching Fallon for days. She'd come back to her cabin and she would imagine Fallon's lips covering her body, imagine her hands covering Fallon's breasts. Her fingers would play in time with the images. She wanted Fallon Foster. She wanted Fallon Foster to throw her up against the wall and take what she wanted. She would not be disappointed.

Fallon practically ripped the blouse from Aubrey's body. It got thrown into a growing heap of clothing. Aubrey reached for Fallon. Fallon grabbed her hands and pressed her against the wall, holding Aubrey's hands over her head. Her mouth crashed into Aubrey's demanding entry. Her teeth toyed with Aubrey's lower lip before descending to her neck and finally to a soft pink nipple.

"Fuck!" Aubrey called out.

Fallon sucked and nipped at the pink flesh until Aubrey strained against her. She pressed her full weight against the younger woman. "I'm going to make you come like you never have."

Warmth flooded Aubrey's veins and pooled between her legs. *Yes.* That's what she wanted.

Fallon unbuttoned Aubrey's jeans and lowered them. She wasted no time. Her fingers found the wet, eager softness she expected. She played for a moment, teasing the woman against her, circling and toying.

"Fuck, Fallon..."

"Fuck?" Fallon asked. "Is that what you want? You want me to fuck you right now?"

"Yes. Fuck yes."

Fallon's fingers thrust into her lover forcefully.

"Yes," Aubrey hissed as Fallon's fingers built a steady rhythm. Her fantasies about Fallon paled by comparison to the woman now moving inside her.

Fallon lost herself. It felt good—all of it. She absorbed the sound of Aubrey's sighs and pleas. She inhaled the scent of arousal and unbridled lust that permeated the room. Everything she felt, everything she questioned she poured into this young woman. This woman wanted nothing more from Fallon than for Fallon to make her feel good, and that is all Fallon desired. She let her thumb press the small sensitive bud that she knew would send Aubrey soaring and pressed her fingers deeper. Aubrey's body trembled. Fallon steadied her with the weight of her body and continued her thrusting.

"Harder!"

A pulse of excitement traveled through Fallon. Harder it would be.

"Fuck yes!"

Fallon devoured Aubrey's cries with her mouth. Aubrey shook violently. Fallon's kiss softened.

"Jesus," Aubrey whispered. "Do I get to return the favor?"

Fallon turned them and led Aubrey to the bed. She shed her remaining clothing and climbed on top of the young woman.

Aubrey let out a primal groan. "I'm going to lick every inch of you."

Fallon grinned. "Do it."

"Thanks for watching Owen."

Marge smiled brightly. "You don't ever have to thank me."

"He loves having you here," Riley said. She wasn't being kind; it was the truth. Owen adored Marge.

"Oh, I almost forgot." Marge ran over to the kitchen table. "This was on the step."

Riley puzzled over the gifts that Marge handed her. "What is this?"

"I don't know. The card is addressed to you. Maybe a present that was missed at Owen's party."

Riley shrugged. "Maybe. Thanks again." She set the boxes on the sofa.

"Did you still want me to come over next Wednesday?"

Riley smiled. "Please."

"Another date with Jerry?"

"No."

"Getting into trouble with Fallon?"

Riley laughed. "It might be Fallon you should worry about. I'm cooking her dinner."

"Another bet?"

"No, an overdue promise."

Marge nodded. "If you need anything before then…"

"You'll be the first to know." Riley bid Marge goodnight and closed the door.

Riley closed her eyes for a second and took a deep breath. A glass of wine was in order, a glass of wine and maybe a good book. She made her way to the kitchen and opened a bottle of Riesling. *Something sweet.* Riley wandered back to the sofa and collapsed onto it, ready for a few moments of complete silence and relaxation. She glanced at the packages she had places there. *Fallon.* The handwriting on the card was unmistakable.

*Riley,*
*I discovered by accident that it's your birthday.*

Riley sighed.

*I'm not sure if there's a reason that you didn't want to celebrate, but I wanted you to know that I think you should be celebrated.*

Riley smiled.

*I know that you probably think what I said in that crazy proposal Andi roped us into was all made up. I really am not very good with words. That was true. You're the aspiring writer. I just serve drinks.*

"You do a lot more than serve drinks," Riley commented.

*It's also true that I don't want to imagine my life without you in it. You've become my best friend. I look forward to our dinners and our late-night conversations.*

"And, sledding down my hill, and me doing your laundry."

*Plus, I get help with my laundry.*

Riley laughed.

*You give to everyone, Riley. You help everyone without ever asking for a thing. I wanted you to have something just for you, something to let you know how special I think you are.*

"Fallon..."

*You mentioned that you like sparkly things. Proposals aside, I thought I'd look for something that fit the bill. I hope you like it. I know that you love Tolstoy, so that's what gave me the idea. You really should write that book you've been talking about. I know I would read it. Maybe this will help. Happy Birthday, Riley.*

*Love,*

*Fallon*

Riley picked up the packages Fallon had left. She tore the paper away from the first and held her breath. Slowly, she opened the lid of the box to reveal a stunning fountain pen, a *Mont Blanc* limited edition honoring Leo Tolstoy. *Oh, my God, Fallon, what did you do?* She'd been looking at them online, daydreaming. Who would spend a thousand dollars on a pen? Apparently, the answer to that question was Fallon Foster. She opened the next gift and smiled. It was a stunning leather journal. Riley's fingertips traced over the cover. *Fallon.* She picked up her phone, pressed the familiar contact and waited.

"Hey, you've reached Fallon. I'm probably pouring at the pub. You know what to do if you don't want to come find me."

"Hi," Riley began softly. "I just opened your gifts." Riley took a breath. "Fallon, they're... They're amazing." *Just like you.* "I don't know how you knew. I didn't tell anyone. It's just... Today isn't an easy day for me. I was going to call you. Jerry called and offered to take me to dinner. I just needed to get out of the house. I never expected you to... I don't know what to say. You are...Well, I feel the same way about you. I don't want to think about not having you in my life." *I don't.* "Call me when you get this. Okay?" Riley's fingers danced over the journal again. She took a deep breath. "Dinner, tomorrow? I'd like to see you. I… I miss you. Call me."

Riley placed the phone beside her and looked at the presents in her lap. *Fallon. What would I do without you?*

Fallon threw her jacket onto the passenger seat and closed the door of her truck. She steadied her breathing and gripped the steering wheel. Why did she suddenly feel worse than she had when she'd walked into *Murphy's Law*? A faint buzzing drew her attention.

"Hi, Mom."

"Hi, Mom?"

"Where are you? And who is Aubrey?"

"What?"

"You called me Fallon, two hours ago—although I'm not sure *why* you called me."

"I didn't call you. Oh, shit. I must've dialed you somehow when I…"

"I don't want to know," Ida said.

"Then why did you call back?"

"What are you doing?" Ida asked.

"Something tells me you already know the answer to that question."

"I thought you were surprising Riley for her birthday."

"Yeah, so did I."

"What happened?"

"Jerry happened."

Ida took a deep breath. "Jerry happened."

"Yeah. I went over, and she was getting in Jerry's car. I guess he rates enough to spend her birthday with."

Ida wished she could crawl through the phone and smack Fallon. "Stop pouting."

"What?"

"You heard me. What makes you think Riley told him it was her birthday?"

"Didn't you hear what I said? She was getting into *his* car."

"So?"

"Mom..."

"I probably should keep my mouth shut."

"Probably."

"Right, probably. I'm not going to."

Fallon groaned.

"If you love Riley, you'd better be prepared to fight for her."

"Fight for her? Why should I have to fight for her?"

"Fallon, honestly. We all have to fight to keep our relationships secure."

Fallon sighed.

"You blame yourself for Olivia. You can say whatever you want; you do. Don't say a word right now, you listen to me. You didn't fight for her. Maybe that was because somewhere inside you knew it wasn't the right relationship for you."

Fallon closed her eyes.

"You didn't fight for Andi either."

"Mom, Andi..."

"I said, listen to me. Andi wouldn't have let you. I know that hurt you."

"Mom, please..."

"Fallon, someone needs to say this to you. It's safest if I do."

"Why? Because you're five-hundred miles away?"

"I'm not scared of you, Fallon."

Fallon chuckled.

"You don't have to say a word. It's written all over your face. You love Riley." She heard Fallon sigh.

"Riley's seeing Jerry."

"Yes, well seeing someone has a different meaning for most people than it does for you."

"What does that mean?"

"Do you really think that sleeping with every moderately attractive woman who passes through is going to make you forget Andi or fall out of love with Riley?"

"Is that what you think I'm doing?"

"Aren't you?"

"It was one night. Mom."

"I know you, Fallon. That's not what you want. Riley's been through a lot."

"And? Riley's straight."

"Oh? Told you that, did she?"

"No, but… Jesus, Mom she was married. She has a kid."

Ida had to shake her head to clear the clouds. "Olivia's married with kids."

"Thanks for reminding me. Olivia is a lesbian."

"Andi's married and has kids." There was no reply. "How do you know what Riley feels if you don't ask her?"

"Ask her? Are you crazy? I don't need to ruin that friendship."

"Well, traipsing off with coeds might just do that for you."

"Mom."

"I think you are underestimating Riley. You might remember that I've had almost forty years to decode your logic. She's had less than six months. Give it some time, Fallon. If you're so worried about Jerry Walker, do something about it."

"I don't want to lose her too."

"None of us want to lose, Fallon. We all wish every ending could be happy. Loving someone ensures that at some point, one of you or both you will have to say goodbye. If it's not life that causes that, it's death."

"Then what's the point?"

"Well, the thing about love is when the ending comes it's all you have left to hold onto. Endings come whether we let ourselves love or not. What you have left to hold onto is what matters."

"Memories? That seems hollow."

"Does it? It's not, Fallon. It's a lot more than memories. Loving someone changes you. It takes time to see that when you're hurting. It's a scary thing—loving someone, giving yourself over to it when you know it could lead you to pain one day. Running from it will hurt as much as following it ever could. Give yourself a chance, Fallon."

"You sound like Andi."

"Andi's a smart woman who happens to love you."

Fallon's eyes welled with tears. "I know."

"Enough to know it was time to let go. Don't make that for nothing."

Fallon took a deep breath. "I do."

"You do?"

"I love Riley."

"You don't say. It's not me who needs to know that."

"I don't think she's ready for that, Mom."

"Then give it the space it needs for now. Just don't give it too much space."

"Mom?"

"Yes?"

"Andi..."

"Fallon, you have to let Andi go now, not just for you, but because she needs you to. She's still a young woman, even if she doesn't think so. She deserves a chance to find out who she is."

Fallon was puzzled by her mother's comment. "Is she..."

"Let it go, Fallon. She'll come to you when she's ready. Give her time."

"I don't know how."

"You do. I haven't told you one thing that you didn't know. You just needed to hear someone say it."

Fallon chuckled. Maybe she did. "I guess I should say thanks."

"You can thank me by not butt dialing me to 'Oh, yes, Fallon' being screamed in my ear."

Fallon cringed. "Promise."

"Thank you. Say hello to Riley and Owen for me."

"I will. If you talk to Andi…"

"She knows, Fallon. Trust me; she knows."

"I'll talk to you soon."

"I certainly hope so."

Fallon disconnected the call. She was about to set down the phone when she noticed the voicemail. Riley's voice came over the line.

*"Hi. I just opened your gifts. Fallon, they're… They're amazing. I don't know how you knew. I didn't tell anyone. It's just… Today isn't an easy day for me. I was going to call you. Jerry called and offered to take me to dinner. I just needed to get out of the house. I never expected you to… I don't know what to say. You are…Well, I feel the same way about you. I don't want to think about not having you in my life. Call me when you get this. Okay. Dinner, tomorrow? I'd like to see you. I… I miss you. Call me."*

Fallon took a deep breath and looked at the time. *It's worth a try.*

"Fallon?" Riley answered her phone.

"Did I wake you up?"

"Not really, I was just lying here."

"I got your voicemail."

"I got your gifts."

"I hope you like them."

"Fallon… They're… I love them."

"I was calling to… I know, I've been kind of an ass the last few days."

"You have?" Riley teased.

"I'm sorry."

"You don't need to apologize. I know you've been hurting."

*Not for all the reasons you think.* "The thing is, I missed you too."

Riley smiled. "Is that so?"

"Yeah, it is."

"Me or Owen and all his new toys?"

Fallon answered honestly. "I miss both of you—and the toys."

"I can't believe it."

"So, um… Is that offer still good for dinner to… Well, later today?"

"It is."

"Great. I'll bring the wine."

"I'll make sure *Super Why* is in the DVD player."

"Who could refuse that offer?"

"Not you."

Fallon laughed. "I'll see you tomorrow."

"You will. Fallon?"

"Yeah?"

"What you wrote in that card… I… You'll never know how much that meant to me—all of it."

*I love you, Riley.* "I meant every word."

Riley closed her eyes. *I know you did.* "I'll see you around six?"

"I'll be there." Fallon set down her phone and closed her eyes. *I'll be there, Riley.*

# CHAPTER ONE

"Why are you pacing?" Carol asked. "It's just dinner at Riley's."

Fallon fidgeted with some glasses behind the bar.

"Would you stop? My God. What's going on with you? Are you feeling guilty about *Aubrey*?"

Fallon sighed.

"Fallon, you aren't with Riley."

"Wasn't it you who was reading me the riot act last night?"

"Well, yes, but that was because I knew you'd feel this way today."

"You're right; it's just dinner."

"What do you want it to be?" Carol asked.

Fallon sighed again.

"Fallon, you need to let her know how you feel."

"How? What am I supposed to do, Carol? You want me to walk into Riley's and say, 'I love you?' Is that it?"

"Pretty good start."

"I can't."

"Why not? Don't you?"

"Don't I what?"

"Love her."

Fallon nodded.

"I understand," Carol said. "I do. Riley's had a rough road. But Fallon, I think you might be missing something here."

"What's that?"

Carol smiled. "You don't see the way she looks at you."

*Actually, I do.*

"What is it?" Carol asked. "What aren't you saying?" She watched as Fallon took a deep breath and wiped the corner of her eye. "Andi," she guessed.

"I miss her."

"I know you do. I know she misses you too."

"How can I think about telling Riley how I feel when I feel so… When I…"

"Feel guilty?"

"I hurt Andi."

"Fallon, Andi loves you. Everyone knows that. She also wants you to be happy."

"I know."

"I don't think anything would hurt Andi more than seeing you hurt," Carol offered.

"Not helping here," Fallon said.

"Well, if it matters at all; I think you and Andi will be fine. You both need a little time."

"She's barely spoken to me. I feel like I lost my best friend."

"What part of *she loves you* don't you understand? She loves Riley too, you know."

"Yeah, I know."

"Give her time."

"You sound like my mom."

"Yeah, well, you should listen to Ida once in a while."

"Why? Do you?"

Carol winked. "All the time."

Fallon chuckled.

"Go to dinner. You don't need to profess your undying love," Carol said. "There are other ways to let her know."

"I'm not hitting on Riley."

"That's not what I meant. Stop overthinking it. If you're not ready to tell her how you feel, then the only thing you can do is be yourself. Don't censor your feelings with her, Fallon."

Fallon shook her head. *Easier said than done.*

Riley opened the front door and instantly wrapped Fallon in a hug. When Fallon tried to pull away, Riley hung on.

"Are you okay?" Fallon asked.

Riley couldn't respond. She wasn't sure what was driving her to hold onto Fallon, all she did know was that she didn't want to let go.

"Riley," Fallon whispered. She let herself submit to the embrace and closed her eyes. Her heart thrummed as she breathed Riley in. If she had any doubt that she was in love with Riley Main, feeling Riley in her arms banished it. She could hold Riley forever. *Oh, God.* "I could." The words fell unconsciously from Fallon's lips.

Riley held on. "What could you do?" Her voice hovered just above a whisper.

Fallon inhaled the scent of Riley's hair. The temptation to feel Riley, to allow her hands to traverse the expanse of Riley's back tenderly overwhelmed her. She forced herself to step back. Riley wasn't ready for that. She couldn't explain how she knew that; she just knew it. "Happy Birthday—a day late," Fallon managed.

"I'm glad you're here," Riley said.

"Me too."

"Well, come in." Riley took Fallon's hand and led her inside. "I know someone who will be happy to see you."

Fallon laughed when Owen screamed her name and ran across the room.

"I told you," Riley said. "I swear the only words I've heard for hours are *when* and *now.*"

Fallon picked up Owen and put him on her back. "When?"

"Yeah. When is Fallon coming? Now? Mommy, when? Mommy, now?"

Fallon laughed. She walked to the sofa and gently dropped down with Owen clinging to her. "Did you miss me?"

Owen giggled. "Fawon, I got da puzzle." He pointed to a wooden puzzle on the floor.

"Ah, I remember those. Did you want me to help you?"

He nodded. "It's a dinosaur."

Fallon looked up at Riley.

"You two complete the dinosaur, I'll see if I can't conquer dinner," Riley said. She winked at Fallon and headed for the kitchen.

Fallon dropped to the floor with Owen. "A dinosaur, huh?"

Owen smiled. "Fawon?"

"Yeah, buddy."

"You stay?"

Fallon was puzzled. "I'm staying for dinner."

Owen shook his head.

"What do you mean, buddy?"

"You stay."

Fallon forced herself not to sigh. She'd been through this with Olivia's daughter, Emily. In Emily's case, since she could talk she had begged Fallon to let her stay at Fallon's house. Emily was seven, and she still cried for hours every time she had to leave Whiskey Springs with her mother. It was one of the reasons that Fallon tended to keep a distance from Olivia's family. She'd visited them a few times in Virginia. Each time, Emily had fallen into an emotional fit when it came time for Fallon to leave. Fallon noted the pain in Olivia's wife's eyes each time it happened. Barb had always accepted the friendship that remained between Olivia and Fallon. Olivia sometimes seemed to lose sight of the fact that her relationship with Fallon had changed. Emily's attachment to Fallon added a layer to a situation that could be emotionally complicated.

"Well," Fallon began as she pointed to the place Owen should set the puzzle piece in his hand. "I might not always stay, buddy."

*Although, I wish I could.* "I'm always thinking about you and your mom, though."

Riley stepped into the doorway just in time to hear Fallon's words. *Fallon.* She held her breath. Fallon's words alone made her heart beat faster. The way Fallon's hand brushed across Owen's head struck Riley with a realization she'd never considered. Could Fallon's feelings for her have changed? She released her breath slowly, forgetting the reason she'd emerged from the kitchen in the first place, and made her way back to the safety of the other room. She gripped the counter and closed her eyes. *Oh, God. What is happening? Riley, calm down. Why are you freaking out? Calm down. You need to get a grip.* Riley took another deep breath. *Maybe you're freaking out because you want her feelings to have changed.* "Oh, God."

"Hey," Fallon peered into the kitchen.

Riley opened her eyes and looked at Fallon.

Fallon's heart plummeted. "Riley? Hey, what's wrong?"

*Nothing. Everything. Oh, God, I wish you would just hold me.*

Fallon had no idea what compelled her to step forward. For the second time in twenty-minutes, Riley was in her arms. This time, Riley's tears escaped. "Whatever it is, it's okay," Fallon promised. "Tell me what I can do."

Riley held on. Her head was spinning, or was it her heart? "Fallon..."

"I'm right here."

Riley gathered herself and pulled away slowly. She'd experienced a million emotions the day before. The memories of her wedding, the gravity of the loss of her husband, perhaps the raw feelings of the prior day were driving what she thought was an irrational emotional outburst. "Yesterday was hard," she told Fallon.

Fallon listened.

"It's not just my birthday. It's... It was my wedding anniversary too."

*Shit. Way to go, Fallon.* Andi had cautioned Fallon that when Riley was ready to explain why it seemed she wanted to avoid celebrating her birthday, she would. Fallon wanted to do something special. Riley deserved it. Now, she wondered if her gifts might have conjured pain for her friend. "I'm sorry, Riley. I didn't mean to bring up sad..."

Riley pressed two fingers to Fallon's lips. "Stop. You... Fallon, your card? It was the one thing that made the day happy."

Fallon was doubtful.

Riley smiled. Her hand cupped Fallon's cheek and Fallon's eyes closed. "Fallon," Riley called. "Look at me."

Fallon opened her eyes reluctantly.

"I don't know what's happening here," Riley confessed.

"Riley, I..."

"I don't," Riley repeated. "But I think we both know something is happening between us." Her thumb caressed Fallon's cheek, and Fallon leaned into the touch. "Let's not pretend there's nothing going on," Riley requested.

"Riley, I don't want you to think that I'm trying to..."

"I think that I feel something right now that I didn't see coming," Riley said. "Or maybe I did."

The last thing that Fallon had expected when she arrived on Riley's doorstep was any conversation about shared feelings. She swallowed hard, unsure of what to say. I love you would be far too much too soon. Riley's eyes seemed to implore her for some reassurance. She smiled. "Let's have dinner," Fallon suggested.

Riley sighed with embarrassment and looked at her feet.

"No." Fallon lifted Riley's chin. "No. Riley, listen, I feel it too. You said it yourself; yesterday was an emotional day for you." She took a deep breath. "It was for me too."

"Why? Did something happen?" Riley asked.

"I saw you leave with Jerry." *There, I said it.*

Riley was confused.

"Shit," Fallon muttered.

"You thought I was interested in Jerry," Riley surmised.

"Are you?"

"No."

Fallon sighed regretfully.

"Fallon? What is it?"

"I... Maybe we should talk about this after dinner."

Riley raised her brow. "No, I don't think so. I think this conversation is overdue."

"Maybe, but Owen is..."

"Owen is playing in the other room. Dinner won't be ready for another forty minutes."

"Can we at least sit?" Fallon requested.

"Do I need to sit?"

"I don't know. I think I do."

Riley chuckled and took a seat at the kitchen table. Fallon began to twist one hand with the other and Riley reached over to still her movements. "What has you so nervous? Is it me?"

"Not the way you think," Fallon replied. The warmth of Riley's hand in hers comforted her. "I... Riley, I..."

"It's just me, Fallon."

Fallon shook her head. "I meant everything I said in that card. I don't want to think about my life without you being part of it."

"That's not going to happen."

"Well, when I found out it was your birthday, I was worried. I asked Andi if you'd said anything. She thought I should... Well, she told me to do what I thought was best."

"And, you bought the present."

"I sort of planned to surprise you."

"Believe me; you did."

"Not by leaving the gifts on the porch."

Riley groaned. "That's how you saw me leave with Jerry."

Fallon nodded.

"Shit. Fallon, I'm sorry."

"No, I am."

"For what?" Riley asked.

Fallon was both embarrassed and ashamed. "I kind of… Well, I went to Murphy's after I left the presents on the porch."

Riley raised a brow to implore Fallon to continue.

Fallon couldn't meet Riley's eyes. *You idiot.*

A smile graced Riley's lips, and she squeezed Fallon's hand. "It's okay, you know? You haven't had the easiest time lately," she observed. "I know you miss Andi."

Fallon looked up. She would never be able to lie to Riley. "I do."

"I know."

"That doesn't mean that I don't feel something…" Fallon's thoughts trailed off.

"I know that too." Riley did know that Fallon's feelings for her ran deeper than friendship. She hadn't wanted to admit it. She realized now that was because Fallon touched her in a way she'd feared no one ever would again. Riley wasn't certain she was ready for what that might mean for either of them. She held Fallon's hand tenderly and spoke softly. "I don't want to know," she admitted. "About who she was. You don't owe me an explanation. I don't have any right to be hurt if you want to be with someone."

Fallon nodded.

"But I'd be lying if I said it doesn't—hurt a little."

"I'm sorry."

"No. I am. Fallon, I don't know what any of this means."

"What about Jerry?"

Riley nearly laughed. The fear in Fallon's eyes stopped her. "I'm not into kissing cardboard."

Fallon smirked.

*Oh, Fallon, you are priceless.* "Can I ask you something?"

"You can ask me anything."

"Andi…"

"I love Andi," Fallon said. "Part of me fell in love with her." *That's the truth.*

Riley's smile failed to reach her eyes.

"I'm not sure what I should say right now."

"Whatever you feel you need to."

*That's exactly what Andi and Mom would say.* "I care about you, you and Owen."

"I know that."

"I don't want to lose you, Riley. I heard you earlier. I don't know what any of this means either. I know what I'd like it to mean."

"What is that?"

"I think that's a discussion for another time. In the meantime, I don't have the desire to see anyone or to..."

"Sleep with anyone?"

"I don't want to be with anyone else; that much I can tell you. Last night? Riley, I felt sick when I got into my truck. And, then my mother called."

"Ida called?"

"Yeah. I guess I dialed her somehow."

"Oh, no."

"Afraid so."

Riley laughed.

"It's not funny."

"It's kind of funny," Riley said.

*Maybe it is.* "Anyway, she set me straight—well, not straight but..."

"I think I catch the drift."

Fallon suddenly faltered. She was used to expressing her feelings with actions, not discussing them. "Tell me what to say," Fallon requested.

"That you'll be patient with me," Riley replied. "Fallon, I feel something I didn't expect to feel..."

"For a woman."

"No. At all, for anyone. I just... I need..."

Fallon gently squeezed the hands still holding hers. "I'll be here."

"Fawon!" Owen's voice boomed through the house.

Riley grinned.

"Fawon!" Owen stomped into the kitchen.

Fallon looked down and forced herself not to laugh at the look of consternation on Owen's face.

"Fawon, I need you."

"You need me?"

"One don't fit."

"You have a piece of the puzzle that doesn't fit?"

Owen nodded and tugged lightly on Fallon's arm. "I need you."

"Owen, what do you say when you want something?" Riley asked.

Owen frowned. Riley raised her brow. He huffed. "Pwease."

Riley smiled. "Now, ask Fallon nicely if she can help you."

Owen pursed his lips and huffed again. "Pwease, Fawon. I need you."

Fallon chuckled. "I'll be right there, okay?"

Owen challenged her with his eyes. She had told him she was going to check on his mommy and would be back in a minute. Owen might not have been able to tell time; he knew a minute was short, and Fallon had been gone a long time. At least, it was a long time in three-year-old terms.

"I promise," Fallon said. "I'll be right behind you."

Owen stared hard at her.

Fallon laughed. "I promise, Owen."

With a deep sigh, Owen left the room.

"He loves you," Riley said.

"I love him too." She turned her attention to Riley. *And, I love you.*

Riley froze. It was strange; the way an ache in your chest could become the most wonderful sensation in life. Falling in love conjured a yearning so powerful it could stop a person's heart from beating for a moment; only to swiftly send it pounding forcefully in the next. As Fallon's eyes held Riley's, Riley felt that familiar ache, the rare longing that existed even in the presence of another person. When did it begin? Was there a moment that she had missed? How could love descend on her without any warning? She struggled to breathe, to summon her voice, to peel her gaze from Fallon's. She had so many questions, and none of them seemed to matter at the moment. Tomorrow, they would surface. Riley knew that. She wasn't prepared to give herself away—not yet. Looking at Fallon, she wondered if she would be given any choice. She forced herself to breathe.

Riley's inner battle was evident to Fallon. She wasn't sure what drove Riley's hesitation. Loss changed a person; that much Fallon did know. There were a million reasons that Fallon should stop what was happening between them in its tracks. She guessed Riley had a million more reasons why venturing past friendship would be a bad idea. Aside from the fact that as far as Fallon knew, Riley was attracted to men, Riley would inevitably be concerned about the implications of a relationship with Fallon for Owen, and for her future. There was also the Andi factor. Fallon didn't require any conversation or confession from Riley to know that Andi was on both their minds. Other than Fallon, Andi was Riley's best friend. Andi and Riley shared an entirely different connection. Andi was the older sister, the mother figure in Riley's life. The bond they shared ran deep. Riley would be worried about Andi. She might feel it was a betrayal to allow herself a chance with Fallon. Fallon understood. She had the benefit of knowing that Andi hoped they might come together. Love was full of constant contradictions. There were so many bridges they needed to cross. All Fallon wanted to do was pull Riley into her arms and kiss her; hold onto her and tell Riley what she felt. If she hoped to build something with Riley—a life with Riley, she would need to wade into the water cautiously.

Fallon offered Riley a smile. "I'd better get back to puzzle duty." She pushed out her chair and stood to leave. Riley grabbed her arm. Fallon smiled again. *You are so beautiful, Riley, and so scared.* "Stop worrying," Fallon said. "I'm not going anywhere."

Riley nodded. Fallon could put her at ease unlike anyone she'd ever known. Her eyes brightened. "I hope you still say that after you eat dinner."

Fallon laughed. She leaned in to place a kiss on Riley's cheek. Instead, Riley's lips found hers. The kiss was soft and sweet, almost chaste—almost. Fallon needed to find her feet again. "We can always order pizza." She winked and began to head off to find Owen.

Riley rolled her eyes and threw a kitchen towel at Fallon's back.

Fallon turned with an impish grin. "Remember, Riley, turnabout is..."

Riley's laughter filled the room before Fallon could finish. *I can only imagine.*

"No!" Owen protested.

Riley steadied her breathing and her temper. She had heard of the terrible twos. She wondered what this new stage Owen had wandered into was called; the tyrannical threes? "Yes," she replied evenly. "It's bedtime."

Owen looked at her and stomped his foot.

"Owen," she warned him gently.

"Fawon weaves."

"You'll see Fallon again soon," Riley promised.

Owen shook his head.

"Owen," Riley began again firmly. "You're overtired."

He huffed.

"Hey," Fallon decided to try. "I promise; I will see you soon, buddy."

"Tomorrow?"

Fallon sighed. She wasn't sure that she would see Owen the next day. She had to work, and she was trying to gauge whether a little space from Riley would be best or if that would increase Riley's fears. The last thing she intended to do was make Owen a promise she wasn't positive she could keep.

"Owen," Riley squatted to her son's height. "What if we invite Fallon to go with us to the pond on Saturday?"

Owen smiled.

"Okay. That's two more sleeps."

"Two?" He asked.

"Two," Riley said. "If Fallon has the time."

"Well..." Fallon pretended to consider the request. "That depends?"

"Oh?" Riley asked.

"Do we get to go fishing?" Fallon asked.

"You two can fish," Riley said. "I don't do worms."

Fallon rolled her eyes. "Owen? What about you?"

"I wuv wums." Owen grinned excitedly.

"Okay, so... maybe wine for Mommy and worms for me and you?"

"Yeah!"

Riley shook her head. "All right, you wormy lovers."

"Wormy lovers?" Fallon whispered in Riley's ear.

Riley giggled. *That didn't come out right at all.* "Off to bed," she instructed Owen. "Say goodnight to Fallon."

"Night, Fawon." Owen threw his hands around Fallon's neck and placed a wet kiss on her cheek.

"Night, buddy."

"I'll be right back," Riley said.

"Wine?" Fallon asked.

"You know where it is," Riley replied.

Fallon watched Riley lead Owen away. *Oh, boy, Fallon. You need to get a grip.* She moved to open a bottle of white wine and pour two glasses. Dinner had been a lively affair. It always was when Owen was present. His vocabulary seemed to increase by the day. Each time he told an animated story, fumbling with pronunciations, Riley gently correcting him, Fallon fell in love with the pair all over again. There would be no running away this time, not from Riley and not from the feelings that Fallon feared might consume her. The memory of Riley's lips touching hers forced her eyelids to flutter and close. It was a sweet kiss, not one meant to convey passion, yet it stoked a fire in Fallon unlike any she'd ever experienced.

Two hands on her hips startled her. Fallon's heart sped up immediately. *Riley, what are you doing?* Her hand trembled when Riley directed her to turn.

Riley took Fallon's hand, which held the bottle of wine and guided it to the counter. Fallon slowly turned to face her. Riley's palm covered Fallon's cheek. "So that there is no question about whether what you are pouring is the reason," she said. Her hand guided Fallon's lips to hers.

Fallon's head spun wildly. Riley's lips met hers tentatively, a quiet admission passing between them.

Riley smiled when she pulled back. Fallon's eyes were still closed, and her teeth had a slight grip on her bottom lip. "Just so there's no mistake," she repeated.

"Riley," Fallon opened her eyes.

"I don't know where this is leading us," Riley said. "I won't pretend I don't feel something." Fallon sighed. "I… Riley…"

"Come on. Let's go sit in the other room."

"And talk?" Fallon asked.

Riley grinned. There were many things she would prefer to engage in, and none involved conversation. A gentle kiss had stirred a potent longing to be closer to Fallon. What had Andi said about sparks igniting? Denying that she was attracted to Fallon was pointless. The flutter she felt in her stomach each time Fallon was close had traveled to points south. *I guess I'm not broken after all.* She would never risk her friendship with Fallon nor any chance they might have at becoming more to each other for the indulgence of a quick romp. The feeling of attraction was less surprising to Riley than the depth of emotion she felt for Fallon; emotion she was not ready to put a name to. And, there was Andi. Riley couldn't think about moving toward an intimate relationship with Fallon until she talked to Andi; not for Andi's permission. Riley knew that as much as it would hurt Andi, she would be supportive and loving when they spoke. That didn't change the fact that Riley felt a degree of guilt. She loved Andi as much as she'd loved anyone in her life. Maybe they had been sisters once upon a time. Maybe Andi had been her mother in another life. Riley couldn't explain it, and explanations mattered little to her. She valued Andi Maguire as a mentor and a friend. The idea that her happiness might come at the expense of someone she loved twisted Riley's heart. Nonetheless, she couldn't walk away from Fallon, not even if part of her wished she could. It would be safer for everyone if she maintained a platonic relationship with Fallon; safer was not fulfilling. Riley knew that. Risking her heart again—that would take courage and time. There were demons to banish, and not just hers. Fallon still had her share of ghosts to confront.

Riley handed Fallon one of the glasses of wine, retrieved the other for herself, and took Fallon's hand. "I hope you might let me kiss you again," she admitted.

Fallon followed Riley the short distance to the living room. "Riley," she began as she took a seat on the sofa.

"Yes?"

"I know this is probably strange for you, maybe kind of unsettling or scary…"

"Fallon, are you referring to the fact that you're a lesbian again?"

"Well, yeah… I mean, it has to be…"

"You wouldn't be my first."

Fallon was stunned.

Riley grinned. "I did have a life before Robert."

"I… I guess I never thought about it."

"Why would you? That's not a part of our lives we've ever shared in any detail, and to be honest; I'd prefer we didn't," Riley said. "I don't want you to think that my… That me needing to take some time here is about the fact that you're a woman. That's not it."

Fallon nodded.

"It's been a long time, Fallon. I'm not talking about sex. And, that's been longer than I sometimes find imaginable." "I understand."

"You're my best friend—you and Andi. I don't want to lose either of you."

"I know. I don't want that either."

"So, please? Just be patient with me. I can't pretend that I don't have feelings for you. I do. I think, if I'm honest, I've felt something for a while. I don't know what to do with that yet. Maybe it shouldn't scare me so much; it does."

Fallon smiled. Riley's honesty and candor were two of the reasons she commanded Fallon's heart. What was that thing she'd always heard—slow and steady wins the race? Fallon had never been particularly adept at slow and steady. She tended toward hot and heavy, in sex and in love. Riley required something new from Fallon. Looking at Riley, one thing was clear; she would give anything to Riley that Riley asked for. For the first time, Fallon wondered if she'd ever been in love before. She loved Olivia. There was no way to deny that she loved Andi—deeply. But her emotions for Riley fell into a different realm altogether. They lacked selfishness. All she desired was to give to Riley.

"Fallon? Are you okay?" Riley asked.

"I'm good," Fallon said. "I told you; I'll be here, Riley. I do have one request."

"What's that?"

"That kiss?"

Riley smiled. "What are you waiting for?"

Fallon took Riley's face in her hands. Her thumbs stroked Riley's cheeks as she slowly brought their lips together. Tenderly,

Fallon coaxed Riley's lips to part. The connection that swelled between them astounded her. *I love her. Riley, I love you.* Maybe she couldn't speak the words. She could pour them into her kiss.

Riley held onto Fallon as their kiss deepened. Passion lay in wait under the surface of Fallon's searching. Riley met it with a silent promise. This was a beginning. When Fallon tried to pull away, Riley refused to relinquish her hold and softly brushed her tongue against Fallon's again. Fallon sighed. Riley could feel the beating of Fallon's heart against her. It told her everything she needed to know. Fallon loved her. Fallon was in love with her. That implored Riley to pull back. She needed to keep her hands on Fallon's arms before they began to search Fallon's body. She needed to stop herself from falling completely into Fallon's grip. It would be easy to let her hormones run away with her head. But then, it wasn't hormones driving her desire. It was something far more powerful. Pulling back from Fallon's kiss was the hardest thing Riley had ever done. She'd battled sadness and grief. As her lips left Fallon's, Riley felt a sense of loss that made her tremble.

"Are you okay?" Fallon asked.

"Yes," Riley promised. Insecurity reflected in Fallon's darkened blue irises. Riley took Fallon's hand and held it. "You need to trust me, Fallon."

"I do."

"You do to a point. I can't make you any promises right now except that I won't run away."

"I told you; I'll be here."

*I know you will be.* "How about we drink that wine and watch a movie? Not *Super Why,*" Riley said.

Fallon laughed. Riley always knew how to ease her fears and tension. They needed to find their way back to being Fallon and Riley, even if that dynamic had shifted. "I like *Super Why.*"

"Why? What's super about it?"

"How about *Friends*?"

Riley's lips curled into a devious smile. "How about Freddy instead?"

"Freddy?"

"Krueger."

"You're sick. You know that; don't you?"

Riley shrugged.

"Horror?" Fallon hated horror movies. She would never admit it to anyone, but she always slept with the light on after watching one.

Riley chuckled. Fallon was transparent. "Don't worry," she said. "I'll hold you if you get scared."

Fallon swallowed hard. Maybe horror wasn't such a bad choice after all.

# CHAPTER TWO

Andi sat calmly as Dave paced the living room frantically. The news that she and Jake were divorcing had been received with mixed reactions. Jacob sat across from his mother in a chair, silently offering his support from a distance. Dave's response was to scream at his parents. How could they do this? Why now? What did they mean that they would be living in different places? Andi had entered the conversation hopeful but without expectation. Historically, Jacob was the child who had shown his emotions outwardly. Dave had always worked to maintain control of his feelings. Apparently, the notion of his parents splitting was the thing that defied his cool exterior.

"Mom?" Dave looked at Andi. "Why?"

"David," Andi began again. "Your father and I are moving in different directions. You and your brother have your lives now. We need to live ours too."

"So, what? Because we are away, you get to just say, 'Fuck it?' That's great, Mom."

Andi stilled her temper. "This isn't easy for your father or for me."

"Right," he said.

"Dave," Jacob tried to calm his brother.

"What? You're okay with this?" Dave shot.

Jacob looked back and forth between his parents. "No," he said. "But it isn't about me or you."

Dave shook his head. "This is fucking bullshit, Mom."

"David," Jake Maguire finally spoke up. "That's enough. Don't speak to your mother that way."

"Oh? Why not? Isn't this because of her?"

Andi held her breath.

"Right?" Dave asked. "I'm right. You and Fallon, right? You were cool with that, Dad?"

"That's enough!" Jake Maguire's voice boomed.

Andi felt sick. How on earth did Dave find out about Fallon? Did Jacob know too? She was surprised to feel her husband's hand take hers. She was even more astounded by the sound of his voice as he addressed their children.

"I said, that's enough. You have no right to make any accusations against your mother or me, David. You're not a little boy any longer. You're in college for God's sake. Act like a man."

"What the hell does that mean?" Dave fought back.

"It means that adults have adult relationships, David. That's what it means. Your mother and I have been together a long time. A lot of things happened in that time. Some of them were great, and some of them not so great. I would imagine most of the not so great things could be blamed on me."

"Jake," Andi whispered.

Jake squeezed Andi's hand and continued. "You can be as angry as you like," he said. "Be angry with both of us. Your mother is right; you both have lives to lead. We do too. The fact that we won't be living together doesn't mean we're not your parents. It sure as hell doesn't give you permission to talk to us the way you are. You may not like it; what happens in our marriage is between us," he said.

Dave's caustic laugh sent a shiver up Andi's spine. "Oh, so what? You fucking around turned Mom into a dyke?"

"That's it!" Jake started to jump up. Andi pulled him back onto the sofa.

With a deep breath, Andi addressed her children. "I have no idea how you found out about Fallon and me. I will tell you this; Fallon is a remarkable woman, and she happens to be someone I care deeply for. Your father and I divorcing is not about Fallon. It's about me and your father. As for your accusation; I don't owe you any explanation about my sexuality or my sex life. You're not ten, David. I'm fully aware of your exploits as well. You can hate me all you want. You can call me any name you like. Whether or not you are happy with your reality, I'm still your mother. I love you, but I won't tolerate your vitriol."

"Whatever. You're both fucked up." Dave shook his head and walked out of the room.

Andi closed her eyes and sighed. *Shit.*

"I'm sorry," Jake said sincerely.

"It's not your fault."

"I'm not sure I'd say that. I'll talk to him."

"No." Jacob looked at his parents. "Let me talk to him."

"Jacob," Andi began. Her tears finally began to surface.

"Mom, don't cry," Jacob said. He took a deep breath. "It's his issue, not yours."

"What about you?" Andi asked.

Jacob smiled. "I wish you weren't splitting up," he admitted. "But I understand. If you mean what do I think about what Dave said to you; I think that was an asshole move."

Andi chuckled.

"Fallon," he started to ask.

"Fallon and I aren't together," Andi said.

Jacob looked at his father and then back to his mother. "I'll talk to Dave." He offered them both a smile and went in search of his brother.

"Well, that went well," Andi said.

Jake looked at his wife sympathetically. "He'll come around."

Andi wasn't so sure. "Maybe."

"Are you afraid that if you end up with a woman, he'll disown you?"

"Honestly, the thought of ending up with anyone is the furthest thing from my mind."

"He'll come around, Andi."

"I hope so."

"He will." Jake pulled Andi into his arms. "I love you; you know?"

"I know you do. I love you too. This is what I need."

"I know it is. Are you going to be okay?"

"Yeah. Can I ask you for something?"

"Anything."

"Just hold me for a little while," Andi requested.

Jake leaned back on the sofa with Andi in his arms. "I'm sorry, Andi—for everything."

"No." Andi pulled back and smiled at him through watery eyes. "I'm not. We had a good run, Jake. We have great kids—mouthy, but great."

Jake chuckled.

"I don't have any regrets. I don't want you to have any either." She fell back into his embrace.

"Mouthy," he chuckled again. "Must get that from you."

Andi laughed. "Probably so."

"What on earth are you doing?" Riley asked.

"Watering the grass," Fallon explained.

"Why?"

Fallon grinned. "So, the worms come out."

Riley shuddered.

"Why don't you go sit on the porch," Fallon suggested. "Me and Owen can handle worm duty without you." Fallon's eyes brightened. "Pay dirt!" She crouched down and picked up a plump earthworm.

Owen squealed with delight. "Wums! Mommy, wook!"

"I see it."

Fallon laughed at Riley's cringe. "Go on the porch and relax. This won't take long. We'll find a few and then I'll make dinner."

"Dinner?" Riley questioned.

"Yeah? I told you I bought steaks for the grill. Well, I got Owen a hot dog."

"Grilling as in touching my food?" Riley questioned.

"Well, yeah. You usually have to touch it to put in on the grill."

"After you touched *that*?"

Fallon looked at the worm dangling from her fingers. She shrugged.

"No," Riley said. "I'll make dinner. You two play in the dirt." She shuddered again and walked away.

Owen looked at Fallon curiously.

"I don't know, buddy. I don't think Mommy likes our worms."

Owen frowned for a second and returned to the hunt. "Fawon! Wum!"

Riley looked over her shoulder. *Gross.*

Riley couldn't stop herself from laughing at the pair of worm hunters in the yard. Fallon had called early in the morning and asked Riley if it would be pushing things to ask her over for dinner. Riley's head was screaming for her to slow things down a pace. She seemed to lack the willpower. She'd fallen asleep against Fallon during a movie the night before. It wasn't the first time she'd drifted off and found her head on Fallon's shoulder. Things had changed. Her heart lurched in her chest when she kissed Fallon goodbye at her front door. Two sleeps were two too many.

"Hey," she called out into the yard.

Two heads turned in unison.

"I hope you have enough bait for tomorrow. Dinner's ready."

"Think we're done for the night, buddy," Fallon said. "Put that last guy in the container and we'll go wash up."

Owen dropped the worm in his fingers into the container of dirt that Fallon had made for their bait. He waved to the worm as she secured the cover.

Fallon chuckled. "Come on." She held out her hand and led Owen through the yard to the deck.

Riley shook her head. "You two look like you could use a bath."

Fallon wiggled her muddy fingers at Riley. "It's just dirt." She moved a pace closer.

"Get away from me!" Riley laughed. "It's worm dirt."

Fallon winked. Owen laughed so hard he fell on his butt.

"I don't believe it. Are you laughing at me?" Riley teased her son.

Owen pointed at his mother. "Mommy, you silwy."

"I'm silly?" Riley shook her head again. "And, you're filthy."

Fallon scooped up Owen. "Let's go, little man. I don't think Mommy's going to feed us until we wash our hands." She carried a giggling Owen into the house.

"Two of a kind," Riley muttered.

"Fawon?"

"Yeah, buddy?"

"We go fishing?"

"Tomorrow, Owen," Fallon said. "We'll see if we can catch a fish."

Owen smiled and turned back to the video on the television.

A knock at the door took Fallon by surprise. She made her way to the door curiously. *Who could that be?* She opened the door and her heart stopped.

Riley had disappeared into the kitchen to get Owen some juice. She turned the corner and saw Fallon standing at the door looking at a handsome young man who resembled Andi considerably. *Jacob.*

"Jacob?" Fallon was confused.

"Hi."

"Come in," Fallon offered.

Jacob looked over Fallon's shoulder and caught a glimpse of Riley handing Owen his juice. "I didn't mean to disturb you."

"You can come here anytime. You know that," Fallon said. "What's wrong? Is your mom…"

"Mom's okay," he said. "She's…. Maybe I should come back."

Fallon looked over her shoulder. Riley's smile gave her instant permission to do what she needed to do. "How about we sit on the deck for a few minutes? Do you want anything? A drink or…"

"No. Fallon, seriously, I didn't know you had company."

Fallon led Jacob outside and around the porch to the deck at the side of her home. "Riley will understand."

"Riley? Mom's friend, Riley?"

"Your mom and Riley are pretty close." Fallon directed Jacob to sit. "What's up?"

"Have you talked to Mom?"

"Not really," Fallon admitted. "It's just… Your mom…"

"You guys split up."

Fallon's face flushed. *Jacob knows?* "Jacob, I…"

"It's cool. I already know."

Fallon groaned. "What did your mom tell you?"

"Only that she cares about you which I already know."

Fallon nodded. "We… Well, let's just say that we're back to being friends—just friends."

"I'm probably out of line here."

Fallon was growing increasingly worried.

"I think Mom could use your friendship right now."

"What's going on?"

Jacob sighed. "She and Dad are getting divorced."

Fallon was stunned into silence.

"You're surprised?"

*That's an understatement. Andi, how could you not tell me?* "You could say that."

"Anyway, I think she's okay. Dad too. Sad, but okay. The thing is—Dave, he sort of blew up."

"Blew up?"

"Yeah, and called her a dyke."

Fallon's heart lurched in her chest. *Shit.*

"I don't know what happened between you and mom."

"Jacob, I love your mom. She's my best friend."

"But you're not in love with her."

"No."

He nodded.

"Look, I don't want to betray her trust," Fallon said. "Or yours. She asked me for some space. I'm trying to give her that."

"Can I ask you something?"

"Sure."

"Did you end it, or did she?"

Fallon sighed. She'd been riding a high since last night. Loving Riley, even if their journey was at its beginning felt amazing. It had been Andi that opened Fallon's heart again. She missed Andi; missed her laughter and her company. She would always want Andi in her life. And, part of her was still reeling from Andi's decision to end their affair. The news that Andi's marriage was ending shocked her. Fallon also loved Jacob. She felt torn. Part of her wanted to sit him down and share everything. She respected Andi. That was Andi's place, not hers.

"Jacob," Fallon began cautiously. "I think you should talk to your mom about this."

"I'm asking you. What happened?"

"I told you; I love your mom." Fallon looked at Jacob and tried to pick her heart up off the floor. "Your mom and I weren't meant to be together forever. I think she'll tell you the same thing."

"But you love her? You know, that doesn't make sense."

"It does. Talk to your mom."

Jacob shook his head. "I don't know what to say." He looked back at Fallon. "I think she could use to hear from you."

*You have no idea how much I want to talk to her.* "I'm trying to respect what she asked me for."

"Please?"

*Shit.* "I'll give her a call."

"Thanks."

"Jacob? Is everything else okay?"

Jacob shifted in his seat.

"Jacob?"

"I don't know how to tell them."

"Tell who?"

"Mom and my dad."

"Tell them what?" Fallon asked.

Jacob took a big breath and let it out slowly. "I'm gay, Fallon."

Fallon smiled. She'd had her suspicions. While she would never pretend to be able to speak for Andi, much less Jake Maguire, Fallon was confident that both would accept Jacob's news with grace and encouragement. Andi would. Fallon had no doubt about that. "Your mom loves you."

"I know, but I think she expects me to get married and have kids. You know, all that stuff."

"Who says you can't have all that stuff?" Fallon asked.

Jacob shrugged. "It's just… The way Dave reacted when Mom and Dad told us they were splitting up—I don't know if I should tell them now."

Fallon was reminded why she had always been drawn to Jacob. He reminded her so much of Andi right now that it took her breath away. Andi was generous and sweet. She'd give a stranger the shirt off her back when it was all she had left to wear. She cared deeply for people, particularly the people closest to her. And, there was no one on earth that Andi Maguire loved more than her two sons; of that, Fallon needed no convincing.

Jacob continued. "I thought I would tell them when I got home this summer; you know? I didn't see this coming."

"And, you think it might be too much for them to handle?"

"Maybe."

"Is that because of you or because you know about your mom and me?" Fallon wanted to know.

"Both."

"Listen, I can't tell you what to do, Jacob. I can tell you that I'm as sure as I can be that your mom will be fine with that information. She's not a judgmental person."

"And, my dad?"

"I don't know," Fallon admitted. "Your dad's an okay guy."

"Not exactly a ringing endorsement." Jacob chuckled.

"Hey, I don't dislike your dad, Jacob. I just want your mom to be happy."

Jacob nodded sadly. "Is she?"

"What?"

"Mom—is she a lesbian?"

Fallon's stomach flipped several times. "I don't know that answer."

"Come on."

"I don't, Jacob. I don't even know how you found out about us."

"It wasn't hard to put together."

"If you say so." Fallon scratched her brow. "Your mom loves your dad."

"She loves you."

*I know.* "In her way, she does."

"So, what does that mean?" Jacob asked.

"I know you want me to give you all the answers," Fallon said. "I don't have them to give you. You need to talk to your mom. Just talk to her, Jacob. Your mom is one of the most compassionate and understanding people I've ever known."

"I know."

"So, talk to her."

He nodded. "Will you? Will you check on her?"

Fallon smiled. "I promise."

Jacob glanced toward the house. "So? Riley and you..."

"I don't know yet," Fallon said honestly.

"Do you love her?"

"Riley?"

Jacob nodded.

*No sense in lying.* "Yeah. I do."

He nodded again. "I'm sorry if I dumped everything on you."

"Jacob, you can come to me anytime about anything."

He shook his head.

"Hey." Fallon took hold of Jacob's arm. "Nothing will change that."

"Thanks," he muttered.

"Don't worry too much about your mom. She's smarter and tougher than you realize."

"I hope so," he said.

"Hey, why don't you come inside for a while and meet Riley. She's heard a lot about you."

"Thanks. Maybe another time."

Fallon detected a note of sadness in his voice. *I'm sorry, Jacob. I really am sorry.* "Call me if you need anything."

He offered her a weak smile and a wave.

*Shit.*

Riley took one look at Fallon's face when the front door closed and made her way across the room. She pulled Fallon close and held her.

Fallon held onto Riley tightly.

"Are you all right?" Riley asked.

"Not really," Fallon whispered.

"Do you want to talk about it?"

Fallon nodded.

"Owen," Riley called for her son's attention. "I'm going to take Fallon and make some popcorn; okay?"

Owen nodded excitedly and turned back to his movie.

Riley tugged on Fallon's hand and led her to the kitchen. The moment they stepped into the room, Riley took Fallon's face in her hands. "What is it?"

Fallon closed her eyes and took a deep breath. "Andi," she admitted.

"Is Andi okay?"

"I don't know. Did she tell you?" Fallon wondered.

"Tell me?"

"She and Jake are getting a divorce."

Riley lost her breath. A myriad of emotions coursed through her all at once—fear, concern, love, disbelief. What if suddenly Fallon changed her mind about what she wanted?

Fallon's hands reached for Riley's and held them. "I know what you're thinking."

"How can you? I don't know what I'm thinking."

"I love Andi," Fallon said.

Riley nodded.

*Fuck it. She needs to know.* "I'm *in* love with you," Fallon said.

Riley's heart fluttered perceptibly. She thought she might cry. It's not as if she didn't know the truth; she did. Hearing Fallon voice it made it suddenly real. She should run. She couldn't; she was suddenly rooted in place.

Fallon couldn't tell what was shining in Riley's eyes. "I don't need you to say anything," Fallon said. "Maybe I shouldn't have told you. I know you need time. But, Riley, I need you to know that as much as I love Andi, I meant what I said to you yesterday. I don't want to be with anyone but you. If that's not what you want, I'll accept that. I can't lie to you."

Riley exhaled. Fallon. "I don't want you to lie to me. I want to tell you..."

Fallon stopped Riley's thought. "You don't need to say anything to me."

*You don't know how much I want to say it.*

"Andi means the world to me," Fallon said. "I'd be lying if I told you that I'm not hurt. I mean, she didn't tell me she was leaving Jake. And, what if he ended it because of me? Jacob knew, Riley. He knew about us." She sucked in a ragged breath. "So, does Dave. Jesus, Jacob said Dave called Andi a dyke." She felt sick. "I don't know how she is, and I don't know how I am supposed to feel. She ends it with me, and *then* they break up? I'm not sure what to feel about that."

Riley nodded. "Fallon, if you want to..."

"I want to be with you right now." A*ctually, I want to be with you all the time.* "I need to talk to her."

"Do you want to cancel tomorrow?"

"What? No," Fallon said. "No. I wouldn't change our plans tomorrow for anything."

"Do you think she's okay?" Riley asked.

Fallon shook her head. *I don't know.*

"Are you okay?"

Fallon smiled at Riley. She leaned in and captured Riley's lips with a tender kiss.

"Fallon..."

"Too much?"

*God, no.* "No," Riley promised. "Maybe I should take Owen home and let you..."

"Stop it," Fallon said. "You promised Owen popcorn."

"And, Andi?"

"I'm not sure what to say to her." *About anything.*

"Is there something else?"

"Jacob came out to me."

Riley sighed. "Wow."

"I know."

"Listen, Owen will understand. We can head out and give you some time to..."

"No." Fallon pulled Riley close. "Please stay for a while," she requested.

Riley let her head rest on Fallon's shoulder. "As long as you want."

*Forever? Is that too much to ask?* "Just for a while," Fallon managed.

"Let me make the popcorn," Riley said. She pulled out of Fallon's embrace. "Go keep Owen company."

Fallon started to leave and stopped. "Riley?"

"Yeah?"

"I'm sorry if I..."

Riley smiled. "You don't have anything to apologize for."

Fallon nodded.

Riley gripped the counter when Fallon left. She'd been tempted to return Fallon's sentiment. She needed time. She loved Fallon. Was she in love with Fallon? She sighed. She wanted to be. She wanted to be able to give Fallon everything. Time—she needed more time. Falling in love had been the furthest thing from Riley's mind when she moved to Whiskey Springs. She'd found a home. She'd formed friendships that meant the world to her. Owen loved it here. She loved it here. Owen loved Fallon. She loved... *Oh, Fallon, please be patient with me. Please.*

Andi opened her door. "Fallon?"

Fallon met Andi's gaze as best she could. She felt angry. She was worried about Andi, and she was hurt.

"Come on." Andi pulled Fallon inside. "What are you doing here?"

"Why didn't you tell me?"

Andi was confused.

"You and Jake?" Fallon clarified.

"How did you..."

"Jacob showed up earlier tonight."

Andi sighed. "Fallon..."

"What happened? I can talk to him if..."

"Fallon." Andi took a deep breath. "I asked him for a divorce."

"What?"

"It's time," Andi said. Fallon's sarcastic chuckle sent a shiver up Andi's spine. "Fallon."

"Let me see if I have this right; you broke it off with me and then decided to leave Jake?"

"That's not what happened."

"Really?"

"Jesus, Fallon!"

"What about him?"

Andi covered her face.

Fallon took a step away. "What the hell, Andi? I thought that we were friends. I thought that we were more than that."

"Do you think this is easy for me?" Andi raised her voice.

Fallon swallowed hard.

"God, Fallon. You don't think after a year that I feel something for you?"

Fallon closed her eyes. This hurt. It all hurt.

"I love you. Do you think I wanted what we had to end? I didn't. I knew it would. It had to. You deserve more than I can give you," Andi said.

Anger rose in Fallon quickly. "Why is it that everyone thinks they know what I deserve? What do I deserve? Jesus, Andi; I'm not some fucking saint. For Christ's sake, I've been sleeping with a married woman for a year."

Andi sighed.

"And, Liv? Well, that wasn't really all her doing; was it? I could've gone with her. Maybe I should have gone with her. I was too fucking selfish. Too damn... What is it she always says? Idealistic?"

"Fallon..."

"What the hell am I doing? Maybe I'm just too selfish."

"Fallon, you may be many things but selfish is not one of them."

"Yes, I am."

"No. If anyone is selfish, it's me," Andi said.

"No. You aren't, Andi. Shit. I'm sorry. You don't owe me anything. Why didn't you tell me?"

"Because you need to do what is best for you now," Andi said. "And, I can't figure in that equation."

"You do figure in it."

"I shouldn't."

"Andi... I thought we agreed we'd remain friends?"

"We did. We are. But, Fallon... What you need and want—I'm not the person who can give you that. As much as I love you, I'm not sure who can give me what I need. I don't even know who I am anymore."

"What's that supposed to mean?"

"It means that I've spent more than half my life being someone's wife and someone's mother. Somewhere along the way, Andi got buried underneath those things."

"Are you okay?" Fallon asked.

"I don't know. I know this is what I need to do if I want to be okay."

Fallon nodded. "And, me?"

"I love you, Fallon. I do. It's not the same way I love Jake. It's not the way you love Riley." She squeezed Fallon's hand. "I miss you. I think a part of me will always miss you, not just the sex. And, trust me; I miss that."

Fallon chuckled. "It was pretty amazing."

"It was." She caressed Fallon's cheek with her fingertips.

Fallon sighed.

"What is it?" Andi asked.

Fallon tried to smile.

"What aren't you telling me?"

Fallon hesitated. She would never divulge Jacob's confession. She appreciated the trust that he put in her. Telling Andi his truth was Jacob's place. She wanted to smile. Fallon's heart hurt. It was that simple. "I told Riley that I'm in love with her."

Andi nodded.

"Andi, I..."

"Don't," Andi warned gently. "I'm glad you told her. She needed to know."

"I'm not so sure."

"Did she run away?"

"No. But, Andi she's scared. I can tell, and not just about being with me. She loves you; you know?"

Andi did know. "I'm okay, Fallon. I just need a little time to make the pieces fit."

"Everybody needs time," Fallon mumbled.

Andi smiled. *You are so sensitive, Fallon.* "Did it ever occur to you that time might be a good thing for you too?"

Fallon was doubtful.

"You rush into everything, Fallon."

One thing about Fallon; she hated the concept of time. When Fallon wanted something, she pursued it unfailingly. Andi was right, and Fallon had no intention of admitting it. She was still angry with Andi. She missed Andi as part of her daily life. Most of all, Fallon was scared. Terrified was a better word to describe what Fallon felt. Time was out of Fallon's control. What if time told Riley to walk away? What if time convinced Andi to leave Whiskey Springs? Olivia had asked for time. When Fallon had gone off to college and then decided to stay in Manhattan, Ida had assured her it was her time to shine. Leaving Whiskey Springs would give Fallon time to discover what she wanted from life. She'd not visited home for six months when the call came that her father had died. As far as Fallon was concerned, time was a thief. It promised clarity and instead stole meaning from life.

"Fallon." Andi took Fallon's hand. "Stop projecting doom in your path."

"Is that what you think I'm doing?"

Andi held her breath for a moment. There was so much pain and uncertainty in Fallon's eyes that it broke her heart. *I love you so much, Fallon. Enough to know that what you need is time.* "Fallon," Andi began gently. "I'm going to be completely honest with you."

"Please."

"It hurts. Knowing that you're in love with Riley; it hurts."

"Andi, I..."

"Please, let me finish."

Fallon sucked in a nervous breath.

"I love you."

"I love you too."

"Fallon! Would you please listen?" Andi chuckled.

"I'm sorry."

"This isn't easy for me. I care about Riley too."

Fallon started to speak, and Andi pressed two fingers to her lips. "Just listen," Andi requested. Fallon nodded. "It hurts. That doesn't mean that I don't want it to work out for you. I do. I want that for you more than anything, Fallon. I want you to be happy, to have someone to share your life with. I want that for Riley too."

Fallon pushed back her tears.

"I can't help that it hurts. I've held you in my arms every week for almost a year. I can't pretend that didn't happen."

"I don't want to pretend it didn't happen," Fallon said.

"I know. But, Fallon, I need to heal. I need to let go, not just of what we had."

"Jake."

"Yes, Jake too. Do you know that when Jake and I sat the boys down, Dave flew off the handle?"

"Jacob might have mentioned that."

Andi closed her eyes. Dave's words and actions remained open wounds. "Do you know the worst part of it?"

Fallon shook her head.

"I wondered if he was right. Jesus, Fallon, I don't even know who I am. Am I? Am I a dyke?"

"Andi." Fallon took hold of Andi's arms. "He had no right to call you that."

"Didn't he?"

"No."

"You sound like Jake."

"Jake is right. No matter how pissed off Dave is, he had no right to call you that."

"But, am I? Who am I, Fallon?"

"You're Andi."

"But who is that? My God, I spent twenty-six years married to someone who wasn't faithful to me from day one. Maybe that was my fault somehow."

"Stop it."

"I'm serious."

"Andi, Jake's infidelity was not your fault. Did he say that?"

"No. He wouldn't. He doesn't want the divorce."

"Then why?"

"Because I need more. You made me realize so many things."

Fallon swallowed hard.

"You made me realize that I could love someone else. You made me believe that I could be enough."

Tears rolled down Fallon's cheeks. "You are enough."

"Maybe. I have to be enough for me before I can think about being enough for anyone else. I have to figure out who I am. You need to take the time to concentrate on Riley, Fallon."

"Riley isn't ready for anything serious."

"Give her…"

"Time?"

"Yes."

Fallon closed her eyes and shook her head. "Time is a funny thing, Andi. It isn't endless. It has a conclusion."

Andi caressed Fallon's cheek. "And, there's that doom again. Yes, it does, sweetheart. It does have a conclusion. Not every ending is tragic."

"Not every ending is happy either."

"No. The good news is that every ending signals a new beginning," Andi said.

"You sound like Mom."

"Your mother's a smart lady."

"Yeah, I know."

"She loves you. We all love you, Fallon. You need to learn to trust that."

"I don't like seeing you hurt."

"I'm okay," Andi said. "Don't look at me like that. I am. I will be."

"Will you promise me something?" Fallon requested.

"If I can."

"If you need anything…"

"We're not saying goodbye," Andi said. "We need to find a new normal. I need to find a new normal."

Fallon nodded. "I'm sorry."

"Don't you dare." Andi smiled. "Love means never having to say you're sorry."

Fallon laughed through her tears. "That was the cheesiest movie you ever made me watch."

Andi grinned. She'd tortured Fallon with a slew of romantic films. She leaned in and kissed Fallon on the cheek. "Don't be so afraid of time, Fallon. It's not your enemy. It's just a reality."

"I love you, Andi. I hope you know that."

"I do know."

"What are you doing here?" Carol asked when Fallon walked in.

"I need a beer. Maybe two—or three." Fallon grabbed a glass and poured herself a pint from the tap. She flopped onto a barstool.

"Jesus, Foster, you look like someone stole your puppy or something," Dale said.

"Or something," Fallon muttered.

"Hey," he said. "How's Riley?"

Fallon's eyes lit up at the sound of Riley's name. "Good."

"Yeah, Jerry is really into her," Pete commented.

Carol glared at Pete.

"What? What did I say?" Pete asked.

"You are a dumbass," Carol commented.

Fallon chuckled and took another sip of her beer.

"Fallon's like her best friend," Pete said. "Do you think she's into Jerry?"

Fallon's hand balled into a fist. She was in no mood to talk to Pete tonight, and not about anything regarding Riley, Jerry's intentions least of all. Her head was spinning in time with her heart. She'd left Andi's feeling guilty. She felt guilty for the way she had approached Andi, remorse for falling in love with Riley. Andi was her best friend. She'd told herself for a year that becoming Andi's lover would never change that. That was before she had entertained the notion that she might ever meet someone she'd want to build a life with. Part of her even felt responsible for what she knew would be Jerry's disappointment. Pete and Dale's antics were the last thing she wanted to deal with tonight. All she wanted was a cold beer.

Fallon picked up her beer. "I guess you'd have to ask Riley." She got up and made her way to a table near the jukebox.

"What's up with her?" Dale wondered.

"You two are the reason they warn against inbreeding," Carol said.

Pete looked at Dale and shrugged.

Carol threw the towel in her hand on the bar and made her way to Fallon.

"Want to talk about it?"

"Not really," Fallon admitted.

"Andi?" Carol guessed.

Fallon sighed. She'd been replaying her conversation with Andi for over an hour. She'd finally given up on sleep and decided to head to Murphy's Law. "Yeah. She's leaving Jake."

"I know."

"You know? Does the entire town know except me?"

"No. Jacob came looking for you earlier. He was upset, Fallon. I took him in back for a minute."

Fallon sighed with regret. "I'm sorry. It's just everything is changing so fast."

"Everything?"

"I sort of told Riley I'm in love with her."

"And?"

"I don't know."

"You do know."

Fallon shook her head. "She needs time," she said. "Everybody needs time," she mumbled.

"Are you saying that Riley's not worth waiting for?"

"What? God, no."

Carol smiled sympathetically. "I know how much you love Andi."

Fallon sighed.

"Riley knows that too, Fallon. You and Andi—you did a great job of fooling yourselves."

"What is that supposed to mean?"

"It means that your relationship was about a lot more than a sexual affair."

"We didn't have a relationship."

"Bullshit."

Fallon's head began to pound. Why did everything have to be so complicated? How did it get so complicated? Wasn't love supposed to be easy? Why couldn't she have a normal relationship without so many obstacles? Why couldn't she fall in love with someone who could give her what she desired? Riley. Would time bring Riley closer to her? Or would time steal Riley from her life as it had everyone else?

"Fallon," Carol grabbed Fallon's hand.

"Is it me?" Fallon asked.

"Is what you?"

"Maybe something is wrong with me. Andi and me… We… I thought she'd be with Jake forever."

Carol regarded her friend thoughtfully. Fallon possessed an incredibly sensitive heart, far more so than many people realized. Long hours at Murphy's Law together had given Carol keen insight into what drove Fallon Foster. She also shared a friendship with Andi and Riley. There were advantages and challenges to living in a small town, and they often stemmed from the basic reality that it *was* a small town. Everyone knew everyone. In most ways, Carol thought that was a blessing. It could feel more like a curse when romantic entanglements were involved. Everyone knew everyone.

"Nothing is wrong with you," Carol said. "You want it so much—to find someone."

Fallon fidgeted in her chair and sipped her beer.

Carol shook her head. Why Fallon was embarrassed by her desire for a relationship confused her. That was Fallon. No one who spent time getting to know Fallon would be able to deny that the one thing Fallon wanted most was to find someone to share her life with. But Fallon feared a broken heart. That was the reason she'd chosen to get involved with Andi. She'd convinced herself that the affair carried no emotional risk. As long as Andi wasn't free, Fallon could keep her heart safe. Carol had always thought the idea was misguided at best. Then came Riley. Carol had to admit that she'd been surprised by the growing affection between Riley and Fallon.

Both were attractive, compassionate, funny women. She hadn't given any thought to the possibility that Riley might be the person that Fallon was waiting for until one day when Riley had strolled into the bar at noon with Owen on her hip. She recalled that Fallon had been arguing with their beer distributor all morning. Fallon's usual roll with the punches attitude had been pressed to its limit. One look at Riley and Owen, and Fallon's entire demeanor changed. What had surprised Carol that day was the way Riley looked at Fallon. There was a sparkle in Riley's eyes that was unmistakable. Carol had learned that sometimes you were the last person to realize you had fallen in love. She guessed that was true in Riley's case. To Carol, Ida, and Andi the feelings that continued to grow between Fallon and Riley had been obvious for months. It was the reason Andi had walked away from her affair with Fallon.

"Fallon," Carol began softly. "Riley's not Olivia or Andi; she's Riley. Just give it…"

"If you say time again, I swear…"

Carol laughed. "Let it be," she said. "As for Andi…"

"She swears she's okay. I can tell she's not."

"She is," Carol said. "You know, you are one of the luckiest people I know."

"Me?"

"Yes, you."

"This should be good. Enlighten me; would you? My best friend is going through hell, and I'm part of the reason, and I'm in love with someone who I don't know will ever be able to love me back."

"Riley does love you."

"You know what I mean."

"I do. She does, Fallon. I know how much you love her. I do. It's written across your face whenever she walks into a room."

"I'm not that obvious."

"You're delusional." Carol laughed.

"Gee thanks."

"You're welcome." Carol glanced over at the bar. "I'd better go back to what you pay me to do."

"Carol?"

"Yeah?"

"Thanks."

"That's what friends are for. And, Fallon? You have more of those than anyone I know."

Fallon watched Carol resume her place behind the bar. She looked into her beer. "What am I doing?" *Feeling sorry for yourself.* Fallon shook her head, grabbed her glass, and made her way to the bar. She poured the rest of her beer down the sink and placed the glass in the dishwasher.

Carol looked at her curiously. Fallon threw her for a loop by placing a kiss on her cheek.

"Thanks," Fallon said. She smiled and strolled out the back door.

Carol stood shell-shocked.

"Is Foster drunk or something?" Pete asked.

Pete's voice snapped Carol back to the present. "Or something," she said.

"Another college girl?" Dale asked.

Carol smiled. "Not even close."

# CHAPTER THREE

**SATURDAY**

Riley sat under a tree watching Fallon help Owen cast his fishing line into the pond. She chuckled. The pole was taller than Owen. He seemed determined to prove he could manage it. Fallon had given up on her pole. As soon as Owen's line made its way into the pond, Fallon collapsed onto a tree stump with Owen on her lap, helping him handle the pole and whispering in his ear. Every so often, Riley would hear Owen giggle uncontrollably. So far, the pair had managed to catch a large branch, a rubber ball, and a mass of leaves. Owen seemed unconcerned. He had Fallon's undivided attention. That seemed to be all that mattered to him. She smiled. Their day at the pond had proved to be exactly what all three needed. Riley was not looking forward to the evening that would follow.

A call from her sister, Mary, had prompted Riley to change plans for her trip home to California. Her niece, Rebecca was going to have a featured solo in a piano recital. Both of Riley's parents were flying in for the event. Riley had reluctantly agreed to make the trip home early. She would be leaving Monday night. She was dreading the need to tell Fallon. It was the worst time imaginable to deliver the news to Fallon. They were only beginning to explore what was developing between them. Riley feared that Fallon would see her departure as running away. And, maybe there was an element of truth to that assessment. Riley needed to breathe; she needed to process the depth of emotion she felt for Fallon. And, she needed to make peace with her past if she ever hoped to build a future in Whiskey Springs. That meant facing down painful memories and the opinions of her family.

"Fawon!" Owen screamed with delight.

Riley jumped.

"You've got something!" Fallon said. "Easy, buddy. We'll reel him in gently."

"God, I hope it's not a shoe or something," Riley mused. She shaded the sun from her eyes with her hand and watched as Fallon directed Owen.

"Easy," Fallon said, doing the work, but allowing Owen to believe he was in control. "Yep. Easy. Here we go." Fallon turned the reel softly.

"A fish!" Owen squealed.

"That's not just a fish," Fallon said. "You got a Large Mouth Bass, buddy."

Riley stood up, still shielding her eyes from the sun. She took a step forward just as Fallon grabbed hold of the fishing line. The size of the fish attached to the line astounded her.

"I got him! I got him!" Owen jumped up and down with excitement. "Hi, fish!"

Fallon spun on her heels. She held up the fish for Riley to see.

The expression of sheer joy on Fallon's face stopped Riley's heart for a second.

"Wook, Mommy!" Owen called with delight.

"I see," Riley said. "That's a big fish. Look at him."

"Yep!"

"We have to throw him back now, okay?" Fallon said.

Owen nodded.

Fallon lifted the hook from the fish's mouth and held him by the lip. "Say goodbye," she said.

Riley nearly fell over when Owen leaned in and kissed the fish. "Bye, bye."

Fallon's laughter carried through the air. She set the fish back in the water and put her arm across Owen's shoulder as he waved goodbye.

Riley's gaze stayed with the pair standing at the edge of the pond. Now, was the worst time for a trip. Maybe she could cancel. Something was happening to her; something was growing minute to minute between her and Fallon. More than a few days away was too long. She bit her lip gently.

Owen ran toward his mother. "I got him!"

"I saw," Riley said.

Fallon strolled up from the pond. She looked at Riley curiously. "Riley?"

Riley took Fallon's hand. "Ask me later," she said.

"Is everything okay?"

Riley smiled and kissed Fallon's cheek. "Please tell me you washed the fish off your hands before you came up here."

"I did," Fallon said. "I'm not sure Owen washed the fish off his lips, though."

Riley couldn't help herself, she laughed and wrapped her arms around Fallon's neck. "I can't believe you let him kiss that fish."

"Bert."

"What?" Riley asked.

"His name was Bert."

"Whose name?"

"The fish," Fallon explained. "His name was Bert. After lunch, we'll try for Ernie."

Riley smiled. "And, what does that make you; Big Bird?"

"Well, I am the tallest one."

"You're incorrigible."

"Probably."

Riley took a deep breath and released her hold on Fallon. "Lunch?"

"Sounds good." Fallon took a seat beside Owen on the blanket Riley had laid out. He crawled into her lap immediately. "You're a real fisherman," she told him.

Owen beamed with pride. "We go again?"

"We can go down to the pond for a little while after we eat and see if we can find Ernie."

Owen smiled at his mother when Riley passed him a peanut butter sandwich.

"Buttah!"

"You're going to turn into peanut butter," Riley said.

Owen munched on his sandwich happily, jelly oozing out onto his cheeks.

Fallon accepted her sandwich and took a bite. Owen had insisted they all have peanut butter and jelly. A squirt of strawberry dribbled onto Fallon's lip.

Riley chuckled. *Two of a kind.*

"What?" Fallon wondered.

"I was just wondering if Owen taught you how to eat."

Fallon's eyes narrowed.

Riley raised her brow.

Fallon reached a finger to her lip, removed the jelly, and sucked it off her fingertip.

"Do we need a bib for you too?" Riley asked with a shake of her head.

"Do you have one?"

Riley shook with laughter. *God, help me.*

"Fawon?"

Fallon smiled from her perch on the side of Owen's bed. "Yeah, buddy?"

"You stay?"

"Not tonight, but I'll see you soon."

Owen frowned. His mother always told him that when he wanted something he needed to ask nicely. "Pwease?"

Fallon's hand brushed through the light brown curls atop Owen's head. "I wish I could," she told him honestly. "We've all had a busy day. I think we could all use a little sleep."

"You stay."

"Oh, Owen; I need to sleep in a bed tonight, buddy."

Owen shifted over on his toddler bed.

Fallon grinned. How she could love any child more than Owen, she wasn't sure. She didn't think she could. He was spirited, loving, and completely adorable. She laid down beside him as best she could, her legs dangling off the end of the bed. "How about this? I will lay here with you until you fall asleep."

Owen settled against Fallon and closed his eyes. Fallon closed hers and sighed.

Riley stepped into the room and froze. How was she going to tell Fallon that she was leaving Monday? How was she going to keep Owen from throwing a fit when they left? If Owen had his way, he'd be with Fallon all day, every day.

Fallon opened one eye and met Riley's affectionate gaze. "I'll be there in a minute," she whispered.

Riley nodded and left the room. She poured two glasses of wine and took them into the living room. "Just tell her, Riley."

"Just tell me what?" Fallon asked.

Riley spun around.

"Oh, that doesn't look good. What's going on? You've been nervous all day long," Fallon observed.

Riley patted the sofa. "Sit with me."

Fallon proceeded hesitantly.

"I… Fallon…"

"Riley, what?"

"I have to leave on Monday."

"Leave?" Fallon's heart stopped.

"I know I wasn't supposed to leave until the tenth, but my niece has this recital, and I promised I would fly there early to see her."

Fallon released the breath she'd been holding. "Your trip home."

"Yeah. I'm sorry. I know with everything..."

"It's okay."

"Is it?" Riley asked.

Fallon sucked in a deep breath and released it slowly. Nothing about Riley leaving Whiskey Springs made Fallon happy. Aside from the fact that she would miss seeing Riley and Owen, she couldn't deny that part of her feared a visit home might change Riley's mind about things—many things. Olivia had taken a trip to Washington DC to visit college friends. Shortly after her return, she had announced that she was accepting a job there. Fallon didn't want to lie to Riley. Her conversation with Andi the night before was still fresh. Andi had said she needed time to figure out who she was. Riley had come to Whiskey Springs to try to do the same thing Andi was now. What might her return home tell her? Where would Fallon fit into either of their lives? One thing Fallon did believe, she needed to love Riley without expectation or conditions. Riley's trip home was inevitable. The timing made Fallon wonder if the universe was conspiring against her.

"Riley, you need to visit your family."

"I do, but I know that now is probably..."

Fallon smiled. "I'll miss you."

"I'll miss you too," Riley promised. A tinge of insecurity flickered in Fallon's eyes. "Fallon, I don't want you to think that this... me having to leave abruptly is about me and you. It's not. It just happened that..."

Fallon kissed Riley lovingly. "I know."

"Can I ask you for something?"

"You can ask me for anything."

"Hold me for a little while."

Fallon wrapped her arms around Riley and settled back into the sofa cushions. "Better?"

Riley sighed contentedly. She couldn't understand the sudden fear she felt. What if a few weeks away changed everything? Deep down she knew Fallon would be waiting for her when she came back. Somehow, that didn't seem to quell her uneasiness. Everything felt out of balance. The only thing that seemed to bring life into focus was the warmth of Fallon's embrace. "I'm so scared, Fallon."

"What are you afraid of?"

"Losing you."

"That's not going to happen, Riley."

"What if it takes me too long to…"

"Shhh." Fallon pulled Riley closer. "Just let me hold you."

Riley closed her eyes. "Stay."

Fallon's heart began to pound. "Riley, I…"

"I don't care if we sleep here, I just…"

"You don't know how much I want to say yes."

"But?"

"I can't," Fallon said. She felt Riley nod against her. "Not for the reasons you think."

"What do I think?"

"Not because I will be tempted to touch you," Fallon said. "I would be. That's not the reason."

"Why?"

"Because," Fallon said. She kissed Riley's temple. "I love you. I hope one day you'll ask me to stay because you can say…"

Riley held onto Fallon tightly. "I understand," she replied, stopping Fallon's words in their tracks. "I…"

"Just relax for right now," Fallon said. "I'll be here when you get back." *Please, come back.*

"Thank you for today."

"There's nothing to thank me for. I'd spend every day with you if I could."

Riley pulled away and looked at Fallon. Nothing but honesty and love reflected in her eyes. "You might change your mind one of these days."

"Even endless peanut butter sandwiches won't do that," Fallon said.

Riley chuckled. "I'll keep that in mind." She fell back into Fallon's arms. *I do love you, Fallon. Why is it so hard for me to tell you?*

Carol enjoyed watching Fallon's nervous pacing. It wasn't because she delighted in seeing her friend's stress. Fallon was head over heels in love. It was written in every move she made, and every word she spoke. If patience was a virtue, Fallon was bankrupt. Giving Riley time, giving Andi the space she'd requested to heal, respecting Ida's decision to spend a month away; all of it challenged Fallon. The three most important people in her life were away from her. There was purpose in Fallon's current reality. In fact, Carol thought the forced distance might be for Fallon's benefit most of all. Fallon wouldn't see it that way. She'd been surprised when Riley had stopped by the pub on her way to the airport. Riley explained that she had something to leave for Fallon. Fallon had yet to open the package.

"Instead of washing windows, maybe you should just open Riley's package," Carol said.

"It'll be there when I'm done."

"When do you think that might be?"

Fallon kept busy with her task.

"Impossible," Carol giggled.

Fallon sprayed and wiped the glass for the hundredth time in a few minutes. She could hear Carol's soft chuckling. Okay, so maybe she was acting neurotic. She needed to move. The next three weeks would entail late nights at Murphy's Law and early mornings working on unnecessary projects at home and at Riley's. Fallon had it all planned out. She would schedule her life. Riley had mentioned that she hoped to cut down some bushes behind the house. Fallon would tackle that. Riley had also pointed out the panels in the backyard fence that were loose and worn. She worried that Owen might get hurt on one of them. Fallon added those to her list. She'd spend tomorrow cleaning out Emily and Summer's room at her house, and the guest bedroom. Both needed to be refreshed, and she had an idea for the spare room that she hoped Riley would receive with excitement. Admittedly, it was presumptuous, but she wanted Owen to have a place he could call his when he and Riley were at Fallon's, which was often. And, Fallon hoped that someday soon, she might wake up beside Riley. "Don't pressure her," Fallon muttered as she wiped the window a final time.

"Who are you pressuring?" Carol asked.

Fallon shook her head.

"What are you up to?"

"Nothing," Fallon replied. "I just have some projects on my mind."

Carol watched as Fallon's eyes drifted to the package Riley had left, and then walked by pretending she was uninterested. She laughed. "Fallon, you are too much."

"Thanks for the ride," Riley said.

"I was happy to escape for a bit," Andi replied. "Do you want to tell me what's on your mind?"

Riley sighed regretfully.

Andi reached across the front seat and squeezed Riley's hand in reassurance. "She loves you."

Riley closed her eyes to keep from crying.

"I don't want you to hold back with Fallon because of me."

"Andi..."

"I mean it, Riley." Andi pulled the car into a parking space and turned to her friend.

"It's not just that."

Andi listened.

"I don't know what it is. I hate leaving. I hate that this hurts you. I hate that I can't seem to bring myself to get as close to her as..."

Andi grinned. "Riley," she said. "Please, listen for a minute. It does hurt a little. I knew Fallon was falling for you a long time ago. And, if I'm hurting, that's my fault, not Fallon's, and certainly not yours."

"How can you say that?"

"Because it's the truth. I love Fallon."

"I know."

Andi nodded. "But I always knew that our time would come to an end, so did she. And... I love you too."

"Andi, you're my best friend. I don't want to lose you."

"No one is going to lose anyone," Andi said. "That doesn't mean things won't change. They already have. That's not a bad thing. Change isn't easy, even the good stuff that changes life. It's not easy. I remember when I had Jacob. I was so excited. I didn't know I could love a human being that much. I thought I was prepared. I wasn't. It was the best change that ever happened in my life—becoming a mom. It wasn't easy, and it wasn't without a lot of fear, and questions, and even some tears."

Riley smiled. "I know what you mean."

"I know you do. All change comes with some loss. I lost my autonomy when I became someone's mother. I lost a degree of that when I married Jake. I wouldn't trade any of it. We've had our ups and downs as a family. Right now, we're going through another change. We all have to adjust. The same is true for you and Owen, and for Fallon. I'm all right, Riley. I promise you; I am."

Riley nodded. "Can I tell you something?"

"You can tell me anything."

"I'm close to my Mom and Mary, but… Sometimes, Andi, I feel like you're the mom I needed. My mom was distant so often. I realize now that was because my dad wasn't present."

It didn't require a genius to see the similarities between Riley's mother and Andi's life. Andi had recognized the kindred nature of their lives from her first few heartfelt conversations with Riley. Brenda Main had two children and had spent years married to a man who had never been faithful. She imagined that they shared other attributes as well. It made Andi relatable to Riley, and Riley special to Andi. What Riley still failed to comprehend was that one of the things that endeared Riley to Andi was how much Fallon loved her. Andi had been Fallon's close friend long before they'd become lovers. She had no doubt that their friendship would find its footing again. And, she looked forward to seeing where Riley and Fallon might travel. That was the truth. She was also looking forward to what the future might hold for her; although, she had a difficult time imagining what that might be.

"I feel the same way," Andi promised. "You already know that. Don't worry so much about everyone else, Riley."

"I feel like I'm being selfish."

"It's not selfish to put yourself first sometimes. You can't give anything to anyone if you're out of balance. Trust me on that. It's why I asked Jake for a divorce. It's why I need to be on my own for a while. I knew it would hurt Fallon. I knew it would hurt Jake and the boys. I even knew it would hurt you in a strange way. I've been so out of balance. Somewhere along the way, I lost track of me. There's always a bit of loss, Riley. It's taken me a long time to accept that. You can't lose yourself. That's the one thing you can't lose. So, you're not selfish. It's not selfish to take the time you need."

Riley sighed. "She's… Fallon… I wish I could…"

"Fallon likes to run head first into things." Andi chuckled. "It's one of the reasons we all love her so much, but she's run into her share of walls over the years. She needs to learn that walking will get her to the same place she's heading. There are a lot of curves in life. She'd fall off fewer ledges if she'd slow down just a touch."

Riley smiled. Andi had the benefit of knowing Fallon nearly a lifetime. Riley didn't need more time with Fallon to understand what Andi was saying. Somewhere along the way in life, Fallon seemed to have developed the belief that if something took time, it would slip away. Riley leaned over and kissed Andi on the cheek. "Thank you."

"You don't need to thank me," Andi said. "Take care of yourself, Riley. Don't try to function on Fallon's time clock. She may not want to admit it, but that's part of the reason you're good for her. You make her take a breath."

"Andi, we haven't... We're not..."

"I know, but it would be okay if you were." Andi glanced in the backseat at a sleeping Owen. She smiled and looked back at her friend. Andi wasn't clairvoyant. No psychic was needed to see the future for Riley and Owen. "Enjoy your visit home," she told Riley. "Don't worry about us."

"I know, you got by for years without me around," Riley tried to joke.

"Mm. Well, things do change," Andi said. "I'm done getting by. I think I'd prefer living." Andi unbuckled her seat belt and started to open her door.

"Andi?"

"Yeah?"

"I..."

"Let's get you on that plane."

Riley nodded. Andi had a unique way of easing her fears. She could confide anything in her friend—anything at all. No matter what she confessed to Andi, Riley was always met with the same pair of twinkling eyes, a smile, and the assurance that somehow life would work out the way it was meant to. Andi wasn't afraid to deliver a dose of truth, but truth always came in the form of compassionate wisdom. Riley often thought that Andi was wise beyond her years.

"Will you do me a favor?" Riley requested.

"If I can."

"I know that you and Fallon are.... But could you..."

"Carol and I will make sure she doesn't do something crazy like build a new house while you're gone or try to exist on pizza and peanut butter sandwiches."

Riley snickered. If anyone would be responsible for Fallon existing on pizza and peanut butter, it'd be Riley. *That's the one thing I'm not worried about.*

"I missed something," Andi said.

Riley winked. Maybe Andi was right; maybe this is exactly what they all needed—a breath. She walked with Andi the short distance to the outdoor counter at airport. "I'll see you in a few weeks," Riley said.

"We'll be here."

Riley nodded. *I hope so.*

Fallon paced around her kitchen aimlessly. She opened a cabinet and closed it. A few steps to the refrigerator and she poked her head inside, rummaging through a drawer and scanning the contents of each shelf before closing the door without removing a single item. Fallon rubbed her face vigorously. Riley had only been gone a few hours. How would she survive the next three weeks? She was about to make her way to the liquor stash when her phone rang.

"Hi," Riley's voice came over the line.

"Hey. How was your flight? Did you get settled at Mary's? How's Owen?"

Riley giggled at the string of questions Fallon fired off without taking a breath. "We're good," she said. "What are you doing?"

"Me?"

"You are the other person on the phone," Riley pointed out.

"Nothing. The usual."

"The usual?" Riley questioned. "So, you're watching *Super Why* and eating pizza?"

Fallon looked at the open pizza box on her kitchen table. "No."

"Really?"

"Yeah, I don't have *Super Why* here. It's at your house."

Riley smiled as she listened to Fallon. "Did Carol give you the package I left?"

"Oh, yeah. Thanks for that."

"Fallon, did you open it?"

"I... Well," Fallon's eyes drifted to the package that sat on the counter.

"Open it," Riley said.

"Now?"

"Yes."

Fallon took a deep breath. She picked up the package and stared at it.

"It won't explode," Riley laughed. "Stop staring at it."

"How do you know I'm staring at it?"

Riley made no reply. She didn't need to see Fallon to picture the scene in Fallon's kitchen. And, she was certain Fallon was in the kitchen. At one in the morning, Fallon would be looking for something to keep herself busy. Riley could easily imagine Fallon deciding to reorganize her cabinets or experiment with new drink recipes. She'd debated for less than a minute whether she should call Fallon so late. "I know you," Riley said. "Just open it."

Fallon looked down at the kitchen table and considered the box. She lifted it and opened it carefully, removing a layer of tissue paper. She laughed.

"Now, you can fall asleep on the couch," Riley said. "As usual."

Fallon pulled out two of Owen's favorite *Super* Why DVDs that she had told Riley to take home. Underneath she found a note.

*Go see Charlie tomorrow. He has something for you. When you get home, make sure you open your refrigerator.*

Fallon stood and made her way to the refrigerator again. She opened it and shook her head.

"You can't live on pizza," Riley said.

"Riley, you didn't need to do that."

"Actually, I had Andi drop it off while you were at work tonight."

Fallon laughed some more. *Figures.*

"You're laughing."

"Would you believe I was looking in the refrigerator right before you called, and I didn't even notice?"

"Yes."

Fallon laughed harder. Her refrigerator was filled with more green items than she'd seen in months, and none of it was mold. "You didn't have to do that."

"Just make sure you eat it," Riley said.

"Worried about me?" Fallon asked playfully.

Riley was worried about Fallon. Fallon still harbored insecurity about their budding relationship. Riley could hardly blame her. "Maybe a little."

"I promise, I won't be a hundred pounds heavier from Tony's pizza when you get back."

"I'll give you a call tomorrow," Riley said.

"You don't have to call me every day," Fallon said. She heard Riley take a breath. "I mean it. Call when you have time. Spend this time with your family. I've got plenty to occupy my time."

"Okay."

"Good. Have a great visit, okay? I'll see you in a few weeks."

"I will."

"And, Riley?"

"Yes?"

Fallon took a deep breath. "Tell Owen I said hi."

"I will."

"Riley?"

Riley chuckled. "Yes?"

"I... I..."

"I'll miss you too, Fallon."

Fallon swallowed hard and put her phone in her pocket. "Why the hell did you tell her not to call?" She admonished herself and opened the refrigerator door again. "Broccoli? That wasn't Andi. What did she do; give Andi a shopping list?" Fallon smiled when her eyes fixed on a cold bottle of UFO White Ale. "Now, *that* was Andi." She grabbed the bottle and was surprised to find a sticky note attached to the back:

*Don't make it a habit.*
*~ A.*

Fallon shook her head. She opened the beer, grabbed a piece of cold pizza, balancing it on one of Owen's DVD's, and made her way to the living room. "When in Rome," she said as she took a bite of her slice of pizza. She snickered again at Andi's note. "Don't make what a habit? The beer or the broccoli?" She swore she heard Andi and Riley answer in unison. "The beer."

"Mommy." Owen stood in front of Riley sporting a face covered in jelly.

"Yes?"

"I call Fawon?"

Riley smiled. Owen had prattled on about Fallon all morning. "I think she's at work, sweetheart."

"I can call?"

What could she say? They'd been gone less than twenty-four hours and Owen was ready to go home. He missed *his* Fallon. That's what he had told his aunt. Riley was sure the feeling was mutual.

"Pwease?" Owen asked nicely.

Riley chuckled. *Who am I kidding? She'd take his call at four in the morning.* "Okay. You say hello when she picks up."

Owen nodded excitedly and held out his hand for the phone.

"Let me dial the number," Riley laughed. She handed him the phone.

Owen waited for Fallon to answer.

"I told you; you don't have to call me," Fallon said, expecting to hear Riley's voice.

"Fawon!"

"Owen?"

"Fawon, you can come here?"

Fallon grinned. "Aww, buddy, I'm working. Aren't you having fun with your aunt and your cousin?"

"You come."

"I wish I could, buddy. Mommy told me you're going to the zoo this week. That will be fun; right? They have rhinos and elephants."

Owen huffed. "With you, Fawon."

"I miss you too, Owen. But I'm working on something special for when you get back."

"Da puzzle?"

"Not a puzzle," Fallon said. "You'll see when you get home."

"Wums?"

"No," Fallon laughed. "I'm not catching worms." She envisioned the expression of horror on Riley's face if they returned home to a worm farm in what Fallon was hoping would be Owen's room at her house. "When you get back, we can catch some worms and go to the pond."

"Fishin'?"

"Yep. We'll go fishing. I promise. What are you doing?" Fallon asked.

"Eatin' buttah."

Fallon snickered. Butter meant peanut butter. "With jelly?"

"Gwape."

"Grape jelly, huh?"

"Yep."

"That sounds good. I might have one of those when I finish what I'm doing."

"Fawon?"

"Yes, Owen?"

"How many sleeps?"

Fallon answered without hesitation. "Seventeen, buddy."

Owen huffed.

"It's not that many," Fallon said. *Who am I kidding? That's a lifetime.* "That's ten plus seven more. Remember how we were counting on our fingers?"

Owen held up a hand and spread fingers. He looked at his mother.

Riley sighed. "Why don't you let me talk to Fallon, sweetie."

Owen frowned. "Mommy wants you," he told Fallon.

"Okay. Give Mommy the phone. I'll talk to you later. You're going to have so much fun there, buddy. You won't even miss me."

Owen handed Riley the phone.

"Ugh," Riley groaned.

"Riley? Everything okay?"

"Yeah. I think I just got peanut butter in my hair."

Fallon laughed.

"Laugh it up, Foster."

"Sorry."

"I hope we didn't disturb you."

Fallon looked at the empty pizza box on her coffee table and the furniture that filled the corner of her living room that she'd removed from the spare room. "You didn't."

"Are you working?" Riley asked.

"Not exactly. Well, not at Murphy's anyway."

"Uh-huh."

"How are you? I didn't think I'd hear from you today."

"I'm sorry if we…"

"You can call me whenever you want," Fallon said.

"He asked you how many sleeps until we're back, didn't he?"

"Yeah."

Riley sighed.

"Riley, give him a couple of days. He'll be fine."

"I don't know."

"He will," Fallon said. "It's good for him. It's good for you too."

*What about you, Fallon? Is it good for you?* "I guess."

"You should probably go get the peanut butter out of your hair."

"I did interrupt you."

"No. Stop worrying about me and Owen," Fallon told Riley. "He'll forget all about me when he gets to the zoo."

"I doubt that."

"Well, he'll forget about me for a little while anyway. Is there something else bothering you?"

Riley wished she was staying anywhere but with her sister. Mary had already pressed her about life in Whiskey Springs. Who was Fallon Foster? Why was she always with Fallon? What about this Jerry person she'd heard about? When did Riley think she might move home? The barrage of questions had landed on Riley like a series of punches in the first round of a boxing match. That had been over breakfast. She hated to imagine what was in store for her when the dinner bell rang. "I've been here less than twenty-four hours and I need a vacation."

"Ahh... Mary's on your case?"

"Understatement. She means well. She always means well."

"She just misses you," Fallon said.

"I know. I feel like no matter what I tell her, she won't be satisfied."

Fallon was familiar with that feeling. As much as she had loved Olivia, she never felt her feelings were considered by her ex-partner. Olivia was adept at asking questions, expressing opinions, and she'd even mastered remaining quiet while Fallon offered her thoughts and feelings. She'd never listened. That's how Olivia had always made Fallon feel—unheard. She still felt that way when they talked. Olivia entered every conversation with an agenda—how she could get the answer she desired. When Fallon failed to deliver, it would all begin again. Olivia would make her point, ask her questions, let Fallon speak, and then explain why she couldn't fathom Fallon's perspective. It had been exhausting. Based on what Riley had shared about her older sister, Fallon suspected Mary and Olivia were a great deal alike. "Just tell her the truth," Fallon suggested.

"You make it sound simple."

"Yeah, well, I probably should take my own advice," Fallon joked. "If you need to talk or..."

"Thanks."

"Sure."

"I'll talk to you soon."

"Have a good time, Riley."

Riley looked up at the sky. "What if I don't know what the truth is?"

"Who are you talking to out here?" Mary asked.

"No one," Riley replied. "Myself, I guess."

"I hope it's a good conversation."

"At least I know what to expect my answers to be."

"How are you, Riley? I mean, really—how are you?"

"I'm good."

"Are you? It must be lonely, I mean; it must get boring being in such a small town."

Riley walked with her sister onto the deck of the house while her niece and Owen played in the yard. "Whiskey Springs is many things; boring is not one of them."

"Really?"

Riley smiled. "Not at all."

"What do you do there?"

"What do you mean?"

"Well, you're not going off to wine tastings."

"Not weekly—no."

"At all?"

"You'd be surprised," Riley said. "Lately, there's been a lot of worm hunting."

"I'm positive I don't want to know."

"Fallon is teaching Owen to fish."

"Like with a pole?"

"No, with his teeth. Of course, with a pole!"

"Don't you just buy bait in one of those little shacks they have?" Mary inquired.

"Shacks?" Riley laughed. There were a handful of gas stations and the corner store that carried live bait. She'd yet to see any "shacks."

"Yeah, you know; those little roadside places for all the rednecks."

Riley laughed again. "It's Vermont, Mary."

"Yeah? In the woods; right?"

"There are trees," Riley replied dryly.

"And, flannel."

"Not so much in June, no."

"Huh."

Riley took a seat on a bench on her sister's deck.

"You still haven't told me," Mary said.

"Told you what?"

"About this guy you've been seeing."

"What guy?"

"The contractor."

"Jerry?"

"Yeah, him."

"Well, I might see Jerry from time to time; I'm not seeing him the way you're suggesting."

"I thought you went out with him a few times?" Mary asked.

"I did." Riley watched her niece, Rebecca chase Owen through the backyard.

"And?"

"He's a nice man." *Very nice, not very interesting.*

"Any other prospects?"

Riley turned her attention to her older sister. "Prospects?"

"For a husband."

Riley rolled her eyes. "Who says I want a husband?"

"I worry about you. Who are you going to meet up there in the wilderness?"

"Wilderness? Where do you think I live, Siberia?"

"Well..."

"You can stop worrying."

"I think you should meet with Derek while you're here."

"Mary, I'm not taking a job in Los Angeles."

"Take it in New York then."

"No." Riley let her gaze fall back on Owen.

"Why on earth not?" Mary asked.

"Owen," Riley called out. "You stay where I can see you."

"I've got him, Aunt Riley!" Rebecca called back.

"Well? Why not? You could keep that house Robert left you as a summer home or something."

Riley sighed. "I don't want to take a job in the city, Mary."

"Riley, you're a young woman...."

"Stop. Can't we just enjoy this time together?"

"You're not enjoying yourself?" Mary asked.

"You mean one-hundred-twenty questions? Not really."

"Just talk to Derek, Riley? What do you have to lose?"

*More than you understand.* Riley shook her head. "I'll talk to him."

# CHAPTER FOUR

**SATURDAY EVENING**

"Riley?" Brenda Main poked her head into the guest room.

"Hi, Mom."

"I wondered where you disappeared to."

Riley smiled half-heartedly. Her mother, father, and stepmother had arrived the day before for Rebecca's recital. They'd cheered Rebecca's solo the previous evening and celebrated with ice cream sundaes afterward. Saturday had been spent with a barbecue in the backyard, a few bottles of wine, and laughing at Owen chasing Rebecca and her friends around the yard. Riley enjoyed the day. She'd missed her family more than she realized. As the evening wore on, Riley had grown contemplative and quiet. She'd given into her sister's nagging and met with Derek Peters about a job at his publishing company. He'd spent over an hour coaxing her to accept a position in the Los Angeles office. It presented Riley with an incredible opportunity. She'd declined repeatedly. He'd countered with arguments and perks. Finally, she'd agreed to "think about it." And, she had been thinking about it. Every consideration she gave the offer collided with a thought of Whiskey Springs. Her heart was upside down. San Diego had been home. If she accepted, her parents would both be within driving distance. She had friends here. Mary, for all her annoying prodding and questions, would be close by. Owen would see his grandparents regularly and get to know his cousin. It would be easy to make a home here. She had done that with Robert. Riley found herself contemplating what he might have to say about everything.

"Are you all right?" Brenda asked. "Don't bother answering. What's wrong?"

"Nothing. I don't know. Everything?"

"Want to talk about it?"

"Derek offered me a job."

"That's terrific, Riley."

"Is it?"

"Why wouldn't it be?"

"It should be."

"But?"

"I don't know. I missed you. I did. I love it here; I do."

Brenda smiled. "Who is he?"

"What?"

"That twinkle in your eyes; Riley, I know that twinkle. You're missing someone."

Riley smiled. "I guess I am."

"So? Who is he?"

"Mom…"

"Is it that contractor that worked on your roof?"

"No, it's the bar owner who took us in as strays."

Brenda let the answer filter through her brain. "Fallon?"

Riley nodded.

"I see."

"Mom…"

"Does she know?"

"That I'm in love with her?" Riley's admission took her breath away. It was the first time she'd permitted herself to speak the truth.

"I'll take that reaction to mean no."

Riley shook her head.

"Does she feel the same way?"

"She does."

"So, you're torn between love and a career?"

"No."

"No?"

"Being here—Mom, it's like I see his ghost everywhere."

"Robert is gone, sweetheart. I know you miss him. You're allowed to love again."

"Am I?"

Brenda took Riley's hand. "Absolutely. And, from what I've seen the last couple of days, you're not the only one in love."

Riley giggled. "He's pretty upfront about that."

"She must be something special for Owen to miss her so much."

"She is," Riley said. She sighed heavily. "I'm sure it's not what anyone expects."

"What's that?"

"You know."

"That you fell in love with a woman?"

Riley shrugged.

"No, I don't suppose it's what any of us expected. None of us expected Robert to die either."

Riley shook her head. "I don't know what to do. I keep wondering what Robert would say."

"Why don't you ask him?"

"I don't think he's accepting calls where he is."

"Well, you might not get the answer the way you'd like. Maybe you need to talk to him just for you, Riley. Maybe you need to say your goodbye."

Riley's tears began to flow. "I don't want to forget."

"Oh, sweetheart." Brenda pulled Riley into her arms. "You're never going to forget him. You do have to let him go, Riley. I know you thought that leaving would accomplish that."

"Didn't it? Mom, I do love her. I know that might sound crazy. How is that not letting him go?"

"You haven't told her."

"No, but..."

"Why haven't you?" Brenda asked.

"I almost did. I wanted to but I..."

"Couldn't?"

"I don't know what's wrong with me. If I can't even tell her... Maybe it would be better for all of us if I just came home."

Brenda smiled.

"Wouldn't it make sense? Fallon has a full life without us. She does. She has family, and she has people who love her there. I have family and people who love me here."

"You don't have her."

Riley thought her heart was about to break. "I promised him, Mom. I promised him forever."

"And, he promised you that too," Brenda said. "Forever is as long as it lasts, Riley. Do you still love him?"

"Of course."

"But he left you."

"Not because he chose to."

"And, you think that being with someone new is choosing someone over him?"

"I don't know. It's not like I didn't know this would happen one day. I thought it would be easier. I thought there could be a forever. What if it doesn't exist, Mom? What if I..."

"What if your forever is Fallon?"

Riley began to sob.

"Riley," Brenda tried to soothe her daughter. "Jobs come and go. Sometimes, people leave. Love is something you have to grab when it appears. It doesn't find you every day. You can run from it, but it won't stop how you feel. And, the truth is, forever might not turn out to be as long as you expect."

"I wish I knew what he would say."

"Just ask him, sweetheart. You knew him best. Tell him what you feel, Riley. He might not answer you. This isn't about Rob; it's about what you need to say to him. Say what you need to."

Riley folded herself in her mother's arms and cried.

"Shhh," Brenda cooed. *Oh, Riley, give yourself a chance, sweetheart. Give yourself a chance.*

❧

"Mom?"

Andi turned to the sound of Jacob's voice and smiled. "Hey, you."

"Can I talk to you for a minute?"

"Sure, you can. Come, have a seat." Andi scooted over on the couch and made room for her son.

Jacob forced himself to smile.

"Jacob? Listen, I know this hasn't been easy. Your father and I…"

"Mom, you don't need to worry about me."

"I know that you've been upset with your brother."

"And, you're not?"

Andi sighed.

"He's acting like a selfish asshole," Jacob said.

"He's hurt."

"Yeah, well, it's not about him."

Andi nodded. "No, it isn't. It feels that way to him, I think. I think he's worried about what his friends will think."

"Why? Half our friends' parents are divorced. It's not like we're little kids."

"I'm not sure it's having divorced parents that concerns him."

"You mean you and Fallon."

"I do."

"Can I ask you something?"

Andi took a deep breath. "Go ahead."

"Did you love her? Fallon, I mean?"

"Very much."

"So, are you a lesbian?"

Andi let out a nervous chuckle. "I'm not sure how to answer that."

"Honestly?"

"No, I mean, I don't know the answer. Jacob, I love your father. God knows, our marriage has not been perfect. I love him."

"And, you love Fallon?"

"Yes. I know, it's crazy."

"Not really."

Andi sat back and regarded Jacob with surprise.

"I don't think it's crazy. Different, maybe. But, did you... I mean, before Fallon..."

"No."

"Did you ever think about it?" Jacob asked.

Andi felt her face flush. The conversation seemed strange to be having with her son. She'd always told her sons that they could talk to her about anything. Talking about her sexual and emotional relationships had not been on her radar. She was wading into murky waters; waters she'd been traversing alone for weeks. She still hadn't been able to see the bottom clearly. Questions and emotions swirled around her everywhere. It seemed no matter how deeply she attempted to dive, regardless of how determined she was to keep her eyes open, she couldn't discern her surroundings amid all the swirling. Murky, that was the best way to describe it.

"Mom?"

"Oh, Jacob, I wish I had an answer for you. Did I know I was attracted to women? Did I think I could fall in love with a woman? Did I think I could love anyone other than your father? I don't know. No matter how many times I ask myself those questions, I get a different answer, or I come up empty. I don't know. I don't know that it matters. I never expected your father and I to split. I never thought Fallon and I... Well, I didn't see that coming. When it did? I held on, probably longer than I should have."

"What if you didn't hold on long enough?"

Andi smiled. Jacob loved Fallon. His affection for her was as plain as the nose on his face. "I wish that were the case; I do. Fallon is in love with someone else."

"Riley."

Andi nodded.

"That doesn't bother you?"

"I wouldn't say that," Andi admitted. "It hurts. Not every relationship is meant to last a lifetime."

"Then why bother? There have to be things that last forever, Mom."

"That's a good question." Andi chuckled at the expression on her son's face. The idealism of youth touched her. "I didn't say that nothing lasts forever. Loving someone changes you forever. Every friendship, every lover, every person you meet changes your life in some way. Not everyone stays in your life. Sometimes, they play a new role. Sometimes they leave altogether. That's just life, Jacob. Maybe some people are bridges. They lead you from one place to the next. And, when you cross them, they get washed away by the changing tide."

Jacob considered his mother's words. She had a softness about her as she spoke. He could detect sadness, hopefulness, love, fear all in her reflective tone. She'd been thinking about her life. That was evident. Fallon flickered in her eyes. Jacob could see Fallon there, far more than he saw the ghost of his father. He wanted to tell her his truth. He needed her to know.

"Mom..."

"What is it, Jacob?" Andi asked. "You can tell me anything."

"That's what Fallon said."

*Fallon – of course, you went to Fallon.* "Fallon loves you, Jacob."

"She loves you too."

"I know. That's not what you want to talk to me about."

Jacob sucked in a nervous breath. "I'm gay."

Andi smiled. "Do you feel better letting it out?"

"You knew?"

"No. I suspected."

"How? Did I…"

"I'm your mother," she replied. "I've been there since the beginning, sweetheart. I remember your crushes, the ones you tried so hard to conceal. I seem to recall the tears in your eyes when Ethan Feldman started dating Katie. That wasn't about Katie."

"Was it that obvious?"

"No," Andi put her son's worries to rest. "Not to anyone but me. People acknowledge what they choose to see," she said. "Sometimes, they only see what they expect to see."

"Are you disappointed?"

"Never," Andi said. She pulled Jacob into her arms. "I love you, Jacob."

Jacob began to cry. "Mom?"

"Yes?"

"Do you think Fallon will still want to see me?"

"Oh, Jacob… Fallon and I may not be lovers; she's my best friend and she always will be. I need a little time, and so does she."

"I'm sorry you're hurt."

Andi felt tears roll over her cheeks. Everyone seemed to be worried about her—Fallon, Riley, Ida, Jacob, even her husband, everyone except her younger son. "I'm all right, sweetie."

"I don't want to tell Dad and Dave yet."

"You don't have to. That's your decision. When you're ready, if you want me to be with you, I will be. You tell me what you need."

"Is it awful?" Jacob asked.

"What's that?"

"I sort of hoped that you and Fallon would…"

"I know."

"It's just, you seemed so happy when she was around."

Andi's heart lurched in her chest. Fallon did make her happy. Fallon made her laugh. Fallon listened. Fallon made her feel alive and special, like she could be more than what everyone expected;

she could be Andi, whoever that turned out to be. "Fallon means the world to me," she admitted. "I'm happy for her."

"Do you think she and Riley are going to get together?"

"I'd bet you a beer."

"A beer?"

"I could use one. You?"

Jacob nodded.

Andi thrust herself off the couch and offered Jacob her hand.

"Mom?"

"Yeah?"

"I love you."

"I love you too, Jacob, more than anything."

Fallon flipped over in her bed, looked at her phone, grumbled and tossed it aside. Why was she freaking out? She'd told Riley to enjoy her visit and not to worry about calling. Apparently, Riley had thought Fallon meant what she said. *Crazy.* That was laughable. It was the right thing to say; wasn't it? The last thing Fallon wanted was to appear needy. Okay, maybe the last thing she wanted was to miss Riley. Why hadn't she told Riley that? Maybe she should pick up the phone and call? Riley wouldn't mind. Maybe Riley would mind. Maybe there was a reason Riley hadn't called in a few days. Maybe Riley didn't know how to tell Fallon that she'd decided home was San Diego. Perhaps Riley had finally met with that family friend at the publishing company. Riley wanted to be a writer. What if she'd decided to accept an offer on the West Coast?

Fallon grabbed her phone again. "Two. That makes it eleven there." She took a deep breath and prepared herself to call Riley. Her head fell back against a pillow in frustration. "Fuck! If she wanted to talk to you, Foster, she would call." Fallon rubbed her eyes. "Fuck it." She threw her legs over the edge of her bed and hopped to her feet. Sleep was not going to come any time soon. That was clear. The pub was closed. It was dark outside. She needed to do something—anything. She'd already erected a new fence off the deck. It made sense. Emily and Summer would be visiting in a few weeks. Owen was at her house often. A fenced-in area would make life for everyone simpler. Besides, she'd been thinking about getting a furry companion. She startled when her phone buzzed.

"Andi?"

"Sorry, I know it's late."

"Are you okay?"

"Jacob came out to me. He just went to bed."

"How is he?" Fallon asked as she slipped a T-shirt over her head.

"Afraid to tell his brother, I think."

"Understandable."

"I feel awful."

"That Jacob is gay?"

"No."

"Andi, what Dave said to you; that was shitty. It's not your fault."

"Then why do I feel like it is?"

"Because you love those boys more than anything. That's why."

Andi sighed. "I'm sorry if I woke you up. I just…"

"Don't be sorry. You know that you can call me no matter what time it is. That's never going to change."

*It probably should.* "I know." Andi heard clunking in the background. "What are you doing?"

"Moving the bed out of the spare room."

"At two in the morning?"

"Yep."

"Why?"

"I can't sleep."

"Want to talk about it?"

"No."

"Haven't heard from Riley?"

Fallon groaned. The bed got stuck in the doorway. "I told her not to worry about calling."

Andi laughed. "Why on earth did you tell her that?"

"Because I don't want her to think I need her to call."

"You are adorable, Fallon."

"What?"

"Well, you are."

"Can we talk about your gay son instead?"

Andi laughed harder. "Funny you should ask."

"Oh?"

"I was hoping maybe you would have something he could help you with at Murphy's."

"Jacob needs a job? All he has to do is ask."

Andi closed her eyes. She missed Fallon more than she would ever let on. "I'm not sure it's a job he needs. I think he might benefit from some time with you."

Fallon scratched her brow. "He can call me whenever he wants."

"I think he feels a bit funny doing that."

"Shit. Because of us?" Andi's lack of a reply gave Fallon her answer. "I told him that you're still my best friend."

"I know. I told him that too. But, he knows things are different now."

"Are they?" Fallon asked. "This feels pretty familiar."

Andi let out a long sigh. "It does but it *is* different."

Fallon sat on the edge of the twin bed in her spare room. "Will it always be?"

"Different?" Andi asked.

"Yeah."

"I'd like to think of it as new."

"New, huh?"

"New—a new chapter, Fallon—for both of us."

"Do you think Jacob might be open to helping me with some things here?"

"What are you up to?" Andi asked.

"It might be all wishful thinking."

"What?"

"Well, Riley's here so much with Owen," Fallon hesitated and took a breath. "I thought I'd convert the spare room into a room for Owen."

Andi smiled as she listened to Fallon. Fallon was hopeful. It still stung—just a little bit. The overriding emotion Andi felt was happiness. Fallon was in love. Fallon deserved to be in love and to be loved.

"Do you think it's a bad idea?" Fallon asked, unnerved by Andi's silence.

"No."

"Shit, I'm sorry, Andi. I'm an insensitive jerk sometimes."

"No." Andi chuckled. "Not at all. I called you; remember?"

"Do you think Riley will be mad?"

"That you want to make room for Owen? Fallon, this is Riley we're talking about. You know the answer to that question."

"She might think I'm…"

"She'll think that you love her and that you love Owen. And, she'll be right. Stop second-guessing everything. I'll have Jacob call you tomorrow."

"Are you really okay?" Fallon asked.

"I am." Andi was surprised by the confidence she felt. She was all right. She was scared. Everything seemed to change in her life overnight. It hadn't been sudden. Change had been slowly creeping into her life, steadily traveling through her veins. She'd resisted it; resisted the pull she felt to let go. Letting go would never be easy. If she hoped to open herself to anything or anyone new, she needed to let go of the past. "I am."

Fallon was struck by the calmness of Andi's voice. "What about Jake and David?"

"Jake is moving to Phoenix. He's already purchased a condo. I imagine Dave will be staying there the rest of the summer."

"I'm sorry, Andi."

"Me too. But David has to go his way right now. I can't force him to understand."

"What about you?"

"Me? This is where I belong, at least, for now."

"I hope it always is," Fallon said.

Andi smiled. "Don't worry so much about Riley," she advised Fallon.

"Have you talked to her?"

"If I did, I wouldn't tell you," Andi said. "You need to trust…"

"I trust her."

"Not Riley. You need to trust what you feel, Fallon."

"Oh, because that always works out."

"It works out more often than it doesn't."

"Are you drunk?" Fallon asked.

Andi laughed. "Goodnight, Fallon."

"Yeah. I love you; you know?"

"I love you too. Don't stay up all night."

"Yes, Mom."

"Funny. I'll talk to you soon."

"I hope so."

"Go to bed, Fallon."

Fallon put her phone on the bed next to her, flopped back and sighed. Talking to Andi always calmed her. She missed seeing Andi. Tonight, she'd felt the first flicker of normalcy return to their conversation. It comforted her. In time, she would have Andi in her daily life again. Fallon smiled as her thoughts turned to Owen. She looked up at the ceiling. "Maybe I should get some of those glow-in-the-dark stars for the ceiling."

The car rumbled slowly along the gravel road. Riley looked in the rear-view mirror at Owen bouncing in his car seat. He gazed out the window, smiling, loving the bumpy ride. She returned her focus to the quiet road. She had seen one car when she pulled through the gates—only one. She shivered and turned the air conditioning down. The temperature was not to blame. Riley knew that. This place always left her feeling cold. She wasn't even sure why she had put Owen in the car and headed here. If Robert was going to be anywhere, it wouldn't be here. For some reason, she felt compelled to visit. Her heart began to race as she pulled the car to the side of the road and turned off the engine. Riley gripped the wheel and closed her eyes. She hated this place.

"Mommy?"

Riley took several deep breaths. "We're going to go leave Daddy your flowers."

Owen grinned. "Okay!"

Riley made her way out of the car and unbuckled Owen. He jumped out of the car excitedly. Riley's stomach revolted. One day, Owen would understand the meaning of this place. One day, he would reflect and wonder about the father he'd never know. She wondered if he had any impressions of his father. Did he see Robert in his dreams? Did some part of Owen remember the sound of his father's voice? She watched as Owen skipped happily toward the tree that stood near his father's resting place, proudly carrying a spray of flowers in his hand. Riley closed her eyes for a moment. How? How many times had she asked how she ended up here? Why? Would she ever understand the reasons why someone with so much life left to live was taken? None of it would ever make sense to her. Everything in life might hold a lesson; Riley wasn't sure that she'd ever believe it all came with reasons. Life held one inevitability—only one; one day life came to an end. The rest was a mixture of chance and choice. She'd long ago thrown away the notion that choice alone dictated life, or that chance held a person's fate hostage. Some things could not be changed or controlled. The choice you had was how to go forward at those moments; maybe even whether you would go forward. Riley had no choice but to keep moving. She watched as Owen picked a small flower from the grass. Death was a strange thing. Amid the silence that came with death, the hum of life continued.

Riley took a deep breath, closed the car door and made her way to Owen. "Owen," she said as she took his hand. "You can put your flowers right here for Daddy."

Owen bent down and laid the small arrangement of roses on his father's grave. "Hi," he said. He put the flower he picked on top of the roses. "I gots you that."

Riley's heart ached.

"Mommy?"

"Yes?"

"I go pway?"

"Owen, this is not a playground; remember?"

Owen huffed. The place was green; greener than most of the places he'd seen since leaving Whiskey Springs. It reminded him of home. There were trees and grass. Around one of the trees, white and yellow flowers like the one he had picked had sprouted. His eyes gleamed with excitement. Fallon had flowers in her yard. Sometimes, he found ladybugs on them. Every so often, he even found a lonely earthworm.

Riley followed Owen's gaze to the tree. "You can go pick some flowers," she said. "Stay at the tree, Owen."

"Okay."

"I mean it. You stay right there."

Owen sprinted toward the tree.

Riley chuckled and looked down at her feet at the small stone etched with her husband's name. "He never stops," she said. She cast her gaze forward again. Owen continued to explore the flowers and grass around the tree. She smiled. "I miss you," Riley confessed. "So much has changed. I don't know what to do, Rob. I feel like I'm going crazy. I thought I had it all worked out. I thought I understood; you know? Whiskey Springs is everything you always said. It's everything Gram told me it would be. It's so much more. Owen, he loves it there. Fallon's been teaching him to fish. I can't pretend to understand what they find enjoyable about catching worms and handling slimy fish." Riley laughed. "But they do. He loves her so much, Rob." Riley closed her eyes and shook her head. "God, help me, so do I. I'm so sorry. I don't know what to do. I wish you could just pick up a damn phone where you are and tell me what to do."

Owen flopped onto his bottom in a plush piece of grass. His fingertips explored the flower petals and stems sprouting from the ground. He studied a soft, white bud curiously, letting his fingers trace the petal gently as if he understood the delicate nature of its existence. His eyes wandered upward to the branches of the tree, considering their height. What would the world look like from above? He could see a few clouds drifting overhead. Fallon liked to look at clouds. She'd find all kinds of things up there. Once, she'd pointed out a bear. Another time, she'd traced the outline of a heart. He tipped his head as a cloud drifted by and reached his hand up to trace its pattern. What did it look like? Owen giggled. It looked like a blob. That's what it was. Fallon said those were just as much fun. They hadn't figured out what they were going to be yet. His eyes tracked back to the ground and his fingers followed, finding the dirt beneath them.

Riley knelt down and traced Robert's name in the stone. "I don't know what I expect. I wish that somehow you could tell me that it's okay. That everything will be all right. You'd like her. I know you would. That much I do know. She thinks she's complicated." Riley smiled. "Fallon isn't complicated at all. Everything is written in her eyes—everything; her fear, her hopes, all that love she wants to give." Riley looked to the sky. Why was it so hard to say goodbye? Robert was never coming back. Tears gathered in her eyes. Could he see her? Could he hear her? Forever was as long as it lasted. Could it ever last a lifetime? Could she let herself believe that again? Robert. Fallon. She missed Robert. She missed Fallon. One was here. One was gone. It should be easy.

"Mommy!"

Riley startled. Owen was hurdling toward her with something dangling from his fingers. Her laughter mixed with a desperate sob, nearly choking her.

"Mommy! I's got one! See? Wike Fawon!"

Riley gripped her chest and closed her eyes. "Thank you," she whispered.

Owen stopped and frowned. He looked at his mother with worry. "Mommy? You want da wum?"

Riley's tears and laughter continued. The last thing she wanted was a worm. She swore she could hear Robert's laughter join with hers. She wrapped her arms around Owen and pulled him close. "No, sweetie."

"You have him." Owen tried to comfort his mother.

Riley sniffled. *Oh, Owen.*

"I show Fawon?"

"I don't think Mr. Worm will make it home, sweetheart. How about we take a picture and you can show her when we get home?"

"Now?"

Riley kept her hand on Owen's shoulders. *Now?*

"Now's as good a time as any," a voice seemed to echo in her ear. "Don't wait, Riley."

Riley's tears seemed endless. "Well, we have to get on a plane, Owen."

Owen's forehead crinkled with frustration.

Riley laughed. She stood to her full height and offered him a hand. "But I'll bet we can find one to take us home tomorrow."

Owen brightened.

"Go put your friend back in his home."

Owen held her gaze.

"Oh, right! The picture." Riley took out her phone and snapped a photo of Owen and his worm. *Oh, Fallon, if you only knew how much we both need you.* She watched Owen run back for the tree. "Thank you," she repeated. "I'll always love you," Riley promised. "Forever."

⁂

"Thanks for coming over," Fallon said.

Jacob pulled up a piece of carpet and tossed it aside. "So, is Riley moving in?"

"What? No."

"Oh."

Fallon sighed. "Jacob, let's go take a break and have a beer."

"It's cool."

"No, it isn't. You and me, we need to talk." Fallon put down the carpet knife in her hand and beckoned Jacob to follow her. She grabbed two beers from the refrigerator. "Let's sit on the deck."

"Fallon, you..."

"Come on," Fallon said. She waited for a few beats to start a conversation.

"This is weird," Jacob said.

"Why is it weird?"

"Because it just is."

Fallon laughed. She recalled Jacob making the same statement years ago when she'd first started to teach him to ski. "Lots of things are weird," she said and then sipped from her beer bottle.

"You and Mom are talking again?"

"I don't think we ever weren't talking," Fallon said. "Jacob, I think I need to make something clear."

Jacob took a long pull from his bottle. "You don't have to say anything."

"Yeah, I do. You know, or maybe you don't; I've kind of always thought of you as a kid brother or something. Not my kid because I'm too young."

Jacob laughed. "You're only six years younger than Mom."

"Be quiet," Fallon advised him.

Jacob snickered.

"I kind of get the feeling you hoped me and your mom might... Well, that we might end up together." Fallon smiled at the shrug and the blush that crept up Jacob's cheeks. He seemed to have transformed into a twelve-year-old. "The thing is, I don't think that's what was supposed to happen."

"Because of Riley?"

"No. Because your mom and I want different things. You and Dave are starting off on your own; you know? I don't think your mom really wants to have another family. I think she wants to explore the world. I know you might not get that. But she was young when she met your dad."

"Yeah, I know. That's sort of what she said the other night after I came out to her."

"And, me? I don't know if it'll ever happen. I don't. I don't know if it will happen with Riley. I still hope maybe someday I will get to do that; you know? Be somebody's mom. I just want to do different things. It doesn't mean I don't love your mom. We're better as friends."

Jacob nodded. "She said that too. You know, you don't have to find things for me to do. I'm sure Mom asked you to talk to me."

"She did." Fallon wasn't in the habit of lying. "I'm glad she did. I miss spending time with you."

Jacob nodded. "I worry about her."

"Your mom?"

"Yeah."

"Me too," Fallon said. "But Andi is probably about the smartest person I know—other than my mom."

"Your mom is everybody's mom."

Fallon chuckled. "She certainly thinks so."

"She seems okay," Jacob said. "She also seems sad."

Fallon sighed. "Your mom is going through a lot right now. That's not all about me. Some of it is," Fallon confessed. "Some of it is your dad and Dave. She's okay, Jacob. One thing about your mother; she's not a liar."

"No, but Mom is always taking care of everyone else," he said honestly. "Like, she's been more worried about Dave than mad that he's acting like an asshole."

"Probably so."

"I don't get it. She keeps worrying about me and Dave, about you, even about Dad. If I tell her I'm worried about her, she tells me not to."

"Yeah, Mom's do that," Fallon said. Her thoughts roamed back to when her father died. "When my dad died, I was a mess. I mean, I was wrecked—completely."

"That had to suck."

"Yeah, it did. It took me a while to see how lost my mom was," Fallon admitted. "Me? I wanted to quit life. I hadn't seen him in almost six months. I'd talked to him the night before. Then he was gone. Boom—just like that, he was gone. I could've come home more. I should have."

"I'm sorry, Fallon."

"No, it's okay. The thing is, my mom poured her energy into me and Dean. Me, mostly. She was broken in a way. Her life changed in a second. When I think about it, her life changed more than mine or Dean's. She lived with my dad every day. She slept beside him every night... Well, unless he was snoring too loud." Fallon chuckled. "Then she'd wander onto the couch with her pillow."

Jacob laughed.

"Her whole life had been my dad in a way. Me and Dean were away. Who was she going to be without him? I think that was the hardest part for her. But I also think that she was more worried about me than about herself. It's a lot like your mom."

"Your mom did okay," Jacob said. "She became the mayor."

Fallon laughed. "Yeah, she discovered all kinds of things after my dad died. Your mom will too."

"Can I ask you something?"

"Depends. How much more beer do I need?"

"Will it bug you? When mom finds someone? Will that bug you at all?"

Fallon pressed down the revolt in her gut. It would hurt a little. No matter how much she loved Riley, it would sting. "Yeah, I'm sure it will. But I want her to. I don't think that's what she's looking for right now, Jacob."

"Do you think I should come back?"

"Move back home?" Fallon asked.

"Yeah."

"As much as I'd love the token gay artist to commiserate with; not unless that's what *you* want; no."

Jacob sighed. "I don't want her to be alone."

Fallon smiled. She understood that. It was one of the reasons she'd been quick to return to Whiskey Springs after her father's death. Recently, she'd found herself pondering that time. She'd found herself musing over the past a lot. After Olivia moved out, Fallon had felt alone. She'd only just begun to realize how much she needed the time to be Fallon, to discover Fallon. She'd never been alone. She had her mother and her friends. She had the pub. Olivia's departure had devastated her. She'd been afraid to open herself again. Loss, no matter how it arrived made a person question. Andi had helped quell all Fallon's questioning. Ironically, Fallon suspected that her presence in Andi's life had accomplished the opposite. Andi was at a point where she questioned everything. That was part of loss too. Loss hurt, but it also revealed a person over time. In its way, loss reminded a person of who they were and what mattered most in life to them. Loss was a catalyst for discovery. Her thoughts drifted to Riley with a new understanding.

"Everyone is on their own journey," Fallon told Jacob. "Follow your gut, Jacob. In my experience, it's usually the best compass for the direction you need to take."

"Yeah. It won't be to Arizona."

"Give it time," she advised. "Dave will come around."

"What if he doesn't? If he could say that to Mom, I don't want to think how he'll feel about my news."

"It's not about you."

"He hates Mom."

"No. He hates the situation."

"Yeah, he wants to save face. Maybe he should become a plastic surgeon."

Fallon laughed. "Don't worry so much about everything. It doesn't help. Trust me; I know."

"So? When is Riley back?"

"Two more weeks."

Jacob took a swig of beer. "You must miss her."

Fallon nodded. "I do."

"I hope it works out," Jacob said.

Fallon's eyes stung with tears. She loved Jacob. She'd never told Andi, and she never would; there were times when she wondered what they might have been together. What if Fallon had found Andi before Olivia, when the boys were still young? What if she'd had the guts to approach Andi years earlier? Andi would say there were no could-have-beens. If it could have been, it would have been. That didn't mean Fallon never contemplated it. Jacob reminded her of Andi in countless ways. "Thanks; me too."

Jacob sniggered. "Maybe you'll let me tag along when you teach Owen to ski."

"You don't need to tag along, Jacob. My door's open any time, just like it's always been."

Jacob stood. "Better get back to work, huh? What are you going to decorate the room with?"

"I don't know. I never had to decorate a kid's room. Liv did the girls' room mostly. Then, they did." She laughed. "What do you think?"

Jacob shrugged. "I think he'll be stoked to have a room."

"I hope so. I was thinking maybe those glow-in-the-dark stars on the ceiling."

"That's cool."

"Hey. What do you say we finish the carpet and take a ride to Burlington?"

"Sure. Why?"

"You can help me pick out the stuff. You're a boy."

Jacob laughed. "You want the gay artist to decorate your kid's room?"

Fallon swallowed hard. "He's not my kid. He's just..."

"Yeah, whatever," Jacob waved off Fallon's words. "From what I've seen, he thinks he is." He laughed.

Fallon felt nauseous. "I just want him to have a place when he's here. Even if Riley and I... Well, they're here a lot is all."

"Right." Jacob opened the front door. He shook his head at the panic in Fallon's eyes.

"What?" Fallon asked.

"Nothing. I just think it's funny."

"What is that?"

"You're scared of a little kid."

Fallon pushed Jacob playfully. "Shut up," she teased him. *No, I'm not scared of him, Jacob. I'm terrified of losing them before I even have the chance to love them.* "If you promise not to bust my ass, I'll even buy you dinner later."

"I have money," he retorted.

Fallon laughed. Having Jacob close eased her fears slightly. She couldn't say why his presence helped. It did. It always had. She'd worried that her relationship with Andi might have destroyed her bond with Jacob. Slowly, things were returning to normal, albeit a new normal as Andi had suggested. Maybe everything would be okay after all. Maybe.

# CHAPTER FIVE

"What are you doing here?" Carol asked.

"I own the place."

"Ha-ha. I thought you had *things to do*. That's what you said when you called yesterday."

"I do. One of those things is checking up on you."

"Fallon," Carol began. She looked at Fallon's hair. "Did you let Dora Bath near your hair?"

"What?"

"Well, the last person I saw who let Dora do her hair was Vera Macmillan before she left to see her daughter in Chicago. It was a faint shade of blue."

Fallon reached up and ran her fingers through her hair. "Must've spattered some paint. And, I wouldn't let Dora Bath near any part of me, much less with scissors."

"What gives? Why are you here?"

"Truthfully, I thought I'd grab something to eat."

"Went through all the groceries Riley and Andi left already?"

"You knew about that?"

"I know about everything."

Fallon rolled her eyes. "You know better than to believe everything you hear."

"Yeah? Well, I heard that Dale asked Marge out."

"On a date?"

"Yep."

"What did Daryl the first say about that?"

Carol laughed. Fallon affectionately deemed Pete and Dale, Daryl and Daryl. They'd yet to find Larry. Marge was Pete's younger sister. Dale was his best friend and a confirmed bachelor. "He was in here grumbling last night."

"Oh boy. Well, maybe it'd be good for them," Fallon offered.

"Marge is a teacher."

"So? Dale could use some instruction."

Carol howled. "Stop."

"I didn't mean *that* kind of instruction." Fallon shuddered. "First, you torture me with Dora Bath and now this? What did I do to you?"

"I could use a raise," Carol bantered.

"Yeah, yeah." Fallon walked into the kitchen where her cook, Don was. "Hey," she greeted him.

"Thought you took today off?"

"Yeah, well; I could use a burger."

"You could go buy some burger," Carol offered from over Fallon's shoulder.

Fallon smirked. "Trying to drum up business for your hubby?"

"Hey, if you don't want to give me a raise..."

"Well, sell more drinks," Fallon teased.

"Stop eating the profits," Carol replied in kind.

"Why do you work for me again?"

Carol shrugged. "I make a better margarita."

"You do not," Fallon said.

"Yeah, I do."

"Oh, really?"

"Yep."

"Care to test that theory?" Fallon challenged.

"What do you suggest? And, before you say it—you cannot have Andi or Riley be a judge."

"Why not?"

"No way," Carol said.

"Scared?"

"No one you've slept with. That should narrow the field."

"I haven't slept with Riley."

"No one you want to sleep with."

Fallon folded her arms across her chest.

"Field just got narrower, huh?" Carol was pleased with herself. "Maybe Daryl and Daryl will play judge."

"You are insane. The only things those two can evaluate are Budweiser and fries. They live on the stuff."

"Okay. It was your challenge. What do you suggest?"

Fallon grinned. "The Cigar Club."

"Excuse me?"

"We'll use the Cigar Club as the judge."

"Oh, no way," Carol said. "I said no one that you've slept with."

"I haven't slept with the Cigar Club."

Carol stared at her friend. "Only Andi and Olivia. No way."

"I haven't slept with my mother, Billie, Deb, or Mabel."

"No one has ever slept with Mabel. And, your mother is your mother. How is that impartial?"

"Well, we'll make them blind."

"Excuse me?"

"We'll get an impartial party to deliver the drinks. Not tell them whose is whose."

"Like who?" Carol asked.

"Don. He can do it." Fallon gestured to their friend.

"No way," Carol said.

"Why not?"

"Don? You pay Don."

Fallon shrugged. "Fine, you pick."

"Okay, I will. When do I need to decide?"

"Liv gets here with the kids on the fifth of July. Cigar Club is that Saturday."

"Fine."

"Good," Fallon said. "It gives you a few weeks to try and perfect your technique."

"It gives you a few weeks to learn how to mix one correctly—boss." Carol winked and headed back to the bar.

"Are you really going to challenge her?" Don asked.

"Sure."

"What if she wins?" He asked.

"She won't."

Don laughed. "You're going to rig it."

Fallon winked. "Just make my burger," she said.

"I can't believe you're leaving already."

Riley closed her suitcase and sat on the bed. "I need to go home."

"What about the job offer?"

"I need to go home, Mary."

"What is going on? This isn't home anymore? You and Mom were up here for hours the other night. You disappeared all morning yesterday and then announced you were leaving. What's the deal?"

Riley took a deep breath. "This isn't home anymore, not for me and not for Owen."

"How can you say that? What happened in the last two days? I thought you were considering Derek's offer? It's not like you don't have roots here."

Riley shook her head. "I don't. I have leaves here, Mary."

"If that's writer speak, you lost me."

"All I'm trying to say is that I left a piece of myself here. It may be where my life started, even where Owen's did. It's not where I want to put down roots, Mary. I know you don't understand that. This isn't where I belong anymore."

"I don't understand it. There are people who love you here."

"There are people who love me in Whiskey Springs—people I love."

"There is someone."

Riley smiled. "There is."

"And, he's important enough to give up your dreams for?"

"Dreams change sometimes. I'm not giving anything up. I'm choosing to give myself a chance with someone I love."

"I thought you weren't into Jerry."

"It's not Jerry." Riley took a deep breath. *Brace yourself.* "I'm in love with Fallon."

"Fallon? Your friend, Fallon?"

"She's a lot more than my friend. At least, I hope that's still what she wants."

"Since when are you a lesbian?"

"I don't know that I *am* a lesbian."

"That makes no sense. So, what? You're bisexual?"

"I really haven't given it much thought."

"Don't you think you should?" Mary asked.

"Not really."

"I don't understand."

"What do you need to understand?" Riley tried to keep the frustration and hurt out of her voice. "I fell in love, Mary. I didn't ask to. I didn't expect to. I did. Owen did." She tried to calm her nerves. "Fallon is an amazing person. She's loving and sensitive. She's funny, and she's intelligent. She loves Owen, and she loves me."

"You're lonely."

"No, I'm not."

"Out there in the woods. That's what this is about."

"No. I'm not lonely. I have friends. Owen has friends. We have Fallon. I left without telling her—without letting her know how much I love her. That was a mistake."

"Well, if she loves you so much, I shouldn't think that a visit to visit your *family* would be a problem."

Riley sighed. "It's not that. It's that I left without telling her."

"I'm sure she can wait two more weeks."

"I'm sure she will wait two more weeks. That doesn't mean she should have to."

"I assume she has a phone. Call her."

Riley smiled. "She deserves more than that, Mary—a lot more than that."

Mary's lips pursed with displeasure. "What about you, Riley? What about Owen? What do you deserve?"

"A chance," Riley replied. "To be happy." She reached out, squeezed her sister's hand, grabbed her suitcase and left the room.

Mary sat shell-shocked.

"Are you planning on sitting here all day or do you want to come downstairs and say goodbye to your sister and Owen?" Brenda asked from the doorway.

"Are you okay with this?" Mary asked.

"I'm not sure I know what you're talking about."

"Riley and a woman out in the boonies—you're okay with that?"

"Riley's a grown woman, Mary. She's no stranger to how cruel the world can be."

"This is hardly like Robert's death."

"No, it isn't. She's in love. Why can't you be happy for her?"

"Maybe because it doesn't make any sense to me."

Brenda nodded. "It doesn't need to make sense to anyone but Riley and Owen."

Mary shook her head.

"You can have whatever opinion you like. Do yourself a favor; don't share it with your sister."

"Why not? That's..."

"If you love Riley, respect her decision."

"Mom, Riley's not a lesbian."

"I never heard her say she was. I heard her say she loved Fallon. Why do you care about that?"

Mary bristled.

"You might ask yourself why you are so eager to have your sister move home."

"I just think she'd be happier here."

"Mm. Then you haven't been paying much attention to Riley's feelings." Brenda smiled at her daughter. "Part of loving people is letting them go, Mary. Riley's learned that lesson."

"Nobody died, Mom."

"I've known people to hang on long after a death," Brenda replied. "Letting go isn't about the person who leaves; it's about the person they leave behind." She watched Mary shake her head again. "You think about it. Right now, I think you ought to come down and wish your sister well."

Mary huffed. "Until disaster strikes," she muttered. She jumped when her mother's head peeked back into the room.

"Who says there will be a disaster?" She laughed. "Maybe you should be the writer. I'll see you in a minute."

Mary sat still for a moment. She tried to process her mother's words, tried to conceive Riley's revelation. "I hope you're right. Who'll be there to pick up the pieces this time?"

Fallon stood back and looked at the wall. Painting the small bedroom for Owen had proved a Herculean task. Why had she ever decided to paint it dark green? That's right; she hadn't; Olivia chose that color. Fallon grimaced. She'd bought primer. Wasn't that supposed to make her life easier? "Apparently not. Good thing she's not back for another two weeks." Fallon scratched her brow and considered the paint pan at her feet. "Round three, I guess." She bent over to pour some paint into the pan when something caught her eye out the window. "What the..."

Fallon squinted to bring an emerging figure into focus. "Riley?" Who was driving Riley's car up the road? Fallon spun on her heels and tripped on the paint pan. Blue paint flew into the air, spatters sticking to everything in its wake. Fallon groaned. "Way to go, Foster." She shed her now blue sneakers, grabbed a cloth, wiped a blob of paint from her cheek, and started the short trek for the front door. "What is going on?"

Riley gripped the steering wheel tightly as Fallon's house came into view. *Deep breaths, Riley.* She'd boarded a plane at eight in the morning. It was just past seven in the evening. She'd stopped by Murphy's Law, expecting that Fallon would be at work. Carol had laughed, explaining that Fallon was immersed in some crazy project. Riley asked what it was.

*"I'm not asking," Carol replied. "She took the last two days off. All I know is she's had Jacob there helping, and she seems to be covered in dirt, dust, or paint every time she comes down here – which is only when she wants food. So, she's not practicing her culinary skills."*

"Fawon!" Owen screamed from the back seat.

Riley's hands began to tremble. *Fallon.*

Fallon walked out onto the front porch just as Riley was closing the car door. Owen barreled ahead, running full tilt for her arms.

"Hey, buddy."

"Fawon!"

"That's me."

Riley took another deep breath. Fallon's eyes met hers. She walked up the steps slowly. Fallon was a mess. Blue paint dripped from her hair. The same shade of blue was spattered across her T-shirt, and a stream of blue ran down her left leg.

"What are you doing home?" Fallon asked as she tried to hug Owen without coating him in paint.

Riley grinned at the pathetic state of the woman she loved. "What were *you* doing?"

"Painting."

"Yourself into a Smurf?"

"I had a little accident," Fallon said. "Seriously, what are you doing here?"

"We missed you."

Fallon's heart skipped.

Riley searched Fallon's eyes and shook her head.

"What is it?" Fallon asked. "Did something happen in San Diego?"

"Fallon..."

"What? Riley, what is it?"

Riley's tears began to fall softly. "I missed home."

Fallon felt sick. Her greatest fear was about to be realized; Riley was going back to San Diego. She nodded.

"No," Riley said, knowing where Fallon's thoughts had traveled. She reached up and cupped Fallon's cheek. She grinned at the fleck of blue paint under her thumb. "No," she repeated. "Here, Fallon." She sucked in a nervous breath. How could she begin to explain what she was feeling? She gently guided Fallon's lips to hers and let her lips brush against Fallon's softly. "*I* missed *you*."

"Riley..."

"We need to talk."

Fallon opened the front door and held it for Riley and Owen.

Owen toddled back to Fallon.

"He missed you," Riley said.

Fallon kissed Owen on the cheek. "Do you want to watch a movie, buddy? I need to clean some things up."

Riley lifted her brow playfully.

"Including myself, apparently. Maybe I can convince Mommy to stay for dinner."

"Fallon, if you have things to do…"

Fallon took a step closer. "Riley, nothing matters to me more than the fact that you are home."

Riley smiled. She believed that, and that was part of the reason they needed to talk.

"Let me get cleaned up," Fallon said. "Maybe you can find something for Owen to watch. He's got some puzzles here."

"Wine?" Riley asked.

"Do I need it?" Fallon asked lightly.

Riley chuckled. "I hope not." *I might.*

"Wine sounds perfect. I'm going to go…"

"DeSmurfify yourself?"

Fallon laughed and kissed Riley's forehead. "It is a bit of a kerfuffle."

Riley giggled. "You do love that word."

"I missed you."

Riley closed her eyes. "I missed you too. Go." She held her breath for a second when Fallon walked away. "I don't intend to miss you again."

Fallon accepted a glass of wine from Riley. She took a deep breath and sat down on the sofa. "So…"

"So," Riley said. Suddenly, she was nervous. Where had her confidence gone?

"Riley?"

"Sorry."

"Talk to me," Fallon said.

Riley let out a long breath. "I missed you, Fallon."

"I missed you too."

"I went back to California and I tried—Fallon, I tried to make the pieces come together. I saw my friends. I saw my mother and Mary. Nothing fit—nothing. I went to visit Robert." Riley sucked in a deep breath.

Fallon reached for Riley's hand. "Riley, you can tell me anything."

"I needed to talk to him. I can't explain it to you. Standing there, talking to him I realized what I need."

Fallon waited.

"To make the pieces fit," Riley explained. "I needed to come home. I need you. What I feel for you—it's... Fallon, I..."

Fallon set her glass down and moved closer to Riley. She took Riley's face in her hands. "You don't need to explain."

Riley's tears began to fall.

"I love you, Riley."

"I love you too. I'm in love with you. It scares me."

"What does?"

"This. I don't want to lose you," Riley said.

"It scares me too. I wasn't sure you would come back."

"I'm not Olivia."

"I know," Fallon replied. *I do know.* "It still scares me, Riley. I can't help that."

"Where do we go from here?" Riley asked.

"One day at a time. We can take this slowly. We probably should. You and Owen are too important to me to screw this up."

"Does that mean I can't ask you to kiss me?"

Fallon chuckled. "You don't need to ask." She brought her lips to Riley's. Gently, she coaxed Riley's lips to part.

Silence—complete silence enveloped Riley. They'd shared kisses; not one had felt like this. Stillness and completion—that's what Riley felt; home, she had come home. She held onto Fallon as the kiss deepened, yearning and tender, speaking the truth without the fumbling of words or sentiment. "Fallon," she whispered when Fallon pulled away.

"Fawon!"

Fallon's forehead fell against Riley's. They both giggled.

"Yes?" Fallon asked.

"I's hungwy."

Fallon pulled back and exchanged a smile with Riley. "Macaroni and cheese or cereal, take your pick."

Riley laughed. "Didn't do any shopping, huh?"

"Nope."

"We need to work on that," Riley offered.

"Mommy, mac n cheese!"

"Guess, you have your answer," Riley said.

"I could run down to the pub and bring something back," Fallon said.

"No. You, me, Owen and a box of mac and cheese," Riley said. She held out her hand.

"Mac n cheese!" Owen danced.

Riley leaned into Fallon as they made their way to the kitchen. "I'll take mine with a kiss," she said.

Fallon smiled. "That, I can handle."

Riley pulled Fallon to a stop. "Fallon?"

"What?"

"I… I heard you—about taking this slowly."

Fallon narrowed her gaze.

"But, tonight… Can we stay here? I need to be close to you."

Fallon pulled Riley close and kissed her forehead tenderly. "Only if you let me hold you."

Riley let out a long sigh. "I missed you so much."

"Let's make that macaroni and cheese. We have all night to talk; okay?"

"I don't want to talk," Riley muttered into Fallon's shoulder.

Fallon chuckled.

"That was out loud, wasn't it?"

"Yeah. But if it's any consolation, I'm glad to know I'm not the only one who feels that way."

Riley stepped back and took a breath. "Not at all."

"Come on." Fallon took Riley's hand. "At least, let me buy you dinner before I take you to bed."

Riley smacked Fallon playfully. "I had to fall in love with a comedienne."

Fallon felt Riley's playful statement in every cell of her body.

"Fawon!"

"We're coming," Fallon laughed. The entire world suddenly felt lighter. *Mac and cheese, a movie, and then I can hold her.*

Owen yawned and rubbed his eyes. Fallon stroked his hair. "You need some sleep, buddy." She looked at Riley apologetically. She had shared her plans, and even let Riley see the *kerfuffle* in the spare room. "I didn't expect you home so soon."

"We can go back," Riley teased.

"Oh, no. I guess it'll be the girls' room for the boy tonight." Fallon lifted Owen into her arms.

Riley reclined on the sofa, content to watch Fallon gently lift Owen into her arms and carry him away. She smiled at the affectionate exchange between her son and the woman she loved. Owen's head rested against Fallon. He mumbled and fell back to sleep.

Fallon looked at Riley curiously. "What?"

"I love you," Riley said. "Put him down so I can show you just how much."

Fallon nearly fell off her feet. *What did she just say?*

Riley giggled. Fallon's face drained of all color and then flushed the deepest shade of red Riley had ever seen. If she got that reaction from a simple statement, she wondered what making love with Fallon might elicit. "Well?" She gently prodded Fallon.

Fallon swallowed hard and nodded.

Riley laughed when Fallon was out of sight. Slow? If by slow, Fallon meant that they shouldn't make love, Riley was about to challenge that idea. She'd enjoyed the evening. A few exchanged kisses and the occasional loving caress stoked her desire to be close to Fallon. She had no intention of sleeping beside Fallon without touching her—none. The thought terrified her. Seeing Fallon falter at mere innuendo, raised her confidence a degree. She wasn't the only one who was nervous.

Fallon laid Owen down on the bottom bunk bed. She covered him lightly and shook her head. "I think your Mommy is trying to kill me." Fallon chuckled. In her wildest dreams, she never expected this day to end with Riley in her home, much less in her arms. Riley's intentions were evident. "Maybe slow is defined differently for her." Fallon chuckled again. "Why am I so nervous?" Fallon's stomach had twisted into knots, her skin tingled with anticipation, and her muscles were already trembling. For someone who prided herself on being "smooth," Fallon was a pathetic mess of angst. She'd been blindsided. Fallon had no time to devise a romantic scenario, no time to plan her words. What if she disappointed Riley? "What is wrong with me?"

Riley waited a few minutes for Fallon to reappear. Deciding that Fallon was taking the opportunity to hide, she made her way to the bedroom Emily and Summer shared when they visited. "Worried he'll escape?" Riley asked from just outside the door.

Fallon spun around. She shook her head.

Riley smiled. *You are truly adorable, Fallon.* Trepidation and hope mingled with love and desire in Fallon's eyes. Riley held out her hand.

Fallon sucked in a shaky breath. She closed her eyes when Riley pulled her close.

"I'm nervous too," Riley confessed. "I need you, Fallon. I feel like I've been waiting forever for you. I don't want to waste any more time."

Fallon took a step back. "Let's go have a glass of wine."

Riley sighed.

"No," Fallon said. She took Riley's face in her hands. "I'm not stalling. Maybe I am." She grinned. "I don't want this to feel pressured for either of us, Riley. Everything between us has always happened naturally. This shouldn't be any different."

Riley nodded. Doubt about her feelings for Fallon was not a problem. She hadn't slept with anyone except Robert in more than eight years. She hadn't been intimate with anyone at all for more than two. Fallon on the other hand—it unnerved Riley—Fallon's experience with women. She didn't want time to think about reality.

Fallon led Riley from the bedroom and shut the door. "You grab our glasses and the bottle of wine. I have something I need to do. I'll meet you on the back deck in a few minutes."

"Fallon..."

"Trust me."

"I do trust you."

"Then get the wine." Fallon kissed Riley sweetly. "Five minutes, Riley. I'll be there in five minutes."

Riley wandered into the living room to retrieve the wine glasses, wondering what Fallon was planning. A quick visit to the kitchen, and Riley was headed to the deck on the back of Fallon's house. She placed the glasses and bottles on the patio table and claimed one of the chairs. Fallon had been gone less than five minutes. To Riley, it felt as if hours had passed. Once she had spoken the words, "I'm in love with you," all Riley seemed to think about was being close to Fallon. More than attraction drove her desire to make love with Fallon. Life was short. Standing at Robert's grave the previous morning reminded Riley how fleeting life was. Her mother's words continued to ring in her ears, "forever is as long as it lasts." It had been a simple statement meant to help Riley cross the bridge from her past into the present. Her mother's sentiment held more truth than any words Riley could recall. She had promised Robert forever. And, she would love him that long. The moment her eyes met Fallon's that evening, Riley understood that

Fallon would hold her heart for the rest of her life, however long that turned out to be. How many people got a second chance at true love? Riley had many friends from the support groups she joined after Robert's death. Many of those people had found someone to share their life with again. She'd seen few whose eyes sparkled with the affection she felt for Fallon. More often, their eyes reflected peace—the peace that comes from quelling loneliness with companionship. Fallon offered companionship. Being with Fallon did quiet the loneliness Riley felt. But Fallon's presence in Riley's life had more than quieted loneliness; it had conjured longing—a yearning so palpable it almost hurt. Time offered no guarantees. Life made no promises for tomorrow. Riley dreamed of sharing tomorrow with Fallon. She understood that tomorrow was a wish. Today was the only place a person could live. She would not let one more day pass without sharing every part of herself with Fallon Foster.

"Pretty night," Fallon said, looking up at the sky.

Riley turned to find Fallon standing behind her with an armload of blankets and pillows.

"I thought we could spend some time out here."

Riley smiled gratefully.

"Grab the wine. I'll lay the blankets out on the grass." Fallon descended three small stairs into the yard and laid a heavy blanket down, then the pillows, placing another blanket on top of the first. She took a seat and patted the ground beside her. "Is this okay?"

Riley nodded.

"Are you all right?" Fallon asked.

"I'm terrified," Riley said.

"Of being with me tonight or of being with me tomorrow?"

"Of disappointing you. Of losing you. Of missing anything with you."

Fallon took Riley's hand. "That's why I wanted to sit out here with some wine. Riley, I'm not going anywhere; I promise."

"You can't promise that, Fallon. Neither can I. I can promise you that I don't want to go anywhere. I can tell you that I don't want to think about one day without talking to you, that I'm so in love with you it takes my breath away. I am. Once, I heard myself say it; that I love you," Riley needed a moment to gather her thoughts. "Fallon, none of us know what tomorrow will bring. I have to live today—right now. And, you need to believe that I won't leave unless I have no choice."

Fallon listened attentively. "I do believe that," Fallon replied. "I know that life is unpredictable. I've lived that reality too."

"I know you have."

"For me, Riley... For me, this—you here with me—it means more to me than anything that has happened in my life."

Tears trailed down Riley's cheeks. "Fallon..."

"I mean it." Fallon reached out and caressed Riley's cheek with her fingertips. She took Riley's face in her hands tenderly and searched Riley's eyes without any further comment. Slowly, she brought their lips together.

Riley's hands reached to hold Fallon's. Fallon's tongue coaxed her lips to part. She sighed at the dance that followed. The soft brush of Fallon's fingertips on her cheek, the tenderness in their kiss sent shivers up and down Riley's spine. Her hands fell from Fallon's hands, gripping Fallon's waist to steady herself.

Fallon's head began to spin pleasantly. Riley's hands moved down the length of her back and lifted her T-shirt. The sensation of Riley's fingertips caressing her skin elicited a desperate sigh from Fallon. Riley's touch was gentler than Fallon had dared imagine. Her heart thrummed in an offbeat rhythm, reverberating in her chest. She pulled back from their kiss in a futile effort to calm a rising storm.

Riley felt the thundering of Fallon's heart pressed against her. She placed a hand on Fallon's chest and looked at her. "I love you, Fallon."

Riley's words were Fallon's undoing. A tear slipped over her cheek. "I can't believe you're here."

"I'm here," Riley replied. "For as long as forever might be, Fallon; this is where I want to be."

Fallon brushed Riley's hair aside and lowered her to the blanket. She hovered over Riley and searched Riley's eyes for any hint of reservation. Seeing a flicker of nervousness, Fallon leaned in and kissed Riley's cheek. "Tell me what you're thinking," she requested.

Riley bit her quivering lower lip. "It's been so long. No one has… No one has seen me, Fallon… No one has touched me in so long. I don't…"

Fallon silenced Riley with a kiss. "I see you," she said. "All you have to do is say stop, Riley. I'll hold you all night if that's what you want."

"I do want that. I want you," Riley said. She couldn't explain her insecurity. No one had seen her naked except Robert in years—no one that she wanted to make love with. It was strange; she'd never felt a shred of worry in the past about her body. Not that Riley viewed herself as any sort of goddess. She'd never given much thought to how a lover might perceive her, not since she'd first taken a lover. Perhaps that had been the naïveté of youth. Or it may have been the stirrings of lust mixed with inexperience that conspired to quash self-doubt. Fallon loved her. Riley believed that. Everything about Fallon made Riley tingle with excitement and emotion. A simple kiss, the faintest touch from Fallon's fingertips set Riley ablaze. Her body was already humming a familiar tune that somehow seemed completely new. She'd felt love. She'd experienced lust and longing. She'd been in love before—made love. Something in Riley's life had shifted. It was as if she could feel gravity itself. When she'd first found herself in Robert's bed, it had been the result of playfulness and exploration. Love had followed sex. It occurred to her as she looked at Fallon that she had never fallen in love before taking someone as her lover. She caressed Fallon's cheek.

Fallon smiled, silent understanding passing between them. In Fallon's eyes, Riley was more than beautiful; she was everything that Fallon had been hoping to find in a partner. Compassion and kindness flowed from Riley. Riley's raw vulnerability made Fallon love her more deeply than Fallon imagined was possible. Fallon had been to bed with people she loved and with women she simply desired. Sex had been a weapon, an escape, and even an expression of emotion. She'd barely touched Riley, and Fallon already understood that life with Riley was going to be something she had never encountered before. Making love would solidify their bond. As Fallon closed the distance between them, she determined to communicate in every way she could that she would hold Riley's heart as if it were glass—gently, with the care and reverence Riley deserved.

Warmth traveled through every part of Riley's body. Fallon's lips tasted the flesh behind Riley's ear, wandering gradually lower to the hollow of her throat. Riley turned her head, inviting Fallon to continue, falling away under Fallon's gentle exploration. Her hands stroked Fallon's back and lifted her T-shirt again. She needed to feel Fallon's skin. Fallon's hand tracked inward, barely brushing her breast over the shirt she wore. She heard herself whimper. Fallon paused. Sensing hesitation, Riley took hold of Fallon's hand and placed it firmly on her breast. Fallon's breath hitched and released in Riley's ear. Riley pulled her closer. "Fallon," she whispered. "Don't stop."

Fallon's brain warred with her body. Owen was asleep in the house. He might come looking for Riley. He might get scared if he couldn't find his mother or Fallon. Worse, he might find them here on the blanket—naked. Because if Fallon didn't stop, she wasn't sure she would be able to. "Owen might wake up," Fallon said.

Riley opened her eyes and directed Fallon to look at her. Could she love a person more? Amid burning desire, Fallon's thoughts had traveled to protecting Owen. "He's asleep," Riley said.

"Maybe we should take this inside," Fallon said. There was a door to her bedroom. She could lock it. They would have time to...

Riley pulled Fallon to her and kissed her soundly. "Don't. Stop."

Fallon's heart hammered violently. Riley's hand caught hers and placed it back over a heaving breast. Fallon's mouth claimed Riley's instantly. Riley's hands slipped under Fallon's shirt and addressed the clasp of her bra in one swift motion. Had she not been so far gone already, Fallon would have laughed. Whatever shyness or reservation Riley might have felt earlier, it had vanished. She sat up and removed her shirt and a dangling bra.

Riley looked up at Fallon. Why did writers always describe sudden wantonness with visions of deserts? How many times had she read the words, "Her mouth went dry?" Her eyes roamed over Fallon's curves and her lips curled into a smile.

Fallon's brow raised in question.

*The things that go through my mind. Hot? Maybe. Dry? Hardly.* Riley's eyes held Fallon's. Her hands caressed Fallon's hips and tugged on the waistline of her jeans.

Fallon unbuttoned her jeans. She was surprised when Riley moved to unzip them.

"You are beautiful," Riley said.

Fallon moved to lie beside Riley. "You think so?"

"You are."

Fallon directed Riley to sit up. She pulled Riley's shirt over her head and tossed it aside. "Have you seen you?" Fallon removed the rest of Riley's clothing one piece at a time until they were pressed against each other, a blanket of warm flesh under a cool summer breeze. "Riley," Fallon called softly.

"Hum?"

Fallon shifted to look into Riley's eyes. She found herself speechless. *It's real. She's here.*

Riley pushed Fallon gently back onto the blanket and climbed on top of her. "You don't need to say anything," she promised. "I already know." Her hands fell to Fallon's breasts, her palms faintly grazing over Fallon's nipples.

"Riley..."

Riley watched in rapt fascination as Fallon's body began to submit to her touch. How had the seductress fallen into Riley's grasp so easily? Her tongue trailed up Fallon's neck to her ear. "I can't get close enough to you."

No part of Fallon could resist Riley's advances. With a ragged breath, her eyelids fluttered and closed. She would relinquish all control, all thought, any reason, and every ounce of restraint—Riley would have all of her. Riley could take all of her, devour her if that is what Riley wished. A sudden warmth surrounding her nipple forced her eyes open. The sight that greeted her took her breath away for an instant. Who needed air? Fallon gasped. Riley's eyes lifted to meet hers, but Riley refused to give up her prize. Her teeth tugged gently at Fallon's nipple. Fallon's hips arched and her hands gripped Riley's shoulders, anything to bring them closer—anything.

Feeling Fallon's frustration, Riley reluctantly brought her lips to Fallon's. A breath away, she traced Fallon's lips with her tongue before kissing her passionately. "Fallon."

Fallon sighed.

"Fallon, look at me. Please."

Fallon opened her eyes again. Suddenly, Riley seemed to falter. A sweet kiss preceded Fallon's remedy. She turned them. Lying side by side, Fallon's fingers traced a delicate trail from Riley's shoulder to her hip. She claimed Riley's lips again, reverently. "Riley," she whispered as her hand moved to cup Riley's breast.

"I need you," Riley said.

"I'm right here," Fallon promised. She kissed her way over Riley's throat to the top of her cleavage and downward until her mouth replaced the warmth of her hand. "Right here," she promised again.

"Fallon." Riley breathed Fallon in. The breeze that caused the branches overhead to sway lifted the scent of Fallon's coconut shampoo and a hint of something floral through the air. Fallon's tongue playfully teased one of Riley's breasts while two fingers tenderly toyed with the other. Had she forgotten what it felt like to be touched? Riley wasn't sure. Tiny prickles erupted over her heated skin. Fallon's body was pressed against her, staving the chill from a steadily cooling breeze. Fallon's fingers drifted lower, circling her navel. Riley's fingers wound themselves in Fallon's hair, urging her to continue. She wanted to touch Fallon. Every cell in her body cried out to feel Fallon. Why had she stopped?

Gently, Fallon's fingers found the warmth of Riley's arousal. Riley's grip tightened. Tenderly, Fallon began to explore the softness that greeted her.

Riley was certain she would explode. Fallon's fingers barely touched her, and she was trembling.

"Shh," Fallon cooed. "I'm right here, Riley."

Riley needed to see Fallon, to stay connected to her. Her hands cupped Fallon's face, her forehead falling gently against Fallon's as Fallon's touch grew more insistent. "I..."

Fallon's lips met Riley's softly, steadily deepening their kiss in time with the rising tide of Riley's arousal. Tonight, Fallon would touch Riley tenderly. Passion would submit to love. When Riley's tongue fought for dominance, Fallon gentled their kiss. "Shh," she whispered. She let her eyes meet Riley's again. She longed to taste Riley, to explore every dip and crevice Riley's body offered. What Riley needed now was to see Fallon, to know that this moment wasn't about physical release. Shared touches were whispered truths, promises, hopes, and dreams. The rise and inevitable fall would crumble the remnants of walls each had erected long ago—nothing would stand between them. The last vestiges of insecurity and fear would banish the ghosts of the past and carry them into a new world; a world shared together.

Riley's body ached pleasantly. Her heart skipped wildly. Still, she needed more. She struggled to voice her desire. Fallon's touch was loving yet timid. It only made Riley want Fallon more. She could say anything, ask for anything, take anything she wanted. Riley understood that. "Fallon," Riley lost her breath before she could continue. "Please… Fallon, I need you closer."

Fallon's finger circled Riley. Again, and again she searched Riley's softness before slipping tenderly inside her lover.

"Fallon!"

Fallon's need was growing by the second. Riley's hips swirled to meet her gentle thrusts. "Oh, God, Riley…" Riley's breasts were pressed against hers. Riley's mouth hovered next to her ear, warm breath washing over her neck. It was delicious. She wanted to feel Riley submit to her. "You feel so good," Fallon muttered. "Perfect."

"Fallon," Riley choked on the name. The trembling in her legs grew steadily. Her mind went silent. Her heart seemed to leap from her chest as her body tensed. It was almost painful—almost. Climbing steadily as if trudging up a mountain; every muscle in her body screaming to reach the top, crying out for relief. One agonizing second to the next, steeped in anticipation, breathless, Fallon pushed Riley higher. How long could she stand to be suspended in this peculiar euphoria? Where was the peak? When would she fall?

Nothing in Fallon's life could compare to the sensation of Riley in her arms, moving against her sensually. If heaven existed, Fallon had found it. Touching Riley made her dizzy. Riley's hands drew her closer. Riley's hips urged Fallon deeper. Pleasant ripples moved through Fallon's core, soft like a flowing stream over smooth rocks. She let her thumb circle Riley's need, pressing softly against the small bud that she was confident would thrust her lover over the ledge she dangled on. Two hands grasped her tightly; a primal sound escaped Riley's throat; a strangled cry of ecstasy released into the summer night like a long-imprisoned soul finally finding its freedom.

Home—Riley thought she had come home when she saw Fallon on the porch earlier. No. Fallon carried her home now. Fallon was home. Riley's body rose to meet Fallon's, shuddering violently, crashing against her will. Memories seemed to stream by at the speed of light, slipping into a distant universe as if Fallon's presence instructed the past to find its rightful place. Just as the thunderous rapture began to subside, Fallon pressed deeper sending Riley spiraling out of control again. All that existed was Fallon. Nothing, no image of the past, no misgiving about the future, no insecurity in the present lived in this place. All that remained was Fallon as Riley plummeted into her final descent. "I love you," she called out. "Fallon..."

Fallon held Riley close until the quaking of Riley's flesh subsided into faint quivering. "I love you, Riley. So much. So much."

Riley had never cried during lovemaking—never. Tears streamed down her cheeks. She'd spent so much time doubting that love would ever touch her life again, that anyone could penetrate her wounded heart. She brushed Fallon's hair aside. "You have no idea..."

"Yes, I do," Fallon said. Her lips caressed Riley's forehead. "I do. Let me hold you."

Riley pushed herself up and grinned.

"What?" Fallon asked.

Riley's lips touched Fallon's briefly. They drifted over Fallon's throat to the swell of her breasts. Riley sighed. She licked her lips. "So beautiful," she muttered. Her mouth tasted a straining nipple. The deep moan that escaped Fallon's throat sent small shock waves through Riley's core, stirring a still rolling tide of pleasure. Back and forth, Riley teased Fallon until Fallon's desperation fell from her mouth.

"Riley... Jesus... You don't know what you're doing to me."

*Yes, I do.* Riley lifted a finger to Fallon's lips, and Fallon sucked it greedily. She couldn't stand it any longer; Riley needed to taste Fallon. That's all she desired. Her body glided against Fallon's, lower, inch by inch, her nipples hard against Fallon's flesh, taunting them both.

*I might die right here.* Fallon's gaze fell on Riley as she descended Fallon's body like a cat on the prowl. *Dear God.*

Intoxicating. Nothing on earth could compare to feeling Fallon beneath her. Riley relished the softness, the curves that were Fallon, the gentle sway of Fallon's hips, and the seductive sighs that passed Fallon's parted lips. For a moment, she had entertained the idea that Fallon moving inside her would define bliss. Yearning unlike anything she'd ever felt encompassed Riley as she touched Fallon. Fallon held nothing back. Riley needed no conversation or explanation to know that Fallon always held herself at a slight distance. She understood. Vulnerability frightened every person. Fallon seemed to open like a blossom in the springtime, offering everything she was, everything she desired, each fear, and all the dreams she kept a secret to Riley's touch. Riley fell into Fallon. Fallon surrounded her, penetrated her. Completion. Amid the torrid stirrings of lust, the throbbing of nerve endings, and the struggle for air, an odd sense of peacefulness encompassed Riley. She glanced up at her lover. Fallon's eyes were pleading. Riley's arms surrounded Fallon's hips, drawing her closer as she ventured to taste the length of Fallon's need.

Fallon opened her mouth to scream. Nothing escaped. She watched as Riley's eyes lifted to hers. Warm, wet, soft strokes seemed to cover every inch of her body. Riley's fingertips pressed into her flesh. Riley's tongue danced over her center, lingering whenever Fallon's breath would hitch and release. The world disappeared. The stars faded into oblivion. The breeze evaporated between them. All that existed was Riley. She let her hands weave into the soft waves of Riley's hair as Riley carried her gently away. Fallon couldn't recall being carried so gently, like a leaf carried by the wind. She managed a deep breath just as the breeze swirled into a powerful wind, taking her to a height Fallon had never known.

Without warning, her descent began. "Riley," she barely managed to call to the woman she loved.

Riley carried Fallon along. She followed Fallon's movements in a perfectly choreographed waltz. Instinctively, Riley understood where Fallon wanted her to go, backward, forward, left, then right. Sensually, they swayed together until Riley felt Fallon's hands lifting her higher. She complied slowly, allowing her body to slide against Fallon's until their lips met.

"Riley..."

Riley pulled back and smiled. She shook her head in awe of the connection they shared. "Are you tired of hearing it yet?"

Fallon's confusion was evident.

"That I love you," Riley explained.

"I don't think I could ever tire of hearing that," Fallon said. "I love you too, Riley."

Riley fell into Fallon's arms, her fingertips tracing circles on Fallon's skin.

"Do you want to go inside?" Fallon asked.

"Not yet," Riley replied. "I just want to be here."

Fallon closed her eyes and delighted in a deep, cleansing breath. "I'm glad you're home."

Riley smiled. *I am home.* "Me too."

# CHAPTER SIX

The bed was bouncing. Why was Fallon's bed bouncing? She rolled onto her back and stretched. Faint giggling greeted her ears, and her lips pursed playfully. "Who's on my bed?" She asked without opening her eyes.

Owen's giggling grew louder.

"Did a coyote slip into my room overnight? Maybe it's a deer." Fallon reached out and grabbed hold of Owen.

"It's me, Fawon!" Owen's giggling turned to a belly laugh.

"An Owen? An Owen slipped into my room?" Fallon tickled Owen playfully.

"Me, Fawon! It's me!"

Fallon laughed and pulled Owen into her arms. "I see that now." She kissed his head. "Where is your mommy?"

"Makin' cakes."

"Making pancakes?" Fallon asked.

"Yep."

Fallon closed her eyes and stretched again. Owen climbed on top of her. She opened one eye.

"Up!" Owen said.

"I'm tired," Fallon countered.

"Mommy's up."

*I have no idea why your mother is not in this bed too. Oh, yes, I do – you.* "Did you get Mommy up?"

"Yep. You was seepin'."

Fallon pulled Owen back down. "Let's take a nap."

"Cakes, Fawon!"

Fallon chuckled. "Okay, okay, I got it. Pancakes prevail." She hoisted herself from the bed with Owen tucked under her arm.

"Fawon!"

Riley turned to the sound of her son squealing with delight.

"I caught something," Fallon said. "A wild Owen."

"Well, look at that. What should we do with him?" Riley played along.

"Mommy!"

Fallon started laughing and placed Owen on his feet. "I guess we have to feed him," she said.

Riley pretended to consider Fallon's words. "What does an Owen eat?"

"Cakes!" Owen laughed.

"Cakes?" Riley asked. "Chocolate cakes?"

"Pancakes, Mommy."

"Oh… Well, I guess you're in luck then. I understand Fallons like those too."

Fallon shrugged. She lifted Owen into his booster seat and leaned in to kiss Riley on the cheek.

Riley surprised her by guiding Fallon's lips to hers. "Good morning," Riley whispered.

Fallon smiled. "Thanks for making breakfast."

Riley winked. "Sit down."

"So, what do you have planned today?" Fallon asked.

"Other than unpacking, nothing." Riley placed a plate of pancakes on the kitchen table. "Why?"

"Well, I kind of wanted to finish painting the room."

"Owen and I can get out of your hair after breakfast."

Fallon frowned. "Well…"

"Fallon, what?" Riley chuckled.

"Maybe for a few hours. I was kind of hoping you might want to go pick out some things for the room. I mean, when I finish painting we could take a ride. Jacob helped me with some stuff, but… I…"

"On one condition."

"What's that?" Fallon asked.

"You are not paying for all of it."

"Why not? It's my house."

Riley challenged Fallon with a stare. Owen looked back and forth between them, curious about the conversation and not fully understanding it.

Fallon groaned. "Okay."

"Good. We'll head home for a few hours after we eat. You call me when you want me to come over."

"How about I just pick you up?"

Riley nodded.

"I'll call first."

"You don't need to call," Riley said.

"Fawon?"

"Yeah, buddy?"

"I got to weave?"

"You'll see Fallon later today," Riley promised.

Owen grinned and stabbed a pancake with his small fork.

Fallon looked over at Riley. Riley could see a hint of fear in her lover's eyes. Would the light of day change things? Riley reached across the table and covered Fallon's hand with hers. "Eat your breakfast," she said.

Fallon nodded and began to pick at the pancakes on her plate. Suddenly, she felt terrified. She should be elated. Everything was suddenly real. What if she pushed too hard? What if Riley had second thoughts? What if, what if, what if…

"Stop worrying," Riley said.

Fallon looked up.

Riley chuckled. "Just think how much easier it will be to get your laundry done now."

Fallon laughed. "I love you for more than your laundry skills, you know?"

Riley smirked causing Fallon to blush. *You are so easy, Fallon.* She laughed. "That's good. So, we're clear; I love you for more than your margarita skills."

Fallon finally relaxed. *She's still here.* She winked at Riley. "Speaking of that…"

"Yes?"

"I have a little bet with Carol."

"Is that so?"

"She seems to think her margaritas are better than mine."

Riley shrugged.

"Wait… Do you think they're better than mine?"

"Of course not."

"You do." Fallon sat back in her chair. "You totally do."

"They're *different* than yours," Riley offered.

"As in better."

"No."

"Right."

"What's the bet?" Riley wanted to know.

"We haven't established what the winner gets. We couldn't agree on an impartial judge, so I suggested we have a blind tasting at the Cigar Club."

"The Cigar Club?" Riley asked.

"Yeah."

"What is this Cigar Club?"

"Oh, right, I forgot; you weren't here this time last year."

"No."

"Well, every summer when Liv is here we have one night that's our Cigar Club at Murphy's. I close the pub down at nine, and it's a women's night of poker, whiskey, and cigars."

"Sounds fun." Riley nearly shuddered. Whiskey and cigars? That sounded almost as bad as worms on hooks and fish out of the pond.

Fallon laughed. "Not your thing, huh?"

"Not really. So, who is in this *club* of yours?"

"Me and Liv, Carol, Mom, Deb Homan, Billie Steele, Marge and then whoever anyone invites."

"Marge is in your Cigar Club?"

"Yep. She usually wins the pot."

"What?"

"From the poker game. Marge is brutal."

Riley laughed raucously. The last thing she ever pictured Marge Lloyd doing was drinking whiskey, smoking cigars, and playing poker. "Marge? I can't picture that."

"Yeah, well, imagine picturing her dating Daryl number two."

"Wait... What? I was only gone a few days."

"Don't ask me. Carol said Dale asked Marge to go out."

"Really?"

"Yeah. Whiskey and cigars doesn't sound so bad now, huh?" Fallon joked.

"Stop," Riley giggled. Daryl and Daryl, as Fallon called them were as much a fixture at Murphy's Law as the beer kegs or bar stools. Riley liked both Pete and Dale. Granted, the pair could easily be characters in a sitcom or a novel. The two played off each other, paid little attention to what was actually being said around them, and according to Fallon were the reason she needed two taps for Budweiser. But Pete and Dale were also kindhearted and amusing. One thing Riley did know; they would walk through fire for Fallon. She'd yet to discover the story behind their evident devotion to.... Her thought stopped midstream. What was Fallon to Riley now? Her girlfriend? Her partner? Riley shook her head to clear the thought.

"Are you okay?" Fallon asked. "I lost you there for a second."

"I was just thinking about something."

"Please tell me it wasn't about Pete or Dale."

"Not exactly, no."

Owen squirmed in his chair. "I get down?"

Riley arched a brow at her son.

"Pwease?"

"You can get down. Let me wipe your hands and face first; okay? Press play on your movie and I'll be there in a bit." Riley proceeded to clean up her son. He climbed down from his seat on the chair and scrambled off toward the living room.

"What were you thinking about?" Fallon asked again.

"It's silly."

"I doubt it unless it was about Daryl and Daryl."

"What is up with the three of you anyway?" Riley wondered.

"What do you mean?"

"Fallon, as much as you love to make fun of Pete and Dale, those two would step in front of a truck for you. I'm not kidding."

"They get free beer."

"Stop. You don't have to tell me..."

Fallon sighed. "I sort of saved Dale's ass once; he sort of saved mine."

"Go on."

"Do you really want to hear this?"

"Only if you want to tell me."

"Riley, there isn't anything I don't want to tell you. I just haven't talked about any of this in a long time."

"You don't have to talk..."

"No." Fallon took a breath. "Before I left for college, Dale got himself in a bit of a jam. I knew him better than Pete back then. He was pretty good friends with Dean at one time. Believe it or not, he was pretty close to Andi once too."

"I believe it."

"Anyway, he and Pete had some crazy ass bet. You know those two."

"I do."

"They decided to try and cross the old rail bridge that runs down behind the pond."

"Oh, no."

"Yeah. I happened to be fishing that day. I wanted to get away from the house; you know? Just sit by the water. I heard yelling. At first, I thought it was kids in the woods. Then I realized it was someone in trouble."

"What happened?"

"They were about halfway across. Pete was ahead of Dale. Dale fell through. I mean, he fell through, Riley. The only thing that stopped him from hitting the ground was that his shirt got caught on some protruding steel. Pete tried to go back to help him, but his weight moving on the tracks started to shake Dale loose."

"Why didn't he..."

"Call someone?" Fallon smiled. "That was twenty-two years ago. None of us had a cell phone."

"Oh, my God."

"I ran toward the sound. There was Dale, hanging by his shirt. There wasn't time to get help. That drop has to be at least sixty feet."

"What did you do?"

"I climbed up."

"You could have been killed!"

"I wasn't really thinking about that. I wasn't thinking about anything except Dale dangling in the air."

Fallon fell into the memory. She hadn't thought back to that day in years. Whenever she did, her heart would beat slightly faster. She still wasn't positive how she'd managed to hoist Dale back up onto the tracks. Fallon was by no means physically weak. Dale stood at least four inches above her, and by her estimation, he had to have been forty or fifty pounds heavier than her back then. Adrenalin was the only answer she'd been able to apply that made sense. The sheer terror in his eyes lodged in Fallon's chest that day. She'd never told anyone the entire story—until now.

"I don't know how I managed to pull him up. He was in a state of panic. When I reached for him, he started to flail. I thought for a split second he was going to fall; I was about to watch my friend die right in front of me."

Riley listened, watching a flurry of emotions play over Fallon's features as if Fallon were reliving the event as she spoke.

Fallon shook her head. "Somehow, I don't know how, I pulled him onto that platform. I don't remember climbing down. Pete met us on the ground. He'd made it to the other side at some point. All I remember after lifting Dale is him in my arms crying like a newborn baby, shaking. I don't remember if I cried. Pete threw up. We agreed we'd never tell anyone about it. We never did."

"I'm sorry you went through that," Riley said. "I'm glad that you were there."

"Yeah, me too. He repaid the favor in spades. He doesn't think so; he did."

"What happened?"

"After Liv came to visit to tell me she and Barb were trying to get pregnant and that Dean was their donor...."

"Fallon, it's okay."

"No. I lost it, Riley. It hurt me when she left. That news? The news that my brother was going to help my ex have a baby with her new partner?" Fallon had to take a beat to calm herself. "He never spoke to me—never said a word. I'm his fucking sister."

Riley winced at the pain in Fallon's voice.

"That's what hurt the most; you know? Not that she had moved on. That he didn't consider my feelings *at all*. I get that it was their decision. I was out of the picture. Neither of them even asked me how I felt about it. Jesus."

"I'm sorry, babe."

Fallon offered Riley a slight smile, enjoying a new term of endearment from her lover. The story she was about to tell remained painful for her. It was a chapter of her life that had forever bonded her to Pete and Dale. "It's okay. It wasn't okay then. I'm telling you, Riley, I've never felt so betrayed in my life. It hurt. This house was built so we'd have a place for *our* children. We'd talked to Dean. He was thrilled to help. It seemed perfect. They'd be a part of both of us in some way; you know?"

"I think I understand."

"I know it sounds awful; I feel like something was stolen from me. Couldn't they have asked someone else? Barb's brother, maybe? Couldn't my brother have at least called me to see how I would feel?"

Riley took Fallon's hand. She suspected that Olivia could have asked someone else. She guessed that Olivia hadn't wanted to. It seemed obvious to Riley that Olivia Nolan still carried a torch for Fallon. Having Dean Foster be Olivia's donor connected her to Fallon in some way for life, even if Fallon wanted to pull away. She wondered if Fallon saw that clearly. She made no comment and simply caressed the hand she held in support.

"I went over the edge," Fallon admitted. "Olivia was all smiles telling me I would be an aunt soon. An aunt? What the fuck was that?" Fallon closed her eyes and took a breath. "I'm sorry."

"Don't be. Go on."

"I don't know. I told her to go back to Washington. I guess I consumed a little too much alcohol." She shook her head. "More like I consumed almost all the alcohol in my house."

Riley braced herself.

"I walked down to the bridge. That same bridge."

"Fallon."

"I don't remember it, Riley. I remember that it hurt so much I just wanted it to stop hurting. I guess plying myself with alcohol wasn't enough."

Riley's chest ached. The mere memory still left Fallon wounded.

"Anyway, Dale was down by the pond with this girl he'd met. He saw me starting to climb up. I don't know what he said to her, but somehow, he must've gotten her to leave. I vaguely remember seeing them." She stopped and gathered herself. "I don't remember him stopping me from getting to the top. I don't remember what he said. I remember waking up in my house with Pete and Dale sitting in my living room. They didn't let me leave for two days. Pete called Carol and told her he'd stopped by to help with something and I was sick. They made me food. They let me cry. Dale told me Liv was a jerk. I laughed. He saved my life, Riley. Not just because he stopped whatever stupid idea I had; because he got Pete and they stayed with me. And, they never told a soul. They might seem like simpletons to a lot of people. They aren't. They're two of the best people I know. And, if you want to know the truth; I love them."

Riley wiped a tear from the corner of her eye. "I know you do," she said. "I always wondered why."

"Not many people see things as they are."

"No, they don't," Riley agreed. "Thank you for telling me."

"There isn't anything I wouldn't tell you. In fact, I don't think there's anything I don't want to tell you. I want this to work—us, together."

"Me too," Riley replied.

"How did we end up talking about this?"

"You asked me if I was okay."

Fallon regarded Riley thoughtfully for a second. "What was that about? You were thinking about Daryl and Daryl?"

"Not exactly."

"What were you thinking about?" Fallon asked.

Riley blushed. "I was wondering what this is; I mean, are you my girlfriend? Are you my lover? Are you my...."

Fallon grinned. She moved from her seat to kneel in front of Riley's chair. "What do you want it to be?"

"Everything," Riley whispered.

"Why does that embarrass you?"

"It doesn't. I know you love me. I just..."

"I think I understand," Fallon said. "Can I make a suggestion?"

"Please."

"Stop worrying about it. I'd like to think you're my girlfriend. Maybe one day... Well, someday I hope maybe you'll be more than that. Someday."

Riley stroked Fallon's cheek.

Fallon's heart raced. A simple touch carried so much more than Fallon could fathom. "Why don't you go get Owen ready. I'll clean up. It shouldn't take me more than a few hours to finish painting the room." She started to pick up the dishes.

"Fallon?"

"Yeah?"

"Someday."

Fallon smiled. *I hope so.*

**FRIDAY EVENING**

"Where has Fallon been?" Pete asked Carol.

Carol smiled.

"What aren't you saying?"

Carol shrugged. "Can't say what I don't know."

"Yeah? So, tell us what you do know."

"I don't *know* anything. You two are nosier than Dora Bath and her Biddy Brigade."

"Come on, Carol; where's Fallon been?" Dale asked.

Dale sounded genuinely concerned. Carol sighed.

"Is she okay?" Dale asked.

"I think she's spending time with Riley," Carol explained.

"Riley?" Pete inquired.

"They're like best friends," Dale commented.

"Andi's her best friend," Pete said. "Everyone knows that."

Carol grinned and shook her head. *True. But you two are clueless sometimes.*

"What are we missing?" Pete asked.

"Besides about a million brain cells?" Carol teased.

Dale didn't laugh.

Carol sighed again. "I think, maybe they've finally…You know…"

"What?" Pete asked.

"You know," Carol said. "Gotten *together*."

"You mean like Riley's moving in there? Why? She's got a place," Pete said.

Carol smacked her forehead.

"No," Dale looked at his friend. "She means they're sleeping together."

Carol looked at Dale compassionately. Few people took the time to see the obvious truth. Carol saw it in Dale's eyes every time he walked up to the bar. He was in love with Fallon. She suspected he had been for most of his adult life, and she was sure that was the reason he'd finally decided to ask Marge out on a date. Pining for a woman who would never return his affection had to be heartbreaking. She didn't think that Fallon realized Dale's feelings transcended friendship. They were closer as friends than most people realized. That much Carol did know.

"Riley?" Pete laughed at the idea.

Dale looked into his beer glass as if it had no bottom.

Pete looked at Carol whose gaze was focused on Dale. "No way," he said. "Riley's seeing Jerry. Besides, Riley's the marrying kind. Foster doesn't do relationships anymore."

Carol turned to shoot daggers at Pete with her eyes.

"What?" Pete asked. "What did I say?"

Carol wondered how someone could be so blind. Pete was Dale's best friend. They'd been inseparable for a lifetime. How could he not see that Dale was in love with Fallon? And, Fallon? Hard as she might try, Fallon wore her heart on her sleeve. She lit up whenever Riley walked into a room. Carol had joked to Ida that Fallon reminded her of E.T. Every time Fallon so much as mentioned Riley's name, she would light up, a bit like the alien in the movie. Carol and Ida would sing, "Turn on your heart light," when the two would walk out of the pub together. She doubted that

Fallon would find it as amusing as she and Ida did. She chuckled, wondering if Ida had any idea what was going on with her daughter and Whiskey Springs' newest resident. Right now, there was a sullen Dale gazing into his beer who needed a bit of cheering up.

Carol squeezed Dale's hand. "Another beer?"

He nodded.

"I think you've been hitting the tap when we aren't looking," Pete commented. "Riley's not gay. She has a kid."

"Oh, my God!" Carol threw her hands up. "Were you dropped on your head as a child?"

Pete lifted his palms and shrugged.

Dale finally chuckled. "Fallon's in love with Riley."

Pete's gaze shifted to his best friend. "What?"

"Guess the feeling's mutual, huh?" Dale directed his question to Carol.

Carol smiled.

"You're both drunk," Pete said.

"I'm not, but I wouldn't blame Dale if he tied one on," Carol commented.

"Why is that?" Pete asked.

"He's got to deal with your sorry ass," Carol said. She flashed the pair a cheesy grin and made her way to the other end of the bar.

"You really think Fallon and Riley are," Pete began.

"You don't?"

"How does Foster land all the women in this town?" Pete asked.

Dale laughed. *More than the women.* "She's Fallon."

"Yeah, you think she's some kind of superhero or something."

"Or something," Dale mumbled.

"Are you sure you want to do this?" Fallon asked.

"Go to the pub with you? Why wouldn't I?" Riley asked.

"Because things have changed, and people will notice they've changed."

Riley kissed Fallon's lips gently. "I told you; I'll meet you there around nine."

"Marge is babysitting?" Fallon asked.

Riley shook her head.

"No? What are you doing with Owen?"

"Fallon, don't ask me that right now."

Fallon let out a long breath. "Andi."

"I need to talk to her."

"I know. I just..."

"She already knows."

"You told her?"

"I didn't have to."

Fallon felt sick. "I should've told her."

"Second thoughts?" Riley asked.

"About what?"

"Me? Andi?"

"No."

"Then relax. I have to see her, Fallon."

"I get it. I'll go."

"You can practice your margaritas on me," Riley said.

"Margaritas, as in plural?"

"Mm-hum. Andi offered to spend the night here with Owen," Riley explained. Fallon's jaw fell so low, Riley thought it might hit the ground. She laughed. "Is that a problem?"

"No..."

"I thought this was a *date* night."

"It is," Fallon agreed.

"I'd like to have some time alone with you—without a three-year-old climbing into our bed first thing in the morning."

Fallon's eyes twinkled. *Our bed, huh?*

Riley giggled. "I can see where your thoughts are." She placed a light kiss on Fallon's lips. "Go. I'll see you in a couple of hours."

"Does this mean we get to sleep in?"

"Why? Do you think we'll need to?" Riley teased.

"God, I hope so."

Riley laughed. "Glad we have that all cleared up."

Fallon shrugged. She and Riley had spent three of the last four nights together. They'd made love twice. Owen had appeared in Fallon's room with a stomach ache on Tuesday. Thursday, Riley had decided she needed to spend some time at home. Fallon hated kissing her goodbye. Riley's remedy to Fallon's pouting was to suggest they have a "date night" on Friday. No kids. No distractions. A drink or two at Murphy's Law and then they could head back to Fallon's house. Between finishing the project that Fallon had started to transform her guest bedroom into a room for Owen, and spending time with Riley, Fallon had barely stopped by the bar. Riley could tell Fallon was itching to check in. And, Riley also thought it was time they make their relationship public. It would be nearly impossible to conceal their new dynamic in Whiskey Springs, and Riley had no inclination to hide her feelings for Fallon. They were together. It might surprise some people. Riley didn't care. She had adopted the philosophy that it was better to live life openly. Her relationship with Fallon would not be fleeting. That much she was sure of. What their life might look like in a month or two or six, Riley couldn't say. She was confident they would be together in a month and two and six.

"I'll see you in a bit," Riley promised again.

"Okay." Fallon kissed Riley deeply. "You know, we could just stay in."

"Fallon..."

"Okay! I'm going."

Riley held her front door open for Fallon and laughed at the downtrodden act Fallon displayed for her benefit. "It's only a couple of hours," Riley giggled.

Fallon climbed into her truck. "What the hell, Foster? You're pathetic. What are you; a sixteen-year-old boy with a crush?" She turned the key in the ignition, looked out the window to where Riley still stood in the doorway. "Sixteen? You're more like thirteen, voice cracking, hormones raging, can't get out of your own way in the heat of puberty kind of mess." She laughed at the next thought that popped into her head. "Hope they don't card me."

"Andi?" Owen grabbed hold of Andi's knees.

"Yes, sweetie?"

"You stay wif me?"

"That's right. Tonight, you are stuck with me while Mommy and Fallon go out."

Owen grinned widely. "Yeah! We can pway?"

"We can play," Andi promised. "Why don't you go see what game you'd like to play when Mommy leaves?"

"Hippos!" Owen scampered off.

Andi laughed. "Hungry Hippos it is. God, I thought I was done with that about fifteen years ago."

"Sorry, no such luck," Riley said. "Thanks for coming over."

"Don't thank me. It'll be nice to have some company." *Other than a bottle of wine and a vibrator.* "I welcome a game of hippos."

Riley nodded. "Andi..."

"Riley, we've been over this. I'm fine."

"Are you?"

"That generally depends on how much wine is in the house." Andi laughed.

"I just want you to know that..."

"Stop. Please, stop. Sit down, Riley."

Riley sat down on her sofa next to Andi and bit her lip nervously.

Andi smiled and patted her friend's knee. "What has you upset?"

"When I was home—back in San Diego..."

"What happened?"

"My mom was great, Andi. She was. I miss her."

"I know you do."

"But the truth is we haven't been close for years. I was always closer to my dad, and his life is... Well, it's different now."

"Did you see him?"

"For a day. He had to fly back home. He didn't really explain."

"And, your sister?" Andi wondered.

Riley wasn't sure how to describe her visit with Mary. "She's Mary."

"Didn't go so well, I take it?"

"Oh, let's just say she's less than thrilled."

"That you didn't take a job offer out there?" Andi asked.

"And, that I told her I'm in love with Fallon."

Andi nodded.

"It doesn't matter."

"It does matter," Andi disagreed. "You love her, and her support is something you would like to have. Of course, it matters."

Riley hung her head in defeat. "I love my family," she said. "There's always been tension. Mary adds to that. I think it's part of the reason my parents have grown distant from both of us."

"What do you mean?"

"Mary, she's great at the guilt-trip."

"I'm familiar with that."

"She was furious when our parents divorced; oddly more at my mother than my father. My mother walks on eggshells. My father avoids visiting. And, me? I always have tried to make her happy."

"And, this time you didn't."

"I couldn't," Riley said. "I almost called you."

"You could have."

"I know, but it didn't feel right."

"Because of Fallon?"

"Partly," Riley admitted. "But I knew that you would understand that."

Andi smiled.

"I didn't want to confide in any of them. If my mother hadn't questioned me, I don't know if I would have said anything about Fallon at all. My head was spinning. I felt like I was betraying Robert. Owen kept asking for Fallon. He talked endlessly about her and his friends, Ida and you. I love my family. I felt so alone."

"And, that made you feel guilty," Andi guessed.

"I wanted to come *home*. I wanted to be *home* – here. They are my family but so are you. I love them but I…"

"Have to live your life for you now," Andi said.

"Yes."

Andi squeezed Riley's knee gently. "You're allowed to, Riley. You're allowed to put *your* happiness first—yours and Owen's."

"Is it selfish?"

"Maybe," Andi confessed. "I understand how you feel; I do. I've rolled through that a million times. Just when I think I've resolved my feelings, it starts all over again. Look at the people I've disappointed in some way—hurt in some way. All people that I love, Riley. I do love them. But I haven't been able to give to any of them the way I want to for longer than I can remember. I don't know what the balance is between being selfless and selfish. Maybe sometimes, self-preservation is the only choice you have. You can't make Mary happy, sweetie. Just like I can't make things all right for Dave. He's disappointed because my choice isn't what *he* expected. Sometimes, people forget that their choices aren't always what we hope for either." Andi offered Riley a wink. "I hate to be the bearer of bad news, but there will be moments when you wrestle with guilt. We all do. Don't let that keep you from what makes you happy, Riley."

"See? This is why I wanted to come home. Are you honestly okay; I mean, with the way things have changed..."

"You are glowing," Andi said. "That makes me happy. I'm sure Fallon resembles a neon sign about now."

"You know, you deserve that too," Riley said.

"Yes, I do." Andi smiled. "But, I need to spend some time with me first. You should get going," she told Riley. "Someone is waiting for you, and I have a date with some hippos. God, that sounds awful!"

Riley laughed. She leaned over and hugged her friend. "I don't know what I'd do without you."

"I do. You and Fallon would be sitting on the floor playing with plastic hippos, and I would be drinking the margaritas you're about to enjoy." She pulled away from Riley's embrace. "Go on your date."

"Andi, I hope you know..."

"I know. Get out of here. I'll see you tomorrow."

"Are you sure that you don't mind staying all night? I can..."

"Get out of here. Jacob thanks you, I'm sure." Andi chuckled. "I think the idea of a night without his mother sitting on the couch devouring ice cream and sipping a glass of wine while watching old movies was the best news he's had in a decade."

"That's what I have to look forward to, huh?" Riley asked.

"You mean Owen wanting the house to himself or the ice cream?"

"Any of it."

Andi shrugged. "If you're lucky, you'll have someone to share it with, and to drive you when you get kicked out of your own house."

"Thank you."

"I'd say anytime, but actually, it's almost anytime."

"Andi!" Owen ran into the room.

"What's wrong?" Andi asked.

"A hippo's broke."

Andi looked at Owen and smiled. "Say goodbye to Mommy. Then we'll go see if we can't fix Mr. Hippo."

"Bye!" Owen hugged his mother's waist for a second and then grabbed Andi's hand.

Riley laughed. "I can see he's devastated that I'm leaving."

"Mommy, I need Andi."

Riley held up her hands. "Don't we all," she said honestly. "Call me if…"

"I will, but I won't need to. I managed to get two into college."

"Well, enjoy your hippos," Riley said.

"Enjoy your margarita," Andi replied.

"Hey, Andi?"

"Hum?" Andi chuckled as Owen tried to pull her forward again.

"What's the deal with this Cigar Club?"

"She told you about that, huh?"

"Somehow, I think she might have left a few things out."

*I'd count on it.* "Ask Fallon."

"I don't like the sound of that."

Andi smirked. "Have a good time, Riley."

"Andi?"

"Goodbye, Riley."

"Mommy!" Owen pointed to the door, eager to have his playtime with Andi.

"Okay! I get it." She looked at Andi. "We'll talk."

Andi shook her head when Riley walked through the door. "Your mother is something else, Owen."

Owen grinned. "Andi?"

"Yes?"

"We has popcorn?"

Andi laughed. "We can have some popcorn."

"Andi?"

Andi chuckled.

"I got a wum."

"You have a worm?"

"He's at home."

"Here?" Andi asked.

"In da gwound."

*Thank God. Popcorn and worms – can't imagine who introduced you to that.*

"Andi?"

"Yes, sunshine?"

"We stay with Fawon."

Andi's heart lurched in her chest. It still hurt. She wondered how long it would take until her heart would mend. Her happiness for Riley and Fallon was genuine. Still, there was a toll to pay for her past, a price for allowing herself to fall in love with Fallon. She would never tell Fallon that, never admit it to Riley. Sometimes, one person's happy ending left another broken-hearted. Andi had learned a few things in her life. The most important lesson she would seek to impart to her sons if they let her, was this: loving someone meant letting them go when it was time. They might fly a few feet, or they might settle on a distant shore. There always came a time for letting go. Love never ceased. Being a mother had taught her that. Loving Fallon, adopting Riley as part of her life had put that lesson to the test. There were moments that she did feel tested. She looked down at Owen and took a deep breath. How strange; Riley was the daughter she'd always wished she's had. And, Owen? He was a light in all of their lives. What could she do? If she hoped to hold onto all of them, she had to let Fallon go. Her hand ruffled the soft waves of Owen's hair. "You like staying at Fallon's, don't you?"

"Yeah. I wuv Fawon."

*Me too, Owen.* "She's easy to love."

Owen beamed and took hold of Andi's hand. Andi was gentle, and she was attentive. She knew things, and she made him feel safe. He looked forward to Andi's visits, and Ida's. He had missed them both. "I wuv you," he said.

Andi fought back her tears. "I love you too, Owen. What do you say we help that hippo?"

Owen nodded.

"Then we'll make some popcorn."

"Buttah!"

"With butter," Andi promised. *Yep, you're under Fallon's spell.* She giggled. *Well, at least, we're all in it together.*

# CHAPTER SEVEN

"Come on," Fallon practically begged Riley.

"No."

"Why not?"

"I am not getting sucked into this crazy competition you have with Carol."

"Because you think hers are better."

"We are still talking about margaritas here; yes?"

Fallon grumbled. "Why? Thinking of stealing her away from Charlie?"

"Think I could?" Riley bantered.

"I'm not answering that."

Carol chose that moment to approach the pair. "Why does Fallon look like someone stole her puppy."

"I don't have a puppy," Fallon said.

"Then why do you look like someone stole it?" Carol countered.

"She wants to use me as a guinea pig," Riley offered.

"*That* is between the two of you," Carol said. "Not my circus."

"Guess that answers the earlier question," Fallon said to Riley.

Riley giggled.

"I don't want to know," Carol said. "Tell me anyway."

"I'm not telling you anything. Buy the video," Fallon said.

"You two are already making videos?" Carol quipped.

Fallon blushed, and Riley erupted in laughter.

"Hey, was Dale okay?" Riley asked. "They took off right after I got here."

Carol's smile was laced with empathy. The moment Riley had walked through the door, the truth was out. Fallon wasted no time greeting the younger woman, and Riley had no hesitation in sealing Fallon's welcome with a kiss.

"Maybe he's getting himself gussied up to see Marge," Fallon said.

"Gussied up?" Carol shook her head. "Riley," she said. "I'm glad you're home. I think Fallon was secretly slipping off to Biddy Brigade meetings while you were gone."

"I like *younger* women," Fallon replied.

"You do now," Carol said.

Fallon glared at her.

Riley took the banter in stride. She wasn't dwelling on the past. "Good thing for me, I guess," she said with a wink.

Fallon smiled.

"So," Riley began. "Since Fallon isn't giving up the goods…"

Carol smirked.

"Not *those* goods," Riley clarified. She delighted in Fallon's blush. Fallon seemed to be blushing a great deal. *I wonder if I can make her blush later?* Riley shook off her inappropriate thought. "About this Cigar Club of yours."

"Invited Riley to the dark side already?" Carol asked Fallon.

Fallon sipped her beer.

"See what I mean?" Riley said.

Carol leaned on the bar. "What *did* she tell you?"

"Cigars, whiskey, poker, and women—not necessarily in that order," Riley replied.

"About right."

"Why do I think there is something missing?"

Carol looked at Fallon. "Do you want to tell her or should I?"

Fallon shifted on the stool.

"Tell me what?" Riley said.

Fallon groaned. "They usually take bets," she said.

"You already told me Marge usually wins at poker."

"Not the card game," Fallon muttered.

Carol turned her attention to Riley. Sooner or later, Riley would find out what the favorite game at the Cigar Club was. "In past years," she began. "There was a pool on how many visitors Fallon would take home from the pub that year."

Riley stared blankly at Carol.

"Guess we'll have to think of a new game," Carol said. She squeezed Riley's hand.

Fallon stared at the contents of her glass, certain the contents of her stomach were about to make an appearance.

Riley took a deep breath. "It's the past, Fallon."

"Yeah, it is."

"Then why won't you look at me?"

Fallon reluctantly met Riley's gaze. "Because I feel like shit; that's why."

"I know they like to tease you."

"Yeah."

Riley smiled. Fallon didn't need to explain a thing. Teasing was something Fallon endured from everyone. Generally, she could give as good as she got. The constant jokes about her exploits bothered Fallon. Riley had recognized that since they'd met. Teasing about the time she spent at the pub, about her singing to the jukebox when she thought no one was listening, about her endless projects, about being a token New Yorker, her love of old sitcoms, or anything at all *except* her trysts with women rolled off Fallon. When it came to Fallon's sexual exploits; she grew uncomfortable. Fallon had been lonely. Some people drank, some people hibernated, some people exercised, some people indulged in food when they were lonely. Fallon took lovers. That had been her escape.

"Hey," Riley called for Fallon's attention. "Maybe they can bet on when Carol will get pregnant this year, or when Marge will get…"

"I swear if you say, 'laid,' I will pee my pants right here."

"Well, run to the bathroom then."

Fallon burst out laughing. "I love you."

Riley winked. "Just remember that when you're smoking cigars."

"Promise."

---

Ida sat across from Olivia listening without comment. She'd always maintained a close relationship with her daughter's former partner. And, Ida would never deny that she loved visiting Dean's family partly because it afforded her time with Olivia's girls. Emily resembled Fallon in ways that sometimes took Ida's breath away. There was no way to deny that Dean was the girls' father. Olivia had allowed him to play an active role in her children's lives. He was Uncle Dean. Fallon was Aunt Fallon, and she was Grandma. The relationship they all shared did have its challenges for Fallon. Ida was cautious on that front. As much as she adored her grandchildren, and as careful as she was to respect the decisions her children made as adults; Olivia's decision to have Dean be her children's biological father, and Dean's failure to consider Fallon's feelings in the equation had never set right with her. She made an effort to remain impartial. Sometimes, impartiality required *great* effort.

"It's something we need to do," Olivia said.

"If you and Barb think it's best to separate, then that's what you should do," Ida replied.

"You don't sound surprised," Olivia observed.

Surprised? Olivia's revelation that she and Barb were, "taking a break," conjured many thoughts and emotions for Ida; surprised was not one of them. She'd always suspected that Olivia had pursued a committed relationship with Barb more in the hope that Fallon's jealously would lead her back to Olivia than because Olivia had fallen head over heels for Barb. It wasn't Ida's place to offer her opinion, and it wasn't her habit to try to make windows into other people's souls. From where Ida sat, the handwriting on the wall had been plain as day. Olivia had never felt comfortable in Whiskey Springs. Ida had heard Olivia's laundry list of reasons why she couldn't envision making a life with Fallon in Vermont. Some of the reasons made sense to her. Some, she thought, were excuses more than deep concerns. Olivia never wanted to be without Fallon. That much had always been obvious to Ida. And, if Olivia's desire to keep Fallon on some type of string was unmistakable to her, she doubted it had escaped Barb's notice. There were times in a person's life when they donned blinders knowingly; at least, they wore blinders as long as life allowed. The fact that Barb had asked for a separation came as no shock to Ida Foster. Few people could spend a lifetime playing second-fiddle in someone's heart much less their life.

"I'm not surprised," Ida admitted. "I am sorry for all of you."

"Well, we'll do our best to make it comfortable for the kids. She's taking a job in Richmond. It won't be easy."

"I don't imagine so."

"Dean mentioned that you thought Beth should move up to Whiskey Springs until he can gets back."

Ida had spent several hours talking with her son about what his family's future might be. Beth was in the midst of a high-risk pregnancy. Dean was away indefinitely. Ida was happy to help, but she missed home. Beth was restless. She needed support; she needed friends that could bolster her spirits. She also needed calm. Evan kept asking when they could go to Vermont. School would be out in a week. She had her suspicions that her grandson was unhappy at school. As a rule, Evan was bright and personable. Most days, he came home from school quiet and sullen. Twelve going on thirteen was a confusing time. It had been for both of Ida's children. Perhaps, Evan would benefit from a change of scenery, and from the support the familiar faces of Whiskey Springs provided. She'd raised the idea with Dean. He had left it in his wife's hands. It shouldn't have taken her back that Dean shared their talk with Olivia. Dean and Olivia seemed to share everything. Ida had evened wondered if they had ever shared more than a friendship. It would explain many things that she sometimes found perplexing about her son's behavior. It was none of her business.

"I do. I think Beth and Evan could both use the getaway."

"You're missing home," Olivia surmised.

"I suppose I am."

"Have you spoken to Fallon?"

*Here we go.* "Yesterday. Have you?" Ida turned the question around.

"Not for a few weeks."

"So, you haven't told her that Barb isn't making the trip with you this summer."

"I thought I should tell her in person about the separation."

*I'm sure you do think that.* Ida nodded.

"How is she? She sounded a little strange when I spoke with her."

Ida wanted to laugh. Fallon sounded strange to Olivia because Fallon was in love with someone new. "She's Fallon," Ida said.

"I hope she doesn't get sick of me. I'm not usually there for an entire week."

Ida smiled. "I'm sure Fallon will manage." *You, on the other hand, might have a few struggles.*

"I hope so."

"Oh," Ida began. "I wouldn't worry too much about Fallon. She's got a busy life."

Olivia smiled. *I wonder if she's open to changing it.*

Fallon stood under a steady stream of hot water, letting her muscles relax. One thing about spending time at Murphy's Law, she seldom got to enjoy it without being put to work. She still hadn't figured out how one of the keg lines had been severed. It didn't matter. She'd fixed it, but not before receiving a partial beer bath. Riley had followed her home, promising to wait while Fallon rid herself of Ode de Budweiser. The sound of the shower door sliding open prompted Fallon to open her eyes. Before she could speak, Riley's arms had slipped around her waist, and a pair of soft lips had found the center of her back. Fallon's eyes closed again.

"You smell like coconut," Riley commented. Her lips kissed their way up Fallon's back to her shoulder.

"Better than Bud." Fallon's hands reached out for the shower wall. Riley's fingertips had found Fallon's nipples. Riley's breasts were pressed against Fallon's back. She could feel Riley's breath against her shoulder, hotter than the steady stream of water from above. "Riley, what are you doing?"

"I thought that would be obvious."

Fallon gripped her lower lip with her teeth. Riley tugged gently at both her nipples, sending shockwaves straight to her center. A warm tongue trailed across the back of her neck, and Fallon feared she might lose her ability to stand. She'd expected that making love with Riley would leave her breathless. She'd failed to consider the possibility that she'd met her match in the bedroom, or in this case, the bathroom. Fallon grinned. Riley seemed to delight in taking Fallon by surprise. Fallon loved it.

Riley loved the feel of Fallon against her. She'd been fantasizing about this moment for days, wondering when the opportunity might present itself. She'd been fantasizing about many things, endless scenarios since they had made love under the stars. Loving Fallon was an adventure in every way. Mornings began with tender caresses. Days were spent enjoying Owen's tales and playful games. When they were apart, Riley found herself anticipating lively laughter over dinner and the closeness of Fallon beside her that nighttime would allow. Being in love meant constant discovery. It seemed to Riley that she learned something new about Fallon in every moment. It might be a painful confession about the past or as simple as finding the spot behind Fallon's ear that made her giggle when Riley let her breath wash over it. Riley could spend a lifetime making discoveries about and with Fallon Foster. Fallon made her body hum and her heart sing. Touching Fallon was sublime; feeling Fallon yield to the faintest caress made Riley ache with desire.

"I've been thinking about this for days," Riley confessed. "Feeling you against me like this. Touching you." Riley nipped the nape of Fallon's neck gently.

"Jesus," Fallon moaned.

Riley giggled. "Let's keep the Biddy's Bible Brigade out of our bedroom—or the shower."

Fallon chuckled.

"Where was I?" Riley asked rhetorically. "Right here, I think." Her tongue lapped at the water droplets pooling on Fallon's back. A faint whimper encouraged her to continue. She let her right hand fall steadily from Fallon's breast to her abdomen. She pressed herself closer, holding Fallon tightly with her left arm as the fingers of her right hand skimmed lower, tracing delicate patterns over Fallon's hip to her thigh and slowly inward.

Fallon's teeth found her bottom lip again. She was tempted to turn in Riley's arms and claim Riley's mouth with a searing kiss. Riley's seduction was more erotic than anything Fallon could recall; which amounted to little at the moment. The more Riley touched her, the less Fallon cared about anything outside the shower walls. God, help her, she was losing her resolve to be reserved. Fallon had yet to whisper anything but sweet endearments to Riley when they touched. Not that more carnal words and images hadn't passed through her brain; they had. Their intimate relationship was new. New often equated to fragile. Fallon would let Riley lead. Evidently, Riley was comfortable with that idea.

Riley inhaled the scent of Fallon's shampoo. She briefly thought that the stuff should come with a warning label. It drove her wild—shampoo. That seemed ridiculous. Who got turned on by the smell of shampoo? Apparently, Riley did. She sucked in a ragged breath when her fingers met the warmth of Fallon's center. "You feel so good," she whispered.

Fallon's heart fluttered. It should have seemed obvious what would come next. Fallon found nothing predictable about this scenario. Riley had taken control, and Fallon couldn't wait to see where Riley was about to take her.

Riley's fingers played for a moment, just a moment. She swiftly returned them to Fallon's nipple, leaving Fallon a whimpering puddle of desperation. She smiled into the flesh of Fallon's shoulder. "Not yet," Riley said. "You drove me crazy the other night."

"I did?"

"You did," Riley said. "You made me wait forever."

Fallon was positive she would either die from a fall or the drowning that would occur once she did fall. There was no way she was going to manage to stay on her feet if Riley continued this game much longer. The sound of Riley's voice alone had her quivering with need.

Riley licked her lips. She'd fantasized about slipping into the shower with Fallon, teasing her relentlessly from behind until Fallon struggled to hold herself upright. Fallon had been timid in their lovemaking. Riley was sure of that. Not that she was complaining. Fallon made her feel things no one had ever managed to. Fallon's inclination was to protect Riley, to love her while making her feel safe. Riley would always feel safe with Fallon. She wanted Fallon to let go. There was no need for caution between them any longer. Riley wanted everything Fallon offered. She desired to give Fallon things she'd never considered allowing another person to take, to reveal about her. Fallon had set something free from Riley; not just her sorrow; Fallon had unleashed her passion.

"You can't have forgotten," Riley said. She certainly hadn't forgotten their last lovemaking session. "You did this," she said. She tugged lightly at Fallon's nipple. "Only with your teeth—over and over and over again."

Wetness pooled between Fallon's legs, and it had nothing to do with the shower. Listening to Riley was making her crazy with lust.

"You know, Fallon," Riley began. "You could've made me come just like that."

Fallon stopped breathing for a second. Heat flooded her veins. *She's going to kill me right here.*

Riley smiled. Fallon was turned on. *Good.* "I seem to recall, you did this." Riley sucked on Fallon's neck.

"Fuck, Riley..."

Riley chuckled. Her center was throbbing already. If she hadn't been so determined to seduce Fallon, Riley would have touched herself. *That could be interesting.* "When you were doing that, I almost touched myself."

Fallon groaned.

"Mm. I guess, you would have approved."

"Completely," Fallon admitted.

"What if I did that right now?"

"Oh, God."

"Is that what you want, Fallon?" Riley asked. "Because I could either," she paused as her hand dropped to explore Fallon's wetness. "Touch you like this," she said. "Or I could..." Riley moved her hand back to Fallon's breast. "Or touch you like this while I touch myself."

Fallon didn't care what Riley did as long as she kept talking. Either way, Fallon was sure she was going to explode without warning.

Riley listened as Fallon's breathing became labored, and her body arched against her will. She let her right-hand fall between her legs and was stunned by the arousal she found there.

"Are you?" Fallon asked. "Shit, you are. I can feel it. You're touching yourself."

"Mmm. Because you make me crazy," Riley panted. It would be easy for her to let go. Seconds—Riley would be able to bring herself to climax in seconds if she allowed herself the indulgence. That's not what she desired most. She wanted to push Fallon to the edge and hold her when she fell over. She moaned in Fallon's ear while her other hand toyed with Fallon's breast.

Was the room spinning? Fallon could hear the spray of water hitting the tile. It sounded far away. Riley's sighs of pleasure produced a steady throb in her core. She wanted Riley to touch her almost as much as she wanted to hear Riley bring herself pleasure. Of all the things she'd imagined experiencing with Riley tonight, this had been nowhere in her wildest fantasies. And, Fallon was positive tonight's shower follies would inspire countless fantasies.

Riley was quickly losing her resolve. Fallon moved against her sensually, seeking contact. Fallon's back arched, begging Riley to tug harder at her nipple. Riley was moving closer and closer to release. She sucked in a breath and returned her hand to Fallon's softness.

"Why did you stop?" Fallon asked.

"You wanted me to keep going?"

"Yes."

"Well, I want to make you come first."

Fallon's heart thundered so violently she could hear it in her ears.

Riley slid two fingers inside Fallon and began to pump slowly.

"Jesus," Fallon moaned again.

Riley continued thrusting in and out of Fallon, tugging and toying with one of Fallon's nipples and then the other, back and forth until Fallon's breathing became desperate panting.

"Yes," Riley whispered. "Come on, babe. Please… Oh, God, Fallon. I want to feel you. Come on, let it go." She bit Fallon's back gently. "Come for me, Fallon."

"Fuck!" Fallon screamed her pleasure. She was astounded at the strength Riley possessed.

Riley's arm surrounded Fallon's waist, supporting her as Fallon's body submitted to her touch. "I love you, Fallon," Riley whispered.

Fallon's body slowly relaxed in Riley's embrace. "Can I kiss you now?"

"You can kiss me whenever you want."

Fallon looked at her lover in awe. "You are full of surprises; aren't you?"

"I hope so," Riley said.

Fallon kissed her tenderly. "I love you too."

"I know. I don't want you to hold back with me, Fallon," Riley said.

"I won't."

"Don't. I want you—all of you."

Fallon's eyes twinkled. She pushed Riley against the back wall of the shower and dropped to her knees. "I'm going to finish what you started," she said.

Riley's head fell softly against the wall. "Thank God."

Fallon laughed lightly. She kissed Riley's stomach and let her tongue trace the outline of Riley's belly button.

Riley's hands held onto Fallon's shoulders.

"Yes," Fallon hissed. Her tongue traveled the length of Riley's need, circling round and round before dipping inside.

"Oh… Fallon…."

Fallon had no time for teasing. She could swear another orgasm was building inside her. Riley's legs were already beginning to tremble against her. Riley's voice echoed in her head—playful, commanding, and seductive all at once. She wished Riley would speak now. *Say anything – anything.*

"Yes… Fallon, yes… Oh… Don't stop. Please…"

*Keep talking, Riley.* Fallon sucked gently on Riley's clit.

Riley had never been overly vocal when she was making love. Fallon's breathing, the way her body moved when Riley spoke told Riley that her words aroused Fallon. It also aroused Riley; knowing the mere sound of her voice held power over Fallon. She would give Fallon anything—everything. Fallon gave everything to her. "Yes...Fallon... There... Oh, yes... I'm going to come... please, babe..."

A series of tremors were set free in Fallon's center, a gentle reminder of Riley's earlier touch elicited by the chorus of sounds that escaped Riley's throat when her body began to shudder. Fallon pressed all her weight against Riley, keeping her steady and drawing out her release until Riley begged her to stop.

"Fallon... I can't.... I..."

Fallon kissed Riley's thigh and pulled herself back to her feet. Riley's arms wrapped around her tightly and held on. "I'm here," Fallon promised. "You're amazing. You make me feel so good."

"I love you, Fallon."

"I love you too." Fallon pulled away and snickered.

"What?"

"Seems kind of strange to say we need a shower."

Riley smacked Fallon playfully. "Might need another one later."

"Thank God we get to sleep in."

Riley awoke to the smell of coffee brewing. She pulled Fallon's pillow to her and breathed in the scent. Leaving the bed was not in any immediate plans Riley had. There were no prying eyes and no toddlers to tug her to her feet. She'd fallen asleep naked against the woman she loved and woken up in the same condition; save Fallon's absence. The sound of distant giggling caused her eyes to fly open. "Owen?"

Fallon kissed Owen on the cheek and handed him a juice box. "You can go in the other room and play. I'm going to check on Mommy."

"Okay." He toddled off happily.

"Are you sure you don't want to stay for a while?" Fallon asked.

Andi shook her head. "No. You enjoy your Saturday with Riley."

"Thanks for bringing him over."

"No thanks necessary." Andi kissed Fallon's cheek. "I'll talk to you later."

"Hey, Andi?"

"Yeah?"

"How's it feel to be a grandma?"

Andi shook her head. "Goodbye, Fallon."

Fallon laughed. "Owen, say goodbye to Andi."

Owen ran back into the hallway and threw his arms around Andi's waist. "Bye, Gwama."

Andi laughed. "Have fun with Fallon," she said. She leaned into Fallon's ear. "Stop encouraging him."

"Why? Riley thinks of you like a mom. Makes sense to me."

"It would." Andi shook her head again and headed for the door. "And, I'm not old enough to be a grandmother."

"Yeah, you are. You *could* be Riley's mom," Fallon teased.

"Not helping, Fallon."

"Her really good looking, young mom."

Andi stepped through the door. "My babysitting fee just increased."

"You'd charge your daughter to babysit?"

"No. I would charge you." Andi walked out the door.

Fallon laughed. Owen had come home with Andi to tell Fallon that she was his new Grandma. Everyone was supposed to have Grandmas. His was far away. He needed one. Andi had taken it in stride, gently correctly him and explaining that his grandmothers were his mommy and daddy's mothers. He shook his head and simply responded, "you!" Fallon found it hilarious and endearing. Owen adored Andi. She was sure that Riley would be touched by Owen's informal adoption of a new grandparent. She chuckled all the way back to the kitchen, poured a cup of coffee, and set out to gently wake her lover.

Riley peered out from beneath the covers when the bedroom door opened. "Is Andi here?" She sat up slowly, stretching and yawning along the way.

"Nope. I'm afraid you missed Grandma this morning." Fallon handed Riley the cup of coffee.

"Should I ask?"

"It seems Owen has decided he needs a grandmother. You'd have to ask him. According to him that would be Andi."

"Oh, no."

Fallon grinned.

"Was she upset?"

"Andi?"

Riley nodded.

Seeing a hint of genuine fear in Riley's eyes, Fallon decided not to tease her. "Upset? No. Why would she be upset? She loves Owen."

"I thought we were picking him up at ten."

"Umm. We were. I wanted to let you sleep in. I called Andi and asked if she'd bring him over."

"What time is it?"

"Eleven."

"What? Why didn't you wake me up?"

"Because you were tired. You were up late... or rather down late."

"I'd smack you for that comment, but I value this coffee too much. Are you sure Andi's not..."

"She loves it. I think she might be worried that you will be upset."

"Me? Why? Andi's like my second mom. She knows that."

Fallon chuckled. "I know. I think the reality of that freaks her out a little."

"What do you mean? Did I..."

"Riley, relax. Andi loves you; you know that. She's raised two kids. She knows how kids are. Be glad; you'll always have free babysitting. She can protest all she likes. I saw her face when Owen hugged her goodbye."

Riley smiled. Owen was attached to Andi. He had many stories to tell his aunt and grandparents on their short trip to California. He'd mentioned Pete and Dale, Carol, Marge, Charlie and his playmates Jenny and Greg. Most of Owen's stories surrounded the time he spent with Fallon, Ida, and Andi. There were two kinds of families in a person's life, the one that was given and the one that was created. Riley decided to change the subject. Home was where you created your family. Home for Riley and Owen was Whiskey Springs.

"I know you have to work tonight," Riley said.

"I do. Carol has the night off. We have all day, though."

"Fallon, I don't want to over stay our welcome."

"Did I miss something?"

"No, but I..."

"Riley, you lived with me when you first got to town."

"For a few weeks."

"And?"

"And, that was different."

Fallon took a deep breath. "So, now that we're lovers you want to spend less time here?"

"No," Riley put the thought to rest. "I love being with you; you know that. God knows, Owen wants to be here twenty-four hours a day. I don't want to jump into something that one of us or both of us aren't ready for."

Fallon took a moment to consider her reply. If she had her way, Riley would never leave again. She had committed to herself that she would let Riley dictate the pace of their relationship. From Fallon's perspective, they were miles ahead of most new couples. They'd already shared a home together. But Riley had a point. Things *had* changed. Anything worth having was worth investing in and waiting for. She chuckled.

"Did I miss something?" Riley asked.

"No," Fallon replied. She reclined on the bed next to Riley. "I was just thinking about investing."

"Uh-huh."

Fallon laughed. "About us," she continued. "Sometimes, I think more in images than in words."

"I'm still lost."

"Well, I was thinking about my past in a way. It's like when I started investing. I chose what I thought were the most interesting companies to invest money in. I guess, in a way they were all a gamble. There's no way to be certain that what you put in is what you'll get out of it. Sometimes, you lose more than your shirt; you lose your shoes too. But I love investing, finding something that I believe in. They don't make me rich right away. You know? The best investments I've made have taken time to mature."

Riley smiled. Fallon understood what she was trying to say. "Fallon? Are you telling me you're rich?" Riley teased.

Fallon surprised Riley by shrugging.

"Fallon?"

"Depends on how you define rich, I guess."

Riley set her coffee on the bedside table.

"I'm not destitute," Fallon offered. "I started buying stock when I turned eighteen, Riley."

"I know; you told me."

"Yeah, but what I didn't tell you is that I have a bit of a talent for it."

"Better than your talent for mixing margaritas?"

"Ah! You do like Carol's better."

"There isn't anything Carol does that I like better."

Fallon laughed. "That's sick, Riley."

Riley winked.

"I might as well get this over with now."

"I don't like the sound of that," Riley said.

"It's not bad. It's just not something I talk about with most people. Andi knows. Mom knows... Liv... But other than ..."

"Knows what?"

Fallon sighed. "Riley, let's just put it this way—I don't need the pub's income."

"Okay."

"Oh shit... Here it is—my net worth is over two million dollars."

Riley stared at Fallon blankly.

"Hello? Earth to Riley?"

"Fallon, did you just tell me that you're a millionaire?"

"Sort of."

"You're sort of a millionaire or you sort of said you are?"

"No, I am. I don't touch that money, Riley. I haven't needed to. It just kind of keeps growing."

Riley shook her head to clear the fog.

"Does that bother you?" Fallon asked.

"No... I just... I'm just... You could be anywhere, Fallon. I mean, you could..."

"I'm exactly where I want to be. Money isn't all that important to me, Riley."

Riley laughed. "You know that sounds ridiculous."

Fallon sighed.

"I didn't mean that as an insult," Riley said. "It's not every day your girlfriend tells you she's wealthy and in the same breath tells you money doesn't matter to her."

"It doesn't—not really. My dad loved everything about playing the stock market. Some people bet on horses, he bet on companies. He did all right too. Not as well as I have, but he left Mom in a position that she never has to worry. He taught both me and Dean. Dean never had any interest in it. Me? I love it. Probably because I it reminds me of spending time with him and how he would get so excited teaching me what to look for—how to gauge when to ride a wave or swim for shore before I drowned. His words, not mine."

"If you love it, why did you ever leave New York?"

"I told you, this is home. I love the pub."

"Yes, I know."

"I don't have to choose between the two. I didn't love doing it for other people. That's the thing. It's my thing with my dad; you know? Just like Murphy's. I can invest from anywhere. I can't be home anywhere."

Riley leaned over and kissed Fallon tenderly. "Thank you for sharing that."

"You might as well know now."

"It doesn't matter to me."

"I know. I understand, Riley. Let's face it, we've both been hurt. I understand that we agreed to take this slowly."

"But?"

"It's not a but. It's more like an intention."

"Go on."

"I know what I want," Fallon said. "I've known what I want with you for longer than you've been ready to hear it. Maybe you're still not ready to hear it. I think I need you to, though."

"I'm listening."

"I want you." Fallon took a deep breath. "The truth is, Riley, you are the one person I would leave this place behind for."

Riley's heart picked up its pace. *Fallon.*

"I realized that when you left to see your family. If you told me that you needed to be closer to them, but you wanted me; I would have left. I would have packed my things and driven to San Diego the next day. That's how I know that you're the person I want to spend the rest of my life with. Maybe we did just admit how we feel. Maybe we've only started this part of our relationship—being lovers. I understand what's at stake. I told you before you left, I'll be here. I'm not going anywhere—not unless you ask me to. I don't want to be any place without you and Owen. That much I do know."

Riley caressed Fallon's cheek with the back of her hand. "I'm not going anywhere, Fallon. Trust me; I already hate sleeping apart from you. I don't think that it's a bad idea to ease into what we both want. And, I want it too. You need to know that."

Fallon nodded. "I'm not good at this."

"What's that?"

"Slow."

Riley laughed. "How about we make an agreement?"

"Okay?"

"We stay together half the week."

"You're not a mathematician; are you?"

"What do you mean?" Riley asked.

"I mean that the week is lopsided." Fallon tapped her lip with a fingertip. "Okay, I agree on one condition."

"Which is?"

"We stay together the larger part of the week—four nights together, three apart."

"You drive a hard bargain, Ms. Foster."

"Yeah?"

"I suppose you want to shake on it," Riley teased.

Fallon kissed Riley tenderly. "Nope."

Riley pulled Fallon close. "I can't believe I fell in love with a millionaire. I'm living a romance novel. Maybe I'll end up being Mrs. Grey. Are you hiding any secret rooms here?"

Fallon pushed Riley away playfully. "Get dressed." She walked to the door.

Riley giggled.

Fallon stopped and looked at Riley. "And, Riley? When the time comes, you won't be Mrs. Grey; you'll be Mrs. Foster." She opened the door and walked through, closing it behind her.

Riley's mouth opened and closed silently several times. She smiled. *Someday.* "I really do have to look for that room."

# CHAPTER EIGHT

**TWO WEEKS LATER**

"I hope this isn't going to be too much for you," Beth said.

Ida squeezed her daughter-in-law's hand. "Not at all."

"What about Fallon? I don't want Evan to impose on her time."

"Don't worry about Fallon."

"I know she loves Evan. But, Ida, she's just starting a new relationship. Having Evan around might…"

"Don't worry about Riley either," Ida said. "You'll see when you meet her."

Beth noted the twinkle in Ida's eyes. "You like this woman."

"Riley?"

"Right, Riley."

"I don't know anyone who doesn't like Riley."

"Do you think this is it?"

Ida shrugged. "Oh, well, I know better than to pretend I'm psychic. I do know that they love each other."

Beth sighed. "Fallon and Liv loved each other too."

"Riley's not Olivia."

"Did something happen when you visited Olivia and the girls?"

"Nothing out of the ordinary."

"Mom, you seem a bit—I don't know; irritated with Liv."

"Olivia is who she is."

Beth chuckled caustically.

Ida looked at the younger woman curiously. "You're not overly fond of her; are you?"

"Olivia?"

Ida nodded.

Beth sighed heavily. She was not fond of her husband's best friend. In fact, she struggled to tolerate the woman for years. As the years wore on, that struggle had become more difficult. "Is it that obvious?"

"To me."

Beth sighed again.

"Beth? What is going on with you and Dean?"

"Mom..."

"Listen, he's my son, and I love him. That doesn't mean I can't listen."

"I don't know," Beth confessed. "I don't know how to say this."

"Just say it. I've been around a while."

"Before this pregnancy, I seriously considered asking for a divorce. This was out of the blue. I can't believe it happened to tell you the truth. We hadn't slept together in almost a year. One night after a heated argument—I don't know; I think we both sensed doom and we..."

"Fell into bed."

"Something like that."

"I'm sure it feels strange talking to me."

"Oh, I don't know. I love him, Mom. I just don't like him very much. I can't seem to get past some of his decisions."

Ida had never asked Beth how she felt about Dean agreeing to be Olivia's donor. Beth had been incredibly supportive of the idea when Olivia and Fallon had been together. She sensed the dynamic in the family caused stress for Beth. As far as Ida was concerned, Beth was her daughter. Beth had been with Dean for over twenty years. "Would this have anything to do with the girls?"

Beth shook her head. She was hesitant to wade into this discussion. She needed to talk to someone. Ida was the least judgmental person she knew. "I love Emily and Summer."

"We all love Emily and Summer. That's not what I'm talking about."

"He didn't ask me, Mom. He just promised Olivia, and that was it. He announced it. He didn't give me a say at all."

Anger bubbled in Ida's veins. She loved her son. He had acted without regard for many of the people who loved him most. Olivia Nolan seemed to hold him under some kind of spell. "Are you telling me that he didn't consult you about being the girls' father?"

"No, he didn't. He said that I agreed when it was Fallon. Why should it matter who Olivia was with?"

Ida grimaced.

"It might not have bothered me as much if they hadn't decided that he should have an active role with the girls. My God, Mom, he spends more time with Emily and Summer than he does with Evan. He might as well be married to Liv. He missed Evan's award ceremony at school in April because Liv needed him to take the girls to their dance lesson."

Ida's face grew hot. "You're not serious."

"I'm totally serious. She has him wrapped around her little finger. I can't take it anymore. When he got his orders—God, help me, I was relieved. If I have to do this by myself, I'd rather do it that way without him around at all."

Ida held Beth's hand "I'm sorry, sweetheart. I love my son, but I can't pretend to understand him sometimes."

"I understand it," Beth said. "He's in love with her. He'll keep her close no matter what."

Beth's observation tore at Ida's heart. It was spot on. She'd recognized it the first time Dean had spoken about Olivia. She understood the attraction. Olivia Nolan was stunning, she was intelligent, she was driven, and she was determined; all characteristics she shared with Dean. Olivia was Dean's equal. And, she was unavailable, which Ida suspected made her all the more alluring to Dean. Dean's inability or unwillingness to place even an inch of distance between himself and Olivia had caused enormous pain for both Beth and Fallon. Until now, Ida had failed to realize how much damage he had done. Worse, after her last visit with Olivia, Ida had come to face a fact she'd long tried to deny. Olivia was using Dean—using him to keep Fallon within reaching distance. Ida sensed a brewing storm. Every person and every situation had a breaking point. A dam could only hold back so much water before it broke. Beth, Fallon, even Evan—they each had erected a dam to hold back the pain and resentment they felt. Ida feared the pressure had reached its limit. She decided to be honest.

"I wish I could tell you that I think you're wrong. I think Olivia has used that to her advantage."

"No kidding. To keep Fallon somehow."

"I'm sorry, Beth. You can stay with me for as long as you want. Don't ever worry about that."

"I hope she doesn't cause problems for Fallon."

"Olivia?"

Beth nodded.

"I hope she doesn't underestimate Riley. I do know this much—Olivia is in for a rude awakening if she thinks she will come between them."

Beth grinned. She was anxious to meet the woman in Fallon's life. Beth adored her sister-in-law. She had little use for Olivia Nolan. Few things would give her more satisfaction than seeing Olivia knocked down a peg, or two... or ten. "I hope you're right."

Ida smiled. "I am."

Fallon paced behind the bar. Carol threw a towel at her. "What is wrong with you?" Carol asked.

"Nothing. Didn't you ever get the feeling something wasn't right?"

"Working here? Daily."

"Ha-ha."

"What is it that feels wrong? Seems to me like your life is going pretty well."

Fallon smiled. Life was going better than Fallon could have hoped. She hated being apart from Riley at all. She had to admit that there was an advantage in the three nights they slept apart each week. It made Fallon realize that she wanted Riley to be with her every night. She was sure that sentiment was shared by her girlfriend. Fallon had always raced into her relationships. She'd been living with Olivia almost immediately. Some of that had been out of practicality. Olivia moved to Vermont to be with Fallon. Fallon had rented a small house close to her mother's home for them. They'd known each other a few years through Dean. She couldn't even make the claim that they had been dating for a while. They'd slept together. Fallon had spent two long weekends with Olivia before asking her to come to Whiskey Springs. Within a month, they'd been living together. There was no way that Fallon intended to lose Riley Main. If keeping separate residences part of the week meant a happy ending, Fallon would find a way to endure Riley's absences. There would come a day when she would ask Riley to change the arrangement. For now, she would continue to follow Riley's lead.

"If you mean me and Riley, things are great."

"You don't say," Carol teased. "I'm happy for you, Fallon."

"Yeah? Me too."

"Good, then don't go asking for the sky to fall."

"I'm not," Fallon said. "I can't explain it. I talked to Mom last night. Something is up."

"Maybe she's just worried about Beth."

"Oh, I'm sure she's worried about Beth. I'm worried about Beth. It's something else. I know her, Carol. You know my mother, cryptic is not her strong suit."

Carol laughed. Ida tended to be forthright to a fault. She meant well. She had never been known to be reserved in her opinions nor sharing them. "Fair enough. All I'm saying is don't project that it signals doom somehow."

"I'm not."

"Good. God knows why, but she seems to be head over heels for you."

"My mother?" Fallon joked.

"Don't be an ass."

Fallon laughed. "You think Riley is head over heels for me?"

Carol rolled her eyes.

The door opened, and Andi strolled in. "Hey."

Fallon put down the glass in her hand and made her way to the other side of the bar. "I thought you were in Arizona?"

"Just got back." Andi waved to Carol. "Hi, Carol."

"Hey, Andi. How was the trip?"

"It was fine. I think we have things worked out," she said.

"Did you see Dave?" Fallon asked. She handed Andi a margarita.

"Jake forced him to have dinner with us the other night," Andi said.

"How'd that go?" Fallon wondered.

"Well, he didn't call me a dyke. So, that was an improvement."

"That good, huh?"

Andi sighed. "I don't know, Fallon. Jake says he'll come around. I have no idea why he's so angry with me. All I can do is give him space."

"Are you sure you don't want me to talk to him? I can take the..."

"Blame?" Andi chuckled. "*You* are not to blame for my divorce. And, you are not to *blame* for who I am."

"I know, but I feel like..."

"You can't fix everything," Andi said. "Neither can I. Whatever is driving his feelings, he's not ready to tell me or his father."

"How's Jacob?" Fallon asked.

"Pissed at his brother. Hurt, I think."

"Yeah, I know. I get that. I was thinking maybe he'd want to go camping with me and Evan."

"I'm sure he'd love that. What about Owen?"

Fallon grinned. "I haven't asked Riley yet."

"Why not?"

"I don't know. I'm asking to take her three-year-old son away for two nights without her. I'm not sure how she'll feel about that."

"Ask her."

Fallon sighed.

"You're pathetic."

"I'm not pathetic."

"Yes, you are. If you had your way, you'd have her walking down the aisle already."

Fallon blushed.

Andi chuckled. "She knows that, Fallon."

Fallon's complexion drained of all color.

"Everyone knows that," Andi said. "She's not going to balk at you taking Owen."

"You don't think so?"

"No. When is Ida supposed to get home?"

"Any time now," Fallon replied.

"How long do you think Beth will stay with her?" Andi wondered.

"I don't know. Something tells me it might be a while."

"Dean's deployment got extended?"

Fallon shook her head. "Something's up, Andi. I could hear it in Mom's voice."

"Don't look at me like that," Andi said. "She hasn't said anything to me except that she was going to make an offer for Beth to spend some time here. That's it."

"Well, she asked me if Evan could stay at my house for a couple of nights when they get here."

"And?"

"Of course, he can. It's just, the spare room is Owen's now. I kind of feel bad making him sleep in the girls' room."

Andi nodded.

"What?"

"Nothing."

"Say it. I can see it in your eyes. What don't you want to say?"

Andi took a deep breath and released it slowly. "Maybe it's time you thought about making the room something else."

"What? Why?"

Andi wasn't sure how Fallon would react to what she was about to say. She did think Fallon needed to hear it. "I just don't know if it's such a great idea to keep a room for your ex's kids when what you want is to live with Riley."

"Riley's not ready for that."

"No, I know she's not. I don't think confronting your past every time she's there is the best way to get her to cross that threshold."

Fallon was speechless.

"I'm sorry, Fallon," Andi said. "I know that you love the girls. I do. I know that you and Liv have this unspoken sort of relationship."

"Friendship," Fallon corrected her.

Andi raised an eyebrow.

"Andi, Liv and I are just friends."

"Uh-huh. A friend whom you've made a permanent room for in your home."

"It's for the kids."

"Who are her kids."

"And Dean's."

Andi held Fallon's gaze firmly.

Carol listened from a slight distance. She respected Andi. Andi was the one person other than Ida who could call Fallon out onto the mat without getting pummeled. And, Carol thought it was long overdue that someone pointed out the obvious conflict in her home. Fallon had a big heart. Sometimes, her generosity was misplaced. That was Carol's opinion.

"Well, they are," Fallon said. "You know they've been raised to know who everyone is."

"And?" Andi challenged her.

"And, what? What am I supposed to do?"

"Put Riley first."

"Riley is first," Fallon said.

"Is she?"

"What is that supposed to mean?" Fallon was growing frustrated.

"Where is Liv staying when they visit?"

"With me; why?"

"You don't see a problem with that?"

"Riley didn't have a problem with it," Fallon said.

"Riley didn't tell you she has a problem with it because that's the way it's always been, and she doesn't live there."

"Did she tell you that?"

"She doesn't need to tell me that," Andi said. "Let me ask you something, Fallon."

"What?"

"What do you want with Riley?"

"You know what I want," Fallon countered.

"Maybe I do. Why is it difficult for you to say it?"

"It's not."

"Good. So? Let's hear it," Andi said.

"Everything," Fallon said.

"Which is what?"

"I want her to move in with Owen."

"And?"

"And, someday maybe I'd like to think that maybe there'll be another Owen."

Andi smiled. "So, where would this future Owen sleep?"

"Andi, if Riley moves in and she wants that too, then we'll have to change some things."

Andi shook her head. "If you want those things with Riley, Fallon, you need to change some things *now*."

"I don't see..."

"No, you don't see it. You need to see it before it bites you in the ass—hard. Emily and Summer are Liv and Barb's daughters."

"I know that."

"Yes, you do. I wonder sometimes if Olivia remembers that."

Fallon sighed. "What am I supposed to tell the kids?"

"The truth."

"The truth?"

"I'd start with telling Olivia."

"Telling her what?"

"That you want to build a life with Riley, and that means making your home Riley and Owen's home. It's not your job to explain things to the girls. It's Liv's. She's their mother. Let her do her job. You do yours."

"Which is?"

"Take care of the family you want, Fallon. Trust me on this one. Start now. If you want all of Riley, make sure she knows she comes first."

Fallon had no argument. Andi was right. Andi usually was right. "You don't like Olivia much, do you?"

"It's not about Olivia. She might think it is. It isn't. It's about you. It's time you made her understand that. I spent years competing with people I never even met in my marriage. You might not think so, that room? This 'arrangement' you have with Olivia? You're asking Riley to compete with your past."

"There's no competition."

Andi smiled. "It's not me you need to make that clear to." She took a long sip of her margarita. "Maybe that feeling you have that something is quote, 'up,' has more to do with someone else planning to visit next week."

Fallon groaned. Right again. She was dreading Olivia's arrival. She'd fallen into a routine with Riley. She wasn't looking forward to anything interfering with that routine. "She'll never understand."

Andi shrugged. *She'll understand. She just won't like it.* "Well, Fallon, that's her problem. You won't always understand the choices people make. If you love them, you have to accept that those are their choices and either live with their decision or let them go. That's her choice; not yours."

Carol turned her back to the pair and smiled. *I couldn't have said it better myself.*

"Are you okay?" Fallon asked Riley.

Riley nodded unconvincingly.

"It's just burgers on the grill with my mom and Beth. You've already met Evan."

"It's the first time I'll see your mom since we..."

"I won't tell her about the shower, or the backyard, or the striptease..."

"Stop!" Riley laughed.

Fallon pulled Riley into her arms. "My mother loves you. She might love you more than me."

"Never."

"Okay, well, she loves you. Beth will love you too."

"I hope so."

"Riley, Beth is probably the nicest person I've ever met aside from you. Seriously. It used to kind of creep me out a little."

"Your sister-in-law creeps you out because she's nice?"

"Super nice. I've never heard her say a bad word about anyone."

Riley wondered if Fallon realized how genuinely caring and kind she was. She might tease her friends relentlessly, but Fallon never spoke ill of anyone. Even when she expressed anger, Riley had never heard Fallon disparage anyone. "It's your family," Riley said. "I'm…"

"You're my family," Fallon said.

Riley swallowed hard.

"Too much?"

Riley shook her head.

"Listen, we keep talking about someday. That's okay." Fallon had been thinking about Andi's advice all day. She decided to take it. "Someday is one day—at least, that's what I believe. It's not a fairy tale; it's what we're working toward."

"I hope so."

"Me too. So, maybe we're not signing mortgage papers or sending out invitations. That's okay. You and Owen are my priority, Riley. If I haven't made that clear, I'm sorry. No one will change that. As far as my mom and Beth go, they'll be thrilled that they have someone new to pick on me with."

"Fallon, it goes both ways."

"Kiss me before my mother gets here."

"That's all you want from me, huh? A kiss?"

"I don't think we have time for a shower."

Riley chuckled and brought her lips to Fallon's.

Ida poked Beth in the car as she pulled up the driveway. "Young love," she said.

Beth laughed. "That's Riley, I assume."

"If it's not, I'd hate to be the woman kissing Fallon who meets Riley in a dark alley."

"She's tough?"

Ida grinned. "Not tough. She is a fighter. More than she realizes."

"You really like her," Beth observed.

"Nope. I love the girl."

---

Owen ran from the small garden Fallon had planted with a tomato in his hand. "Fawon!"

"Oh, he found another tomato," Riley said.

"At least it isn't a hot pepper this time," Fallon said.

"A hot pepper?" Beth asked.

"Yeah, I wasn't thinking about three-year-olds in the house, or the yard when I chose my produce," Fallon said with a grimace.

Riley laughed. "Owen discovered one last week. He knows everything growing on the vine is okay to eat in there. We sort of forgot there was anything hot he could find."

"Yeah, I did make up for it with ice cream, though," Fallon said.

"And, a movie."

"Well, I felt bad."

"And, you took him out for pizza the next day."

"He was traumatized. Plus, it was my fault."

Riley rolled her eyes. "Traumatized? You don't take me to dinner and buy me ice cream when you subject me to worms."

"Did you *eat* a worm? You won't even touch a worm," Fallon said.

"Because looking at them is bad enough," Riley countered.

Beth laughed. "You two are like an old married couple."

"She's older," Riley teased.

"Hey!"

"Fawon!" Owen barreled into Fallon's legs.

"You found a tomato. Why don't you go see if Evan will help you put it in the basket in the kitchen?" Fallon suggested.

"Okay. Eban!" Owen yelled, and ran to the house.

"Does he ever stop?" Ida asked.

"No," Fallon said. "Last night, I went in his room to check on him and his feet were moving in the bed like he was running."

Riley laughed.

"He's adorable," Beth said.

"Thank you," Riley replied.

"Are you sure that you two are okay with Evan staying here tonight? All he's talked about is Fallon since we left."

Riley smiled. "Sounds familiar."

"I think the question is are you all right with him staying here with us," Fallon said.

"Why wouldn't I be?" Beth asked.

"If you're not," Riley said. "Owen and I can go back to our house."

"Why would you do that?" Beth wondered.

Fallon cleared her throat. "Well, you know Riley and I..."

Beth's laughter startled everyone on the deck. "I'm sorry. Fallon, Evan knows you're a lesbian. For heaven's sake, he's been staying here for years. He's around Emily and Summer all the time."

"Still, we just want to be sure," Fallon said.

"That's one thing you never have to worry about," Beth assured Fallon. "He might eat you out of house and home. I would be more worried about that if I were you."

"If you will all excuse me, I'm going to head inside and find some more wine," Ida said.

Fallon watched her mother leave curiously. When Ida was out of sight, she turned to Beth. "Is Mom okay?"

"I think so. Why?"

"I don't know. I can't put my finger on it."

Beth sipped her iced tea. "I didn't want to say anything to you tonight."

"About?"

"I'm going to go help Ida," Riley said.

"You don't have to leave," Fallon said.

"Let me make my graceful exit," Riley replied. She squeezed Fallon's shoulder. "Besides, I want to make sure Owen isn't jumping on his bed again."

Fallon nodded.

"She's terrific, Fallon."

"Yeah, she is," Fallon agreed.

"She loves you. That much is obvious."

Fallon beamed. "To tell you the truth, I still can't believe it."

"What's that?"

"That Riley is here. I'd pretty much given up on finding someone again."

Beth looked at the ground.

"Beth? Hey..."

"Oh, Fallon, I don't know what to say."

"About?"

"About everything—to you."

"We've been friends forever. You can say anything."

"I'm not sure I want to stay married to Dean."

Fallon tried to take the information in.

"I shouldn't be telling you..."

"No, you should. Did something happen?"

"A lot of things have happened." Beth sighed. "I don't want to spoil tonight."

"You're not spoiling anything."

"It's just... With Olivia getting here this week..."

"What does Liv have to do with you and Dean?"

Beth's face fell into her hands. "I'm so tired, Fallon."

"Do you want to go lay down?"

"Not that kind of tired."

Fallon felt helpless. Something was bothering her sister-in-law. She wasn't sure why Beth seemed reluctant to talk about it. "Dean may be my brother, that doesn't mean I always agree with him, and no matter what, I think of you as a sister."

"Fallon, I can't compete with her."

"Who?"

"Olivia."

"Olivia? Why would..."

"He's in love with her."

"Who?"

"Dean. Fallon, Dean is in love with Olivia."

Fallon felt gut-punched; as if the world just delivered the truth with one mind-altering blow. *Of course, he is.*

"Ida?"

"Checking up on me?" Ida asked Riley.

"More like giving Fallon and Beth some space."

"Wise woman, you are. How are you, Riley?"

"Honestly?"

"No, lie to me." Ida laughed.

"Happy."

"It shows."

"Does it?"

"Like that little wrinkly alien in the basket."

"What?" Riley asked.

"You and Fallon. You remind me of that little alien, E.T. Don't look at me like I'm drunk. I know you're young. Don't you know who E.T. is?"

Riley chuckled. *I'm going with the drunk scenario. What did Fallon put in her wine?* "I know who E.T. is. I don't know why either of us reminds you of E.T."

"Carol is the one who pointed it out."

"What are you talking about?" Riley kept chuckling. *She has to be drunk.*

"Carol."

"Uh-huh."

"Every time you would walk into the bar, Fallon would get goofy. You both get goofy. Maybe we should've called you Goofy."

"I have no idea where this is going. I'm an alien or am I a dog?" Riley wanted to know.

"You remember in the movie, *E.T.* when he was ready to go home, his chest lit up?"

"Yeah?"

"Well, that's Fallon—and you. You light up with each other."

Riley smiled. "How much did you and Carol have to drink before coming up with this idea?"

"Who knows? Doesn't mean we're wrong."

"I've been called some strange things. I can't say E.T. was one of them. Until now, anyway," Riley said. "You realize that she's worried about you."

"Fallon ought to worry more about Fallon and less about everyone else."

"Ida?"

Ida groaned. "I worry about her."

"Fallon?"

"Just remember, Riley, she loves you."

"I know."

"Mm. Fallon has one major blind spot in her life."

Riley knew exactly what Ida was referring to. "Olivia."

Ida grinned. *Very astute.* "Olivia. Believe me when I tell you this; she's not in love with Olivia, hasn't been for a long, long time."

"I know that too." Riley sighed. "Olivia still hasn't gotten that message."

"I don't think so. She's never had to confront seeing Fallon with anyone else—not really."

"Maybe Owen and I should vacate while she's here with the girls."

"You most certainly should not."

"I trust Fallon."

"You should. Don't you go putting yourself in any backseats on account of Olivia Nolan. Too many people have let her have the driver's seat over the years. That's her way. She's smart and she's," Ida stopped herself before she said something unkind. She'd accepted Olivia into her family, loved her like a daughter. And, she cherished her granddaughters. But, after a long visit with Fallon's former partner and hearing Beth's painful revelations, Ida had been forced to face facts about who Olivia Nolan was; what lengths she was willing to go to in a quest to get her way. Olivia had manipulated Dean and Barb for her purpose. That purpose was Fallon. "It's cost them, Riley."

Riley nodded. "Is that why Beth is here? Olivia?"

"Oh, it's part of it. Dean's an equal part. They've made some decisions over the years that have caused a lot of people a lot of hurt. More than I realized." She sighed. "I love my grandchildren, Riley—all of them."

"Of course, you do."

Ida smiled. "That includes Owen."

Riley thought she might cry.

Ida grasped Riley's hand. "What you and Fallon have; it's not as new as you both want to pretend. I think we all know this isn't a passing fancy. She loves Owen too."

"I know."

"Mmm."

"I think I understand what you're trying to say."

"Fallon means well. Sometimes she means too well. She has a hard time saying no."

Ida's message was clear. Riley wondered what might have prompted Ida's cryptic warning. She had a few suspicions. Riley had recognized Olivia's possessiveness where Fallon was concerned from the moment they'd met. She'd felt Fallon's pain when it came to the parentage of Olivia's children. It didn't require a crystal ball to see the anguish behind Beth Foster's smile. All of it amounted to one simple conclusion for Riley; Olivia had not given up on Fallon, and if she was gauging things correctly; Dean had never given up on Olivia. In three days, Olivia would descend on Whiskey Springs whether Riley was ready for that or not. One thing Riley did know, she was not going to give Olivia control of the steering wheel. She leaned over and kissed Ida on the cheek. "Thank you."

Fallon landed on the bed with a thud.

"Are you okay?" Riley asked.

"Just thinking about my day."

"Anything you want to share?"

Fallon turned on her side. "You know; don't you? That this—you and me—that's the most important thing to me. You know that."

"Must've been some day if you need to ask that."

Fallon groaned. "Do you think it's possible that Dean is in love with Olivia?"

"I don't know Dean."

"Yeah, but do you think it's possible?"

"What do you think?" Riley asked.

"I think it makes sense. Explains why he's been pissed off at me for years."

"Do you think that's why he didn't ask you how you'd feel about him being Olivia's donor?"

"Hurting me; you mean?"

"Yeah."

"I think that was just a bonus." Fallon sighed.

"Fallon..."

"Beth told me some things tonight, Riley. Honestly, I don't know what to do with them."

"Do you want to talk about it?"

"Yeah. Not tonight," Fallon said.

"Okay."

"That's it? You're not going to question me?"

"No. I'm not her, Fallon. I'm not Olivia."

"No, you are not."

Riley smiled. "Make sure you remember that."

Fallon pulled Riley into her arms. "That's not something I could ever forget."

"Remember something else."

"What's that?"

"I love you, Fallon."

Fallon kissed Riley's temple and pulled her closer. "I love you too."

# CHAPTER NINE

**WEDNESDAY**

"Mommy!"

"Yes?!"

"We go now?"

"In a bit."

"When?"

"Soon."

"When, Mommy?"

Riley's forehead fell onto her kitchen table gently. *Give me strength.*

"Mommy," an indignant Owen stood before Riley's chair.

*Help? Please? Anyone?* "Owen, we'll go to Fallon's in a little while."

"Two sleeps. You said two sleeps."

"Yes, I did." Riley pulled Owen into her lap.

"Now, Mommy?"

"Owen, Fallon has company. We're going to see her after they have dinner. We'll have our dinner here. Let Fallon have a little time with Emily and Summer. They haven't seen her in a while. You see her every day."

"No. Only two."

"Owen, you saw Fallon yesterday and the day before."

"My room, Mommy."

Riley was at a loss. Owen hated to be away from Fallon's house. He wanted his room. He wanted to play in the garden. He wanted to watch movies on her sofa. He wanted Fallon. Fallon had worked late the previous two nights. Owen was at the foot of Riley's bed first thing each morning asking when he could go home. *When did Fallon's house become home*? She was ready to address Owen again when her phone rang.

"Hi," Riley answered.

"You sound exhausted. Are you okay?"

Riley hesitated to respond.

"Riley? What's going on?"

"Owen, it's Fallon."

"Fawon!"

Riley sighed. "He wants to talk to you, I think."

"Okay."

"Fawon?"

"Hey, little man. How's your day going?"

"I come home."

Fallon immediately understood the tone she'd heard in Riley's voice. "You'll be here later tonight, buddy."

"Now, Fawon."

"Owen…"

"Two sleeps!"

"Okay, buddy. Let me talk to Mommy."

Owen held out the phone for his mother.

"Why don't you go play in your room for a minute?"

Owen huffed. He hopped off Riley's lap and stomped lightly from the room.

"Hi," Riley began again.

"Come home, Riley."

Riley sat shell-shocked.

"I'm serious," Fallon said. "Just come home."

"Fallon, I am home."

"Okay, I know this is not the time for this conversation. Are you?"

"What does that mean?"

"I know we have an agreement. I respect how you feel. Please, right now, just come home."

Riley rubbed her eyes. She wanted to. "We can't just give into him."

"I get that. You're coming over later anyway."

"Are they there yet?"

"They're unpacking."

"You need some time…"

"I need you," Fallon said.

"Fallon, I have to stick to my guns with Owen. We have to."

Fallon was growing frustrated. "You're right."

"You're mad."

"I miss you, Riley."

"I'll be there in a few hours. Spend some time with the girls."

Fallon groaned in protest. "He's going to hate me."

Riley laughed. "When pigs fly."

"They can."

"Stop," Riley said. "We'll see you in a few hours like we planned."

"Now would be better."

"Fallon…"

"All right, I get it; let it go."

"Why did you call?"

"Do I need a reason?"

Riley sighed. Fallon was testy. "Never."

"I'm sorry. I'm just tired."

Riley didn't buy Fallon's excuse. Fallon was seldom short-tempered. For a split second, Riley considered giving in to Fallon's request. Regardless of how much she wanted to, and no matter where she thought their relationship was headed, Owen needed to respect the boundaries she placed—the boundaries they placed. He was developing a strong will along with the confidence and vocabulary to voice his opinions. Riley had no desire to quash that. She did want her son to understand who was driving the car. That thought led her directly to Fallon's guest. Olivia's presence had Fallon rattled. Fallon had been stressed for several days. After hearing a bit about Fallon's conversation with Beth, and her interaction with Ida, Riley was sure that Fallon was struggling with how to handle Olivia. And, she suspected that Fallon was wrestling with questions she needed to ask but was afraid to get the answers to.

"I'll be there in a couple of hours," Riley promised.

"You're staying; right?"

Riley tried not to laugh. Fallon was as bad as Owen at times. Riley didn't relish the nights they spent apart. She needed to keep a space that she could use as an escape. She wasn't sure she could explain that to herself, much less to Fallon. When Riley closed her eyes at night, her thoughts traveled to a life with Fallon. She dreamed of all the things she knew Fallon was hoping for. She wanted to wake up with Fallon each morning, argue with her over the grocery list, watch her chase Owen through the yard, and cringe when Fallon left her shoes in the middle of the floor just like Owen did. She'd let her daydreams wander to the possibility that one day she might hold Fallon's hand as they brought a new life into the world. All of it—every, single thing—Riley wanted to share with Fallon. Fear wasn't holding her back; awareness was. Riley had faced her past; at least, she had as much as any person could. She'd said the goodbye she needed to. She'd moved squarely into the present so that she could plan for a future; one she hoped would keep Fallon at its center. Riley had needed to hop on a plane and travel a distance to let go of the weights that had been clinging to her ankles, holding her down. Fallon's past existed here in Whiskey Springs. It came in the form of a person named Olivia Nolan. Riley had come to understand that it was not Olivia's exit from Fallon's life that had caused the most damage to Fallon's heart; it was Olivia's insistence—at nearly any price—to remain at the center of Fallon's world that had left Fallon wounded and wary of attachments for years. Fallon was staring down that reality now.

"We agreed," Riley said. "Two sleeps; remember?"

"I remember. I just thought that you might be leery of being here with..."

"I'll see you in a bit," Riley promised. She set down her phone. "Olivia doesn't scare me, Fallon—not even a little bit."

Andi sipped her margarita, content to listen to the usual banter at the bar. Pete was egging Dale on about his first date with Marge. Charlie had wandered in and was making puppy eyes at Carol while she mixed drinks for a table of tourists. She was happy to sit amid the familiar chatter and faces. It comforted her. An early morning call from her husband to inform her that their younger son would be moving to an off-campus apartment in Connecticut year-round had sent her heart into a rapid free-fall. Dave's anger with her still perplexed her. She was positive both her sons knew about their father's affairs. They'd not been raised by bigoted parents. Both Andi and Jake Maguire had gay and lesbian friends. Dave and Jacob Jr. had spent many days skiing with Fallon. Andi had run through a million possibilities that might be driving Dave's reaction. Nothing added up for her. She was grateful that Jake was supportive. He'd called that morning to tell her that Dave wanted distance from both his parents. Andi closed her eyes and savored her drink. Loving someone didn't mean you could fix the world for them. There were days when Andi struggled to make herself get out of bed. She did. She was determined not to let the people in her life see the battle raging within her—so many questions, few that seemed to have answers. Andi had made her choices. She was confident that she'd made the best decisions she could. Sometimes, there was no "best" decision. Sometimes, she thought, there wasn't even a "better" choice. There were times in a person's life when the road forked in multiple directions. None of the paths were clearly marked. That's where Andi had been standing. She'd selected the path of solitude and self-discovery. Daily, she discovered it was a road full of curves and rocks. *One day at a time.*

"Fancy meeting you here, stranger."

Andi smiled at the sound of Ida's voice. "I thought you'd be at Fallon's."

"Nope. That's a mess I don't need to clean up."

"That sounds like a cause for another margarita."

"Yeah, better make mine heavy on the tequila," Ida said.

"Everything okay?" Andi asked.

"With me? Yes. With my kids? I swear, Andi; I don't know what Dean is thinking sometimes."

"Oh, boy."

"More like, oh, Olivia."

"Oh, no."

"Can I ask you something?"

"If I said no, would it stop you?" Andi asked.

"No."

Andi chuckled. "Then proceed."

"What do you think of Olivia?"

Andi sucked down the last bit of fluid in her glass. "Carol?"

Carol strolled over to the pair. "Double trouble," she said affectionately. "Hi, Ida."

"Carol. How goes the war?"

"Currently winning. Ask me again in an hour. Let me guess; two margaritas, heavy on the tequila and salt, low on the 'rita."

"Very low," Andi said.

"You've got it."

"Do I need to wait for your answer until she makes those drinks?" Ida asked. "I'm not getting any younger, you know."

Andi laughed. "What do I think of Olivia?"

"Yes."

Andi took a deep breath. *Truth time.* "I can't stand her."

The fact that Andi didn't care for Olivia Nolan didn't surprise Ida. Andi's blunt reply did.

"I'm sorry, Ida. It takes every ounce of strength I have not to throttle her when she's here."

Ida nodded. "Can I ask why? And, please; don't hold back."

"She's a manipulative bitch. That's why."

Carol placed the drinks in front of her friends and attempted not to smirk.

"You too?" Ida asked Carol.

Carol shrugged.

"Carol?" Ida questioned. "You don't like her either."

Carol sighed. "I know she's your family."

"Forget that. I feel like an old fool," Ida admitted. "I always knew she was carrying a torch for Fallon. I never wanted to believe those girls figured into that equation."

Andi looked at Ida compassionately. "They're terrific kids, Ida. And, they're your granddaughters."

"Beth told me that Dean agreed to that arrangement without talking to her."

Andi and Carol were both stunned. Andi's face grew hot.

"That was my reaction," Ida said. "It was bad enough that neither of them talked to Fallon. I think that just about killed her."

Andi shook her head. *It did.*

"But for him to go ahead with that without talking to his *wife*? Honestly, I'm not sure I could have survived that in a marriage."

"I don't know if I could either," Andi said. "Affairs are painful. Deciding to have children with someone..."

"I think I might need one of those now," Carol said, pointing to the margaritas.

"Do it," Andi said. "We won't snitch."

"It'd be different if he had just been a donor," Ida said. "That's not the way it's ever been."

Andi nodded. "It keeps Fallon on a string," she said. "Even if it kills Fallon."

"I think Beth is going to divorce him," Ida said.

"Oh, Ida," Andi began. "I'm sorry for all of you."

"I'm sorry for Beth and Evan. The more I learn, the more I want to hop on a plane and throttle his ass."

Andi chuckled.

"I love him. I do. I can't pretend to understand what the hell he's thinking where Olivia is concerned."

"Love does strange things to people," Andi said.

"Well, it doesn't excuse selfishness."

"No, it doesn't," Andi agreed with a sigh.

"Oh, now, don't you go taking this on yourself," Ida advised. "You are not selfish, Andi. Human? Yes? Selfish? No."

"I wish I believed that."

"Well, you should."

"Tell that to David."

"He'll come around, Andi," Carol said.

"I don't know."

"Carol's right. Don't let him off the hook so quick when he does wander back," Ida said. "You let him know that he hurt you."

"I just hope he does come back." She closed her eyes. "I'm tired of losing people."

Ida put an arm around her friend. "Well, you haven't lost me," she said. "And, that's a bonus because I'm buying."

"You don't pay for drinks," Carol reminded her.

"Exactly. Which means Fallon is buying. Which, I think is exactly what we all deserve. Keep 'em coming," Ida said.

Carol laughed. *Something tells me I'll be calling Jacob in a few hours.*

Riley kept a close eye on Olivia all evening. A brush against Fallon in the kitchen, a seemingly innocent comment laced with sexual innuendo, a memory of days gone by, offering Riley insight about the house and its design; Riley noted everything. She sat and smiled, laughed at the appropriate moments, and did little to assert her relationship with Fallon. Olivia seemed to delight in what she perceived as Riley's innocence. Inside, Riley's blood boiled. She respected Fallon's past, accepted that the woman seated across the room had once shared every aspect of Fallon's life including her bed. She'd let Olivia play her game. Fallon's eyes rarely left Riley. Something, Riley was certain Olivia found maddening.

The kids had been in bed for nearly two hours. It was approaching eleven-thirty, and Riley decided it was time to gracefully make her exit. What Olivia perceived as Riley's innocence was confidence. She leaned over and placed a gentle kiss on Fallon's cheek. "I'm going to turn in."

Fallon startled. "Oh... Okay, I'll just..."

Riley smiled at Fallon and then offered the same gesture to Olivia. "You two catch up," she said, reaching her feet. "I'm sure Owen will be up bright and early looking for the girls, and probably pancakes." She winked at Fallon. "Goodnight."

"Goodnight, Riley," Olivia said.

"I won't be too long," Fallon promised. "But I'll try not to wake you."

"You can," Riley said flirtatiously. She walked down the hall.

Fallon swallowed hard, wondering how she could make an exit without being too obvious.

"She's a nice girl," Olivia said.

"Huh?"

"Riley."

Fallon grinned like a teenager in love. "She's the best."

"Really?"

"Would you stop?" Fallon chuckled. "Get your mind out of the gutter."

"Why? Isn't that where yours is?"

"No," Fallon said. Nothing about being with Riley resembled a gutter and that included sex.

"I'm just teasing you."

Fallon decided a change of topic was in order. "How come Barb isn't coming up?"

Olivia brought the glass of wine in her hand to her lips. "She's decided to take a job in Richmond."

"Wow. So, are you moving or doing the commuter thing?"

"Neither."

Fallon was confused.

"She isn't interested in commuting—either way."

"I'm missing something."

"She left, Fallon."

"Barb left you? Come on. Barb? Barb is crazy about you."

"Things change, Fallon."

Fallon nodded. *Yes, they do.* "I'm sorry, Liv."

"Seems like there's a lot of turmoil lately."

"What do you mean?"

"Look at us all, Fallon. Here we all are entering our forties, and not one of us is settled."

"Who is *we all?*"

"Me, Barb, Beth and Dean—look at Andi. I would have thought we'd all be married and fat by now."

"Umm… Beth and Dean are married."

"Not an easy situation, Fallon; being away from the people you love. Dean's having a hard time being so far away from the kids. But from what he's told me, that's likely to be the case permanently where Evan is concerned soon. Beth has intimated that she wants a divorce."

Fallon bristled. What was the deal with her brother and Olivia? Why did Dean seem to think it was okay to tell Liv everything and his wife and sister nothing? And, Beth would never keep him from Evan. Olivia's observations irked Fallon.

"You didn't know?" Olivia asked.

"Not until the other night, no. And, not from Dean. Not that I should be surprised by that."

"What does that mean?" Olivia asked.

"Forget it."

Olivia sipped some more wine from her glass. "How's Andi?"

"She's all right."

"You two are still speaking?"

"Why wouldn't we be?"

"How does Riley feel about that?"

Fallon smiled. "Riley loves Andi and vice versa."

"Must be strange."

"Not really," Fallon said.

"You were always good at keeping a distance from your lovers."

Fallon pressed down her anger. "What the hell, Liv?"

"What? All I'm saying is that you don't get involved."

"That's not true."

"Anymore?"

Fallon had no desire to banter or argue with Olivia. She'd hoped they would be able to catch up. The last things she wanted to delve into were her feelings about her brother or her past with Andi. Both Andi and Dean would always hold a place in her life and her heart. Andi would always be Fallon's best friend, no matter what had passed between them or where either was headed. Dean would always be her brother. That didn't mean that Dean would ever be her close friend. And, Fallon had no intention of discussing her growing relationship with Riley; not late at night with Riley down the hall. There were things she needed to tell Olivia. Tonight was not the time.

"Riley and I are taking it slow."

"Slow?"

"Liv, let it go."

Olivia held up a hand. "I just worry about you."

"You don't need to." Fallon stretched and stood. "I think I'm going to turn in too. Riley's right; Owen will be in our bed before the sun is all the way up."

Olivia nodded. *Our bed?* "Well, get some rest. I'm going to finish my wine and make myself cozy on the sofa."

"We'll try to be quiet in the morning."

"You know me, Fallon; I can sleep through an earthquake."

Fallon nodded. *True.* "Goodnight."

Olivia waved and sipped her wine when Fallon disappeared into the hallway. *Playing house, Fallon?* She finished the glass of wine and set it aside. *In our house.* She laid down on the sofa. *Things do change, Fallon. They do.*

Riley rolled over when Fallon walked into the room. "That was quick."

Fallon replaced her jeans with a pair of shorts and grabbed a T-shirt. "I don't know how to talk to her anymore."

Riley pulled Fallon into her arms when Fallon slid into the bed. "I'm not sure it's such a great idea that she stays here. And, before you say anything, that's not because of you."

"Okay..."

"Well, it is, but not because I care what she thinks."

Riley smiled.

"I care what you think, though."

"I think that Olivia is someone you will always care about, and I think you love Emily and Summer."

"And?"

"And, I think that while you may have moved on; she never has."

"That's nuts. She was with Barb for years."

"Was?"

"Yeah. I guess that's over."

Riley sighed deeply. "Fallon..."

Fallon turned so she could look at Riley. "I need to tell her."

"Tell her what?"

"I know you aren't ready to hear this."

Riley waited.

"I don't know when you will be ready. I do know that I want this to be our home, not my house. I know I should keep my mouth shut, that you want to take things slowly, and I get that... Well, I sort of get it. Even if you aren't here every day, I want you to feel that this is home as much as..."

"Fallon!"

"What?"

Riley smiled and kissed Fallon gently. "Relax. I'm not threatened by Olivia."

"You shouldn't be."

"I'm not."

"That's not why I'm telling you..."

"I know," Riley silenced Fallon with another kiss. "I know. I don't know how to explain this to you; I need a little time before we take that step. Not forever, Fallon—just a little time."

"Are you afraid I'll change my mind?"

"No." Riley had been mulling over her feelings for days. "I'm afraid of losing you, though."

"You're not going to lose me; not anytime soon."

"That's probably true," Riley admitted. "When Robert died, everywhere I turned he was still there. I could smell his after-shave in the bathroom. It took me months to throw it out. His clothes were in the closet. His books were on the bedside table. His favorite baseball cap was hanging behind the bedroom door.

Everywhere I turned, there he was. Sometimes, it was comforting—like I could hold him close for a minute again. But every time I tried, it wound up feeling empty—an empty shirt, an empty shower, a lonely baseball hat. Still, I couldn't part with any of it," Riley said.

"Riley..."

"The thought of that... Fallon, of touching your robe without you to fill it... Smelling your shampoo and knowing I'll never see you standing in the shower again... I can't bear it. I don't know if I could survive that. Losing you? It would be unfathomable. But having you linger everywhere with no escape? Fallon..."

Fallon pulled Riley close. "I'm sorry. I'm so sorry that you ever had to go through that. I wish I could tell you that neither of us will have to go through that. I can't. I know I can't. I can only promise you that I'll do everything I can to keep that from happening until we are so old, our kids are grandparents."

Riley laughed through some tears. "Kids, huh?"

"Have to keep the town going somehow."

Riley looked into Fallon's eyes. "I'll get there. I just need a little time."

Fallon nodded. "Promise me one thing?"

"Anything."

"No matter if its four nights or every night here, you know that it's home."

Riley held Fallon's face in her hands. "I promise." She collapsed beside Fallon and held onto her waist. "Just tell Olivia the truth," she said.

"I'm not sure she'll understand."

"It doesn't matter if she understands, Fallon. It doesn't even matter if she listens. It's not about Olivia. It's about you."

Fallon took a deep breath. "I love you."

"I love you too."

"Are you sure you don't want to come to the Cigar Club Saturday?"

"Positive."

"I am sorry I'll miss your margarita show-down."

"You won't."

"Why not?"

"Carol says it's a stacked deck. She's plotting something; I know it."

Riley sniggered.

"I feel bad. You shouldn't be stuck babysitting."

"But you don't feel bad that you'll be climbing in bed with me reeking of cigars and whiskey?"

"You could reek of cigars and whiskey if you came."

Riley laughed. "I think I might prefer baiting a hook."

Fallon laughed. "I'll remember that."

"I've no doubt. Goodnight, babe."

"Goodnight.... Would you really rather bait a hook?"

"Go to sleep."

Fallon chuckled. *I'm going to have to test that theory.*

"Fallon?"

"Hey, Em."

"What are you doing?" Emily asked.

Fallon put down the drill in her hand. "I was just fixing the fence. What are you doing?"

Emily shrugged.

"Something bothering you?"

"Ma left."

Fallon nodded. "Come on; what do you say you and me take a walk down the hill?"

"Mom will...."

"Go run and tell your mother we're going for a walk. I'll wait here."

Emily ran off. Fallon tried to mentally prepare herself. She'd immersed herself in time with the kids the last two days hoping to avoid Olivia. Riley had gone home for two more sleeps. That would end tonight after Cigar Club. That was *if* Riley let Fallon into bed. She snickered at the likelihood that Riley would make her shower and brush her teeth for an hour before Fallon would be allowed within an inch of the bed. Usually, Fallon looked forward to the Cigar Club follies. Ida had avoided coming to Fallon's house, evidence of her displeasure with Olivia. Fallon guessed her mother was less than pleased to learn Dean hadn't been upfront with his wife about many things. Andi had made it abundantly clear in the unique way she possessed that she did not trust Olivia. Fallon was finding it increasingly difficult to deny the truth that was staring her down.

"Ready!" Emily yelled as she ran toward Fallon. "Where are we going?"

"I was going to drive down to Murphy's to check on some things. Why don't we walk? I'll spring for a Shirley Temple."

"Can I play the jukebox?"

"Sure." Fallon directed Emily toward the winding road that led from Fallon's house to the pub she owned. "So? What's on your mind, kiddo?"

"How come Ma moved?"

"I don't really know, Em. Sometimes, grown-ups just need to take a little break from each other."

"Is that why you don't live with Mom?"

"What?"

"You did before."

Fallon felt blindsided. "A long time ago, yeah, your mom lived here."

"I wish I lived here."

"You have lots of friends at home," Fallon said.

"Yeah, but Grandma is here and you're here. Mom's never home. Ma always was. And, Uncle Dean, I mean, he's our dad but I don't know. It's just weird."

"What's weird about Uncle Dean?"

"I don't think Ma likes him much."

"Oh, I don't think that's true. She probably just wants to make sure she lets you have alone time with Uncle Dean too." *Yeah, I'm sure that's it.*

Emily shook her head. "She cries a lot."

"Barb cries?"

Emily nodded.

"Well, you know, she loves you and your sister. It was probably hard for her to leave, even if it isn't that far."

"Mom says it's far."

*Jesus, Liv. What the hell?* "I wish I could make it easier, Em."

"Are you going to live with Riley?"

Fallon sucked in a deep breath. "I hope so."

"She's nice."

Fallon smiled. "You like Riley, huh?"

"Yeah. You do too, huh?"

"Yeah, I do, Em. I like her a lot."

"Evan says Owen is like your kid now."

Fallon coughed. "Evan said that?"

"Is he?"

"Owen's dad died when he was a baby," Fallon explained. "He had a dad and a mom."

Emily shrugged. "I have a dad and two moms."

*Didn't see that coming.* "That's kind of different."

"Why? You're gonna live with them."

"Well, someday I hope that will happen."

"Like we live with Mom and Ma."

"Yeah…"

"So, you're like his Aunt?"

"I don't really know," Fallon said. "I'm just Fallon, like with you."

Emily kicked a rock down the road. "Are you gonna get married?"

Fallon coughed again. *Where are these questions coming from?* "I don't know, Em. Why do you ask?"

"Evan says you should."

*Evan has a lot to say.* "He does, huh?"

"Yeah, he said Aunt Beth and Grandma said so."

*What?* Fallon laughed. "I think Riley might have something to say about that."

"You should ask her."

Fallon laughed harder as they approached Murphy's Law. "What do you say we misbehave? I'll have Don make us some nachos." Fallon opened the door for Emily.

"I love nachos."

"I know."

"Hey, look what the kid dragged in," Ida said.

"Hi, Grandma!"

Ida accepted a hug from Emily.

"What are you doing here at two in the afternoon?" Fallon asked.

"Dropping off some things for tonight," Ida replied. "You?"

Fallon grinned. She reached into her pocket and handed Emily a five-dollar bill. "You go ahead and play some songs. I'll order us those nachos."

"Feeding time at the zoo?" Ida asked.

"More like a way to keep her mouth busy with something other than my love life."

"Huh?"

"Evan seems to think I'm getting married. You wouldn't know anything about that, would you?"

"Me?" Ida shook her head. "Nope."

Fallon shook her head. "What is it; you need to compensate for a divorce with a wedding?"

"Not funny, Fallon."

"I'm sorry. I feel horrible for Beth. But, really? What on earth would make you two think I'm getting married?"

"What *on earth* are you talking about?" Ida asked.

"Em said that Evan told her he heard you and Beth saying Riley and I were getting hitched."

Ida laughed. "That was a mouthful. No. Beth said you and Riley might as well be married."

Fallon rolled her eyes and stepped behind the bar to make a Shirley Temple for Emily.

"Think she's wrong?" Ida asked.

"I think that's a long way off."

"Probably so," Ida agreed. "How are things at the zoo?"

"I escaped."

"I see that."

Fallon shrugged. "I need to talk to Liv."

"About?"

"About some changes."

"What changes?"

"I want Riley to move in."

"How does Riley feel about that?"

"She's not ready."

"Mmm."

"You've been talking to Andi," Fallon surmised.

"I don't need to talk to Andi to know that Olivia still wants her hooks in you, Fallon."

Fallon stepped back slack-jawed.

"Oh, everyone knows it except you."

Fallon sighed. "I know it. I guess I just didn't want to see it."

"Maybe because a part of you hoped one day she'd succeed."

"Maybe," Fallon admitted, surprising her mother. "Well, maybe I did. At least, when she would visit with the kids I felt like it wasn't all a waste."

"A waste?"

"The house. My life. I don't know."

"Oh, Fallon."

"I know. It's pathetic."

"A little," Ida teased gently.

"Thanks, Mom."

"Do you think it was a waste now?"

Fallon smiled. "I think that I was waiting for Riley to show up. I think I was waiting for her to wander down the street in the snow and land on my doorstep. That's what I think."

"If I didn't love Riley so much, I'd be yelling at you right now."

"Why?" Fallon asked.

"What the hell are we going to bet on tonight? Can't be how many coeds will visit the top of the hill this ski season."

"I don't know how I feel about my mother placing bets on my sex life."

"My winnings paid for a few drinks."

"You don't pay for drinks, Mom."

"I do when I'm not here."

Fallon laughed. "Riley suggested that we bet on when Marge and Dale might do the deed."

"The deed? What deed?"

"Mom..."

"Dale and Marge?"

"Yep."

"Holy shit. I'll be damned."

"Keep talking like that and you will be; damned that is."

"You really are funny, Fallon. Maybe you should've become a comedienne instead of an investment broker. I'm out of here. I need to take a nap before tonight's festivities. Bye, Em!"

"Bye, Grandma!"

Fallon laughed at her mother as she left the bar.

"Didn't think I'd see you until closing time," Don said as he emerged from the kitchen.

"Kinda slow, huh?" Fallon observed.

"Yeah, well, everybody knows we're closed later."

"Do me a favor and make Em and me some nachos," Fallon requested.

"Sure thing. Hey, I almost forgot." Don reached under the bar. "Riley said to give you this when I saw you."

"Riley was here?"

"For about two seconds this morning. Said she was on her way to Burlington."

"Huh." Fallon looked at the envelope in her hand. She tore it open and found forty-dollars wrapped in a note.

*Hi Babe,*

*I can't stand the smell of cigars. But here's my contribution to the pool. If you bet on Carol's womb, go for news by Christmas. If you bet on Marge, bet on next week.*

"Next week? What does she know that I don't?" Fallon laughed. Riley made her laugh more than any person Fallon had ever known. *Just another reason to love her.*

# CHAPTER TEN

## CIGAR CLUB

Fallon shuffled the cards in her hand and chewed on the end of a cigar.

"How does she make that look sexy?" Marge whispered to Andi. "Lucky cigar. I'm not even a lesbian and I want to fuck her."

Andi spewed the whiskey in her mouth across the table.

"Hey!" Billie Steele yelled.

Andi kept laughing. "Who knew dating Dale would bring out your wild side?"

Marge shrugged and sipped her whiskey. "Tell me you weren't thinking the same thing."

"I'm trying not to think. And, you just caused me to lose my mind eraser," Andi replied.

"What are we betting on this year?" Billie asked.

"Riley thinks we should bet on Marge's love life." Fallon wiggled her eyebrows.

"You might want to be careful with *that* wager, Fallon," Andi said.

Marge shrugged and grinned. "Go ahead."

"Aw, shit! No way, you and Dale already…"

"No," Marge said. "I hope I haven't forgotten how."

Andi snickered. "Keep watching Fallon with that cigar; you'll remember," she said.

Fallon looked at Andi and laughed. "Is that a compliment?"

"It's not an insult," Andi said.

Ida tossed back the whiskey in her glass. "Why do I come to this party?"

"Because you love it," Fallon said.

"It's disturbing," Ida replied. "Deal the cards, Casanova."

"Not anymore," Deb Homan said. "Fallon's been whipped." She made the sound of a crack with her hand on the table.

Olivia picked up a cigar and lit it. "Must be a change of pace," she commented.

"What's that?" Fallon asked as she dealt the cards around the table.

"You're usually the one holding the whip," Olivia said.

Ida threw back another glass of whiskey. Andi did the same.

"This could get ugly," Billie whispered to Marge.

Marge coughed a bit from the cigar in her mouth.

Fallon took everything in stride. She ignored Olivia's comment and sipped her whiskey. "All right ladies and lesbians in waiting." She winked at Marge. Marge coughed again. Andi chuckled. "Five card stud—that's why I'm dealing."

Ida rolled her eyes. "Why do you all encourage her?"

"Riley?"

Riley turned to find Emily and Evan standing behind her. "I thought you two were in bed?"

Both kids looked at their feet.

"What's going on?" Riley asked.

"Can we stay here?" Evan asked.

Riley was perplexed. "Stay here? You are staying here."

"No, like forever," Emily said.

Riley sighed. *Oh, boy. How do you handle this one, Riley?* She threw the dishtowel in her hand on the counter and directed the pair to follow her into the other room. "How about we talk on the couch?" Riley took a seat and inhaled a deep breath. Fallon had shared a bit about her talk with Emily that afternoon. *Diving in.* "I know you both love visiting. You'd miss home and your parents if you stayed here all the time."

Evan shook his head. "I want Mom to stay here," he told Riley.

"I want to stay with Evan," Emily said. "Summer too."

*You are way over your head on this one.* Riley smiled gently. "You don't think you'd miss your friends? What about your dad… and your other mom, Emily?"

"They're not there anyway," Evan said. "Em sees Dad more than me."

Emily put her arm around Evan. "I don't know why we can't just be together," she said. "Evan's our brother."

"Yes, I guess that's true," Riley admitted. *No sense in dodging that.*

"And, Ma moved away. Mom is always working. We'll just end up at Aunt Beth's anyway," Emily offered.

Riley tried to take everything in. She had many conversations with her niece and understood that kids often needed someone they regarded as an impartial adult with whom they could confide their feelings. The family that Evan and Emily shared was complicated. It didn't have to be. Riley didn't think so. Everyone loved the kids. Everyone wanted to be a part of their lives. From where Riley sat, Olivia had used her daughters as a pawn in a twisted game of chess. That not only unnerved her, it also disgusted her. They knew who their father was. All three children knew who was raising them, and yet it seemed that Emily and Evan felt incredibly insecure about where they belonged. They all clung to Beth and Fallon as anchors. It made sense. Riley had only just met Fallon's sister-in-law and she already considered Beth a friend. Beth

Foster was easy-going, nurturing, and honest. She was a bit like Andi when Riley thought about it. She could see a lingering sadness in Beth's eyes. It was the ache that accompanied betrayal. In some way, the girls were a reminder of that for both Beth and Fallon. Ironic—they were the two adults that all three children trusted the most. For Riley, it spoke volumes about the woman she loved and Beth. It also told a story about who Olivia Nolan was. Riley thought it resembled a twisted fairytale; the original kind that ended in tragedy rather than glass slippers and pumpkin coaches. Her inclination was to end the discussion and tell Evan and Emily to wait for their parents. That would equate to a betrayal for them. They'd sought her out. They'd placed trust in her. She would need to navigate carefully through the rocky waters of childhood confusion and emotion.

"I'm sorry that your mom, and that your dad, Evan are both away right now."

"I wish we could be here," Emily mumbled.

Evan looked at Riley. "Are you gonna marry Aunt Fallon?"

Riley's eyes grew wider. She took a breath. "Someday, if she decides to ask me; I will."

Evan nodded. "So, Owen will be her kid, right?"

Riley's heart began to pound. She'd never heard that reality spoken to her. It threw her off balance.

"If you get married," Evan tried to explain his reasoning.

Owen already thought of Fallon as his parent. She was *his* Fallon. That's what he'd told Riley's mother and sister. Listening to Evan and Emily, Riley realized what Owen meant by that. "I think that he already is."

"But he doesn't call her Mom," Emily pointed out.

"No, he doesn't. He loves her that way. Just like you love both your moms."

"His dad is really far away, huh?" Emily asked hesitantly.

Riley smiled. "Owen's dad is in heaven. So, Owen can't *see* him, but I think he's still close by."

"How?" Evan asked. "That's so far. My dad is in another country and I only get to talk to him once a week."

"But you think about him; don't you?"

Emily and Evan nodded.

"Just like you think about Fallon and your grandmother when you are home," Riley said.

"Yeah."

"Do you ever think about them and then they call?" Riley asked.

Emily smiled. "Once, I was talking about Fallon and she called to say happy birthday."

Riley nodded. "Well, that's kind of what I mean. Just because you can't see someone or even talk to them doesn't mean they aren't missing you too."

"Then how come they leave?" Emily asked.

*Oh, Emily, I wish I had that answer.* "I don't know," Riley answered honestly. "They never leave here," she said, pointing to her heart. "No matter where you live."

"Riley?" Evan looked at Riley and then cast his eyes downward.

"What is it, Evan?"

"What if they don't?"

"What if they don't what?"

Evan pointed to his heart.

Riley thought hers would break. She pulled both kids close. "They do, Evan. Sometimes, people have a funny way of letting you know they love you. That doesn't mean they don't. I know that's hard to understand. You both have a lot of people who love you."

"Do you?" Emily asked.

Riley pushed back her tears. No child should ever worry about their parents' love. "Of course, I do."

Andi was off-kilter. In other words, Andi was drunk. She was not alone in her predicament. Several poker games down, she'd lost track of the number of whiskey glasses she'd drained. Ida, Marge, and Billie had all slipped into a bout of silliness. It was a typical Cigar Club gathering that felt anything but ordinary to Andi. Olivia had spent the night making loosely veiled comments about Fallon and Andi's affair. Andi had noticed that Fallon was measuring her alcohol consumption. That was not for Riley's benefit. Andy guessed that Fallon was close to decking her ex-girlfriend. Olivia had also been a slow sipper all evening, hardly able to make an excuse that her comments were the result of inebriation. Andi slapped her cards down on the table. "I fold. And, I've got to pee."

"You should never have broken the seal!" Fallon called after her.

Andi waved her off.

"I'm out too," Olivia said, throwing her cards on the table. She stood and followed the path Andi had taken.

"You too?" Fallon asked Olivia.

"You know the drill, Fallon. We travel in pairs."

Fallon glared at Olivia's back as she walked away, knowing exactly what Oliva had meant by that comment. *She'd better not start shit with Andi.*

Ida grabbed hold of Fallon's hand. "Andi can handle herself."

"I'm missing something," Marge said.

The table laughed. "The question for all of us, Marge, is how long you'll be missing it," Billie said.

Fallon sipped from her glass, feeling a sense of unease creep over her skin. *Andi can handle herself.*

Andi emerged from a stall and washed her hands. She startled at the feel of two hands on her waist and looked into the mirror. Olivia's eyes met hers. "What are you doing?" Andi asked.

"That's not obvious?"

Andi turned and pushed Olivia away. "Have you lost your mind, Liv?"

"Pining over Fallon is pointless, Andi."

"Oh? Who are we talking about?"

Olivia stepped closer. "If I had known that you were open to this, I might have made some different choices when I visited Whiskey Springs."

Andi laughed. "You are unfucking believable."

"I am." Olivia reached a fingertip over to trace Andi's cleavage.

"What the fuck?" Fallon's voice boomed.

Andi stepped away, and into Fallon's arms.

"What the hell are you doing, Liv?"

"Well, if you hadn't interrupted, I might have been doing something a lot more fun."

Fallon looked at Andi. "Are you okay?"

Andi nodded. She took a deep breath and put her hands on Fallon's chest. "Go. I'm all right."

"Andi..."

"Maybe you should leave, Fallon. Last I checked, you didn't have any claim to either of us."

Andi felt Fallon tense. "Fallon." She forced Fallon's eyes to hers. "Go. Trust me."

Fallon sucked in a slow breath. She turned slowly and left.

"She really needs to get over her Lancelot complex," Olivia said. "Where were we?"

Andi shook her head. "You have; you've lost your mind."

"Oh, come on, Andi. We're both adults, both single last I checked, and we both know what we like."

"Stop," Andi said. "Olivia, I would marry my vibrator before I would sleep with you."

Olivia chuckled.

"You think this is a game? You think it's funny?"

"Isn't it?"

Andi had sobered quickly. "You know, I used to think that you loved Fallon and you were so afraid to admit you fucked up that you did crazy things to hold onto her."

Olivia crossed her arms.

"Now, I think you're so in love with yourself you can't see anyone else. You left, Liv. In case you forgot, that broke her heart."

"How could I forget with all of you constantly reminding me?"

"She's happy. Let her be happy. If you ever loved her at all, let her go."

"Like you did?" Olivia asked. "Do you? Love her?"

Andi swallowed the lump in her throat. *More than I thought possible.* "I love her. That doesn't mean I belong with her."

"Do you know where you belong?" Olivia shot.

"No. I know where you don't." Andi stepped up and brought her face within an inch of Olivia's. "Watch it, Liv. You underestimate how many people have your number."

"What does that mean?"

"You know what? You do what you want."

"Thank you for the permission slip."

Andi shook her head. She was about to open the door when she heard a loud crash. She ran toward the sound. "Fallon!"

Fallon sat in the backseat of Charlie's car without comment. Olivia stared forward silently. Carol looked ahead to where Riley was standing on the front porch. She wasn't sure if it was the right thing to do. It seemed like the only thing she could do. If the annual Cigar Club continued after tonight, Carol was confident it would be minus one of its founding members. She'd never seen Fallon out of control. Fallon had made the excuse she wanted to check on Andi because she was drunk. Carol knew that was bullshit when Fallon approached the bathroom. She and Ida had shared an exchanged glance that expressed mutual concern. Andi could hold her alcohol as well as anyone Carol had ever seen. Andi might've wavered in her stride; she was not one to waver in her senses because of a few drinks. Fallon had walked out of the bathroom and strolled to the bar without a word. Her silent walk had been the calm before the storm. Fallon gripped the bar trying to calm her anger. When that failed, Fallon swiped her hand through a line of bottles, sending several on a collision course with the floor and a few directly at the wall. Despite the distance between them, Andi had been the first to reach Fallon. Carol counted that a blessing. She felt sure that Andi was the only person in the room with the ability to calm Fallon at that moment. Even Ida stepped aside until Andi had managed to drag Fallon into the kitchen.

Carol's inner debate lasted less than a minute when she saw the blood dripping down Fallon's hand. She called Riley. More than a shitty hand of cards had made the night a bust. For once, Carol was glad she didn't have to be a fly on the wall in Fallon's house.

"I'll be down in the morning to clean the rest up," Fallon said evenly.

"Fallon, don't worry about it," Carol said. "Call me when you get up."

Fallon nodded and stepped out of the car. Olivia followed.

"What the hell happened?" Charlie asked when both women had closed their doors.

"Olivia happened. What else is new?"

"Fallon looks pissed."

Carol sighed. "I think it's a lot more than that."

Riley moved to the steps and greeted Fallon. She ignored the woman trailing a foot or so behind. Riley shook her head and wrapped an arm around Fallon's waist. "Come on, let's get you inside."

Fallon let Riley lead her to the bedroom. She said nothing, embarrassed and regretful for her outburst. She'd been simmering all night. Who was she kidding? Her patience had been slowly reaching boiling point for days. Olivia was famous for crossing all kinds of lines. Cornering Andi, trying to seduce Andi, thinking that Andi was an easy target—a way to hurt Fallon again, a way to distract Fallon from Riley—that was Olivia's fatal mistake. If there was one silver lining, it was that Fallon had broken some bottles and not Olivia's nose.

"I'm sorry," Fallon muttered.

Riley looked at Fallon's hand. "It's not me who needs an apology. Good thing Billie is a nurse, huh?"

Fallon groaned.

Riley directed Fallon to sit on the bed. She sat beside her. "Talk to me."

"I can't have her in my life, Riley, and I can't kick her out of my life. She made sure of that when she had the girls with Dean."

Riley sighed. "No, you can't. They need you, Fallon."

Fallon looked at Riley curiously.

"Emily and Evan wanted to talk to me tonight."

"About?"

"Living here in Whiskey Springs, living with you."

Fallon threw her head back. "Fuck."

"What happened?"

"Carol didn't tell you?"

"Only that something happened."

"She tried to put the moves on Andi."

Riley was dumbfounded.

"Yeah. I can't believe it. I mean, I can understand wanting to be with Andi. That's not why she did it."

"No, I don't imagine it was."

"That's shitty to do to me, Riley. To Andi? I can't even..."

"I know."

"She just doesn't know when to stop."

"No, she doesn't. Fallon, she knows you've moved on. She's in a bind. Her partner left her. Dean's away. She's alone."

"You don't seriously feel sorry for her?"

"No. I feel for the kids. I feel for you. I feel for Beth, for everyone that she's hurt. And, unfortunately, you're right. As much as I want to tell you that I never want to see her in this house again, that would hurt all those people in some way. Because all of you love each other, and those kids need you, Fallon—whatever role you play for them, that much I do know."

"She can't stay here."

"Well, I might have a solution to that."

"Really?"

"There is an empty house a couple of miles away."

Fallon stared at Riley in disbelief. "It does have two bedrooms. Maybe it's time you set some different ground rules."

"She's here for another week, Riley. That will break the arrangement you and I have."

Riley nodded. "Well, maybe we need to talk some more about that *arrangement*."

"What are you saying?"

"Only that we need to talk some more about it," Riley said. "The kids made me realize something tonight."

"Oh?"

"You and I are the only parents Owen has ever known."

"Riley, I..."

"Just listen. He'll never know Robert. I don't know if he has impressions of his father. Robert is a face on paper, a story people tell him. You're real. You're *his* Fallon. When he says that, that's because you're not the fun adult friend who entertains him, you're the person he trusts to protect him. You're the person *I* trust to protect him. He's lucky, Fallon. He'll have loss someday. Right now, all Owen knows is that people love him. He's secure."

"That's because of you," Fallon said.

"Partly. It's because of you too. And, Ida, and Andi... and Carol, and all the people he *knows* he can count on. But most of all it *is* because of you and me. And, Fallon, that's also because he sees how much we love each other."

"Must've been some conversation."

"It was," Riley said.

"I'd better go talk to her," Fallon said.

"No." Riley kissed Fallon's cheek. "I will."

Fallon tipped her head.

"Did you mean it when you said you wanted me to consider this home?"

"Completely."

"Then she's in my home. You're my partner, Fallon."

Fallon grinned.

"What are you going to say?"

Riley winked. "That's between Olivia and me."

"I'm glad you decided to stay here tonight," Ida said.

"Thanks for the offer," Andi replied.

"Are you okay?"

"I am. I wish I could say that I can't believe it."

Ida rolled her eyes. "I have a feeling she's not going to like where this all leads."

"Safe bet," Andi agreed. "Riley might seem naïve; she's not a pushover."

Ida chuckled. That was the truth if ever she'd heard it. She poured them each some whiskey. "I noticed Billie was casting a lot of glances in your direction."

"What?" Andi took a sip of her drink. "Billie? You're imagining things."

"I don't think so."

"Billie's not a lesbian."

"Neither were you a year ago."

Andi laughed. "I still don't know who I am."

"I like Billie."

"Oh, my God. Are you trying to play matchmaker?"

"You don't?" Ida asked.

"I like Billie."

"Do you think you might *like* Billie?"

Andi laughed so hard she coughed. "Are we in sixth grade?"

"After tonight, we'd be lucky to classify as kindergartners."

"Touché."

"Well?" Ida prodded.

"I don't fancy making a fool of myself—again."

"So, you did notice the glances."

Andi grinned. "Maybe."

"Just don't close yourself off."

"Alcohol makes people do strange things, Ida."

"Alcohol reveals the strange things people want to do, Andi."

Andi sighed. "I don't think I'm ready for that." The mere thought of dating anyone, much less Billie caused her to down her whiskey.

Ida sipped from her glass to keep from laughing. Andi still loved Fallon. She'd caught a few long stares between the affable nurse and her friend. No one was ever ready for love. Maybe it had been the haze of alcohol, cigar smoke, and innuendo. Ida had a strange feeling that something more was starting to brew between the pair. She'd suspected for years that Billie was a lesbian. She also guessed Fallon knew that. She never asked. As much as people liked to accuse her of being nosy, she wasn't. She simply paid attention. Andi wasn't attached to anyone, and while it remained something people murmured about, everyone was aware of her affair with Fallon. She looked at Andi with a devious smile. "You're not ready for *that?*" Ida asked.

"Anything," Andi replied.

Ida shrugged. "Well, not that anyone listens to me, but Billie is a thirty-eight-year-old single woman who I've yet to see involved with a man. You do the math. One plus one equals two."

"That doesn't mean it equals Andi."

"Never know 'til you jump into the equation."

Andi chuckled. "Pour the whiskey."

Riley made her way into the kitchen. Olivia was sipping a glass of wine.

"Come to read me the riot act?" Olivia asked.

Riley leaned against the counter. "No."

"Really?"

"Should I?"

"I figured Fallon filled you in."

Riley nodded. "What is it that you hope to accomplish here, Olivia?"

"Accomplish?"

"Yes."

"I'd hoped that my daughters could visit their family."

"Meaning their grandmother and their aunt," Riley said.

"Yes?"

"Mm. You do realize that Fallon is their aunt; not their parent?"

"I think I would be aware of that."

Riley waited for a beat to continue. "Fallon cares about you, Olivia."

"Thank you for letting me know."

"Because you were a big part of her life."

"Were?"

"Yes, were." Riley sensed Olivia's desire to bait her into an argument. She remained calm. "The truth is, you'll always be a part of her life."

"And, that doesn't sit well with you, I'm guessing."

Riley smiled. "What doesn't sit well with me is seeing anyone I love hurting."

"And, I would be responsible for that hurt."

"I don't need to answer that. You just answered it yourself. Here's what you need to understand."

"I'm listening."

Olivia's sly grin made Riley want to choke her. She refused to allow her disdain to show. "I don't care if you like me. I don't care if you hate me. I don't care what you say *about* me. When you're here in this house; you're in my home."

"Is that so? Moving in already?"

Riley ignored the question. "The girls are Fallon's family. That makes you a reality. That's all you are to me. I know all the reasons this house was built. I know what every room was intended for. I know that a piece of Fallon broke when you left, and another shattered when you and Dean decided he'd father your children. None of that's a secret to me. It's also no secret to me that all of it, everything you do is to try and keep Fallon dangling on a line, just waiting for the moment you can reel her in."

Olivia grinned and sipped her wine.

"You'll be waiting on the shore until the end of time to catch that fish."

"Because you have."

"No. Fallon's not a prize to me," Riley said. "She's the person I share my life with. There's a difference. She's ready to send you packing. Tell you to go back to DC."

"I'm sure she is."

Riley nodded. "That's your choice."

"That's kind of you."

"Not really. I haven't given you the choice yet. Emily and Summer are welcome to stay here anytime. You are not," Riley said. "That presents an issue for you. I doubt very much that Beth feels like sharing her quarters with you right now. So, that leaves out Ida's. And, I don't need clairvoyance to know that you won't be bunking down with Andi."

Olivia's skin was beginning to flush.

"There is a house not too far away that will be vacant for the next week. You are welcome to stay there. As a mother, I know I would want my son close. There's an extra room if you want the girls to stay with you. That's up to you."

"You think I'm disrespecting you in your home?"

"I don't think you possess enough self-respect to be able to *respect* anyone. What I think isn't the point. You don't need to decide tonight. You can let us know in the morning." Riley pushed off the counter that had been supporting her and walked to the doorway. "And, Olivia?"

Olivia looked up.

"So, we're clear; Fallon and Andi are both a part of my family. I know what it's like to lose family. There isn't anything I won't do to protect mine. Just so we're clear. Goodnight." Riley left the room.

Olivia looked into her glass of wine before downing it in one gulp. *Shit.*

Riley climbed into the bed and wrapped herself around Fallon.

"Well, you survived," Fallon said. "Did she?"

"She'll live to see another day."

"What did you say?"

"Nothing that wasn't true."

"I really am sorry."

"For what? Messing up your bar, cutting your hand, or the fact that you still stink of cigar smoke?"

"I'm sorry. I can shower."

Riley pressed her weight against Fallon. "You're not going anywhere. Neither am I."

Fallon took the first deep breath she had in hours. "I think Billie has a crush on Andi."

"What?"

"Yeah."

"Billie's not a lesbian."

"Yeah, she is."

Riley sat up. "You're joking."

Fallon shook her head.

"Huh. She's cute."

"She's cute? Thinking you jumped too soon?" Fallon teased.

Riley laughed. "Not a chance." She laid back down. "Evan thinks we're getting married."

"Yeah, I heard. I think my mother and Beth helped in that department."

"Crazy."

"Insane," Fallon said.

Riley closed her eyes.

"Is it?" Fallon asked.

"What?"

"A crazy idea—us married."

Riley smiled. "It is if you think we're doing it tomorrow."

"What about Monday?"

"Which Monday?"

"You pick."

"Fallon, if this is your idea of a proposal, I think you need to be getting lessons, not giving them."

"I'm not proposing."

"Glad we cleared that up," Riley said.

"But if I were to decide... You know, at some date in the very distant future..."

"How distant?"

Fallon chuckled. "Pick a Monday."

Riley laughed. "I'll look at the calendar in the morning." She yawned.

"You do that." Fallon closed her eyes.

"I will. Goodnight, babe."

"Riley?"

"Hum?"

"It doesn't have to be a Monday, does it?"

Riley kissed Fallon's chest. "Go to sleep, Fallon."

"I love you, Riley."

"I love you too."

"I really love you."

Riley gigged. Fallon was a bit intoxicated. "I *really* love you too."

"Okay."

A few moments passed.

"Are you really going to look at the calendar?" Fallon asked.

Riley shook with silent laughter. *This could be fun.* "If I can find one long enough."

"Okay. Wait... What does that mean?"

"Go to sleep, Fallon."

"Sorry." Fallon sighed. She started to drift off. "I have a calendar," she muttered before falling asleep.

Riley smiled. *I wonder when she'll pencil me in.* She closed her eyes and held on to Fallon. *Maybe on a Monday.*

CPSIA information can be obtained
at www.ICGtesting.com
Printed in the USA
LVHW051307180623
750108LV00003B/721

9 780692 083710